Dark Tidings on the Thames

The Kier and Levett Mystery Series
Book 7

DEB MARLOWE

ARE YOU SIGNED UP FOR DRAGONBLADE'S BLOG?

You'll get the latest news and information on exclusive giveaways, exclusive excerpts, coming releases, sales, free books, cover reveals and more.

Check out our complete list of authors, too!

No spam, no junk. That's a promise!

Sign Up Here

www.dragonbladepublishing.com

Dearest Reader;

Thank you for your support of a small press. At Dragonblade Publishing, we strive to bring you the highest quality Historical Romance from some of the best authors in the business. Without your support, there is no 'us', so we sincerely hope you adore these stories and find some new favorite authors along the way.

Happy Reading!

CEO, Dragonblade Publishing

To *my* Melissa,
for being a great friend and supporter.

Prologue

Covent Garden
London

MISS GLYNN FOULGER stretched and put down her sewing. The crowds were thin, this late in the afternoon. She'd made a little progress on her project, but now the light was fading. Cool evening air brushed her cheek, bringing the stink of the Thames with it. Flinching from thoughts of the river, she stood to survey the goods she had left after a long day's work.

Not so many blooms remained, thank goodness. Her stall was a prime location, located as it was just outside the flower market building in Covent Garden. The farmer she worked for expected top results. He would be happy with today's take, but she still expected to make a few sales to the girls who sold flowers at night—those who frequented the areas outside the theatres and music halls. Ah, and here they were, starting to trickle into the Garden.

Glynn had sold nearly everything when a pretty brunette stopped at her stall.

"Jeanette says she wants one of your specials, as nice as ye can make it. But she's running late and says please don't leave till she comes."

Glynn closed her eyes. "Did she say *how* late? Jeannette knows I like to be gone from here before dark." All the night girls knew it, but they came early to buy from her because she always kept some of her nicest blooms back for them.

"She didn't say. Jeanette's got something going on, though. She particularly asked you to wait. She thinks your specials are good luck."

Glynn gave a reluctant nod. "I'll wait. Have a good night, Doris."

The brunette scampered off with an armful of wallflowers. Glynn set to work making a special bouquet, shaping up a bunch of lavender, hyacinths, and violets, all tied prettily with a fancy lattice of lace ribbon. Once it was finished, she tried to take up her sewing to ease the wait. She was fashioning a smock again, the sort she often put together and donated to the Waif's Wardrobe, a charity that donated decent clothing to those in need.

The Wardrobe was a fine enterprise, smoothly run and well organized. Their work made a difference for some of London's poorest, and the people who volunteered there had become her friends—the only true friends she'd found since coming to London.

Squinting, she carefully examined the embroidery that would make this smock unique. Usually her donations were anonymous, given over to the society and distributed by the workers specially chosen to seek out the needy, but this smock was different. She was making this one for a girl she knew. One with circumstances that required a few alterations, like a warm lining and a snug jacket to go over it all.

The light was too far gone, though. She packed the smock away in her carry bag, along with the day's earnings and a last, lonely potted tulip—and she waited. And waited. Glynn lingered far past the time she normally would have departed to spend the evening at home, or perhaps to enjoy the camaraderie of the volunteers at the Wardrobe. She fought back impatience and anxiety as the shadows lengthened. Covent Garden at night was an entirely different place—and she had business to do tomorrow morning. Business that would keep the dark stink of corruption from the light that was the Waif's Wardrobe.

At last Jeanette came running over the cobblestones, breathlessly apologizing as she came. "I'm so sorry. Glynn. Ye're a gem, ye are. Thank ye for waiting." The flower seller's eyes lit up when Glynn produced the bouquet. "*Cor!* What a beauty! Here." Jeanette tossed coins at her. "Oh, the gent will pay big for this 'un, so it's only fair ye get some extra, too. Keep a bit for yerself, aye?"

Jeanette did not linger, but was quickly off, to Glynn's relief. It was full dark now. Taking up her bag, she set out, her nerves on edge. Moving quickly, she reached the edge of the Garden— and jumped when someone addressed her out of the darkness.

"Sorry, Glynn! Didn't mean to startle you. Just sayin'—ye're here late tonight."

"Good evening, Bertie. Yes. I've been waiting on a sale. But you've stayed later than usual, too?"

The vegetable vendor sighed. "Aye. 'opin' to make a little extra to take home to the missus. It's her birthday, innit? But the cabbages didn't much move today."

Glynn reached into her bag and pulled out the potted tulip. "Take this for her—and don't tell her it's from me." The woman's husband had thought of her, after all. Glynn would have to give over the extra coins from Jeanette, but Bertie's wife was a sweet lady.

"Truly? My thanks to you, Glynn. She will love it. Here, now!" He tossed her a cabbage. "Take that in exchange."

She caught it. "Thank you, Bertie." She tucked it away in her bag.

"'eadin home, then?"

"No." She didn't want to be alone with her nerves about tomorrow's meeting. "I think I'll go and see who might be hanging about the work rooms at the Wardrobe tonight."

"See ye tomorrow, then. And thanks again to ye."

"Tomorrow." Glynn headed for the steps of St. Paul's and went into the church. The chapel lay quiet tonight. She saw only one lone woman before the altar as she headed for the back and the door into the churchyard. The garden back there was an oasis of peace and quiet greenery in the bustle of the Garden. The end of the space butted up to the back of the Waif's Wardrobe. The main entrance, on Bedford Street, would be locked up tight by now, but there were sure to be a few souls lingering in the workrooms, being social, and having a cuppa while they sewed, folded, or sorted.

Her steps slowed as she breathed in the quiet and calm, but the light from the backroom beckoned. She headed for the door—only to pull up short as a figure stepped out of the shadows.

"You!" She took a step back. "No. You had your chance. Leave me alone and let me pass."

"I had *my* chance?" A soft growl sounded out of the darkness. "I warned you, Glynn."

"Warned me? That's rich. You are the one who is acting in an utterly inappropriate manner."

"My manner is none of your business."

"Your reprehensible behavior is the business of everyone who works for the Wardrobe! So many people striving to do some good in this world. So many poor men, women, and children who are no longer shoeless, cold, or wearing rags. You put all of that in jeopardy!"

"It is you who will be in jeopardy, if you do not call off your meeting with the duchess and learn to keep your mouth shut."

Glynn raised her chin. "I won't be silenced. You are sick. Vile. The Wardrobe is not your hunting ground. You will be stopped."

A low laugh taunted her. "I won't be stopped, but you will be silenced—one way or another." A shift in the shadows. A glint of faint light on dark metal—and Glynn saw what her opponent held.

She stepped back. "Is that...?"

It was. Suddenly she understood the full extent of what was about to occur.

"No!" She turned to run. She made it only a few steps before the blow came. A flash of blinding light, then instant darkness.

She never felt it when she hit the soft grass.

She was already gone.

Chapter One

A week earlier
Scotland

Kara Kier, the Duchess of Sedwick, clutched her husband's hand. Pride swelled in her chest as she watched her ward grin at the group assembled in the entry hall at Tallenford Priory.

"Thank you all for coming to see my knight," the boy said without a trace of bashfulness.

Harold had come a long way from the scrawny street rat she and Niall had first encountered at the Crystal Palace. He stood tall and proud and bright eyed—and tears threatened. Kara blinked them away and smiled widely at the boy instead. Niall, glancing down at her, tugged her close and wrapped an arm around her. She leaned into her husband's embrace and listened.

"This is the largest and most complicated piece I have ever made, but I could never have got it done without the help of everyone here." Harold grinned at her and Kara's heart skipped a happy beat. "I first must thank Kara for sharing with me how she works, for explaining arbors and gears and lantern pinions, but also for telling me all about Green Knights when I found the one hiding behind the ivy in the walled garden. We decided together to make a Green Knight my next project, but she let me design and put him together myself. She always helps me when I need it, but lets me work alone, too—and she never laughs at my mistakes."

Harold turned to look up at Niall. "Thank you to Niall, who finally showed me how to make a sword, even if it is a small one. He didn't laugh, either, even when my first one looked more like a corkscrew." Everyone gathered laughed outright at that. Grinning, Harold forged on. "Thank you to Gyda for showing me how to etch the vines and blossoms into his sword and armor."

Gyda, standing near the stairs, gave the boy a nod. Kara noted the dark circles under her eyes and the shallow nature of her friend's smile, and exchanged a look with her husband.

"Thank you to Ailsa for telling me about the spirits of the forest, and many thanks to Mrs. Pollock for clootie dumplings and cherry crumble."

"Hear, hear!" Niall called.

Mrs. Pollock reddened. "No cook was ever so happy as when feeding a boy with a hollow leg," she called out.

More laughter, but next to the cook, Turner—Kara's butler, friend, and lab assistant—took out his pocket watch and raised a brow at the boy.

"And thanks to Turner, for always keeping me on track—especially when I forget to leave the lab or forge." Harold's expression softened. "And for teaching me how important it is to care for others."

Kara wasn't the only one blinking back tears of pride now.

Harold stepped close and grabbed a corner of the cloth covering his creation. "And here it is!"

His pride was obvious and justifiable as he whipped the cloth away. The piece had been kept under wraps in their new workroom at the priory, so there were gasps of surprise all around. Harold had done a remarkable job. Kara had never accomplished anything so involved at his age. The Green Knight stood two feet tall. The armor, with the etching Harold had inscribed with Gyda's help, was well done, but it was the face that caught and held attention at first. The boy had painstakingly rolled out different thicknesses of metal vines, curling and twisting them into magnificent hair and a beard surrounding a weathered face. Metal oak leaves and pine cones were interspersed throughout.

"Now, watch," Harold said, excited. He inserted a key and wound the piece.

Everyone breathed out in awe as the figure lifted its head. One knee bent forward and the sword arm lifted, the forearm bending to put the figure in a defensive stance.

"Bravo! Well done!" Cries of wonder and congratulations echoed in the entry hall. Everyone surrounded Harold and the piece, proclaiming their awe.

"Did it truly look like a corkscrew?" Kara asked Niall quietly.

"No. It merely had a warp or two. Everyone's first blades do. It takes time to develop the skill." He raised a brow in her direction. "Would you care to make the announcement?"

"No. You do it."

Kara let him go, and Niall stepped forward. "I know you are all as proud of Harold as Kara and I are," he began.

Everyone quieted down to listen.

"We are very pleased to say that Harold has agreed to allow his knight to be permanently displayed in the main parlor here at Tallenford. We've commissioned a special pedestal for it and you will all be able to examine it at your leisure." He raised a hand to quell a spout of applause. "But in the meantime, once you have had a look, we invite you to come outside to the garden to help us celebrate Harold's accomplishment with biscuits, lemonade, and good company."

Thirty minutes later, Kara took another square of spiced shortbread and tried to convince Mrs. Pollock to stay outside with them a little longer.

"No, no," the cook said, shaking her head. "I've a shank roasting, and it will be needing a good basting." She nodded to where her kitchen assistant was darting among the rosebushes with the other maids. "Let the young ones stay and frolic a bit. I'll go and take care of kitchen business."

Relenting, Kara sat back with a sigh. She watched Mrs. Pollock pass Niall, Harold, and Turner hovering near the colonnade, then turned to where Gyda sat nearby, just outside the shade from the tent they had erected over the seating and the table of food and drinks. She started to speak, but her friend had her eyes closed and her face tilted into the sun. Kara closed her mouth. She knew Gyda hadn't been sleeping well.

One of the young footmen approached, carrying the post. Kara frowned and waved him away as he headed for Gyda.

"But there's a letter for Miss Winther, ma'am," he said quietly.

"I'll take it," Kara told him.

"No. I'm awake," Gyda said, sitting straighter. "I'll take it."

The footman handed it over and turned to move toward the men. He left both Niall and Harold with a letter each.

"It's from Darrow!" the boy exclaimed, ripping open his own. He read on. "He's caught up in court but wants to come and see my knight soon."

"That was thoughtful," Kara murmured to Gyda. They had met Mr. Darrow, the procurator fiscal, when they first came to Scotland. They had come to inspect Tallenford Priory and the estate the Crown had gifted Niall, to go along with his new dukedom. Somehow, as per usual, they had ended up in an adventure as well.

Her friend was frowning down at her own letter.

"Bad news?" Kara asked.

Gyda sighed. "Beth fears there is trouble in the wind at that charity she's been volunteering at. You know how nervous she gets when conflict starts brewing."

"Yes, but you have always been able to bolster her confidence. I'm glad she's comfortable enough to write and ask for your advice."

"Yes." Gyda gazed into the distance, her mind clearly occupied with her faraway friend.

Kara stood as Harold approached, with Niall on his heels.

"What project should I work on next, Kara?" the boy asked, coming to lean into her.

"I thought you might want a break from the lab. Practice your blade forging, perhaps?"

"I will," the boy said with a nod. "But I like to have two projects going at once. I like having one in the forge and one in the lab—especially here at Tallenford, since I don't have the gymnasium or special lessons," he added with a sigh.

Gyda looked over. "Are you wishing to return to London, Harold?"

The boy looked instantly contrite. "No, of course not. I love the priory. I have plenty to occupy me here."

Kara's heart melted a little. Harold knew the main reason they had come to spend these last months at Tallenford was to give Gyda, who had recently suffered a difficult loss, the peace and quiet she needed to grieve.

Gyda nodded slowly. "I just thought everyone might be getting a little restless, missing all the bustle of the city, or all the occupations we cannot pursue here."

"We are all perfectly content, Gyda," Niall told her. "We will all stay as long as you like."

"Well, that's just it," she said. She looked to the letter in her lap. "Beth seems a little more distraught every time she writes. And I've been thinking. I might be ready to stop ... wallowing. Perhaps it might do me good to get back to at least a bit of normal life."

Kara exchanged glances with Niall.

He shrugged. "Well, I have finished the extra standing screen that Mr. Blundel added to his order. It would be helpful to get up a meeting in London with my next client."

"Gyda, are you sure you are ready?" Kara asked gently.

Her friend looked about, taking in the garden, the colonnade, and the house. She nodded. "The quiet here has been exactly what I needed. I needed to think. And feel. I appreciate the chance. Thank you." Gyda looked between Kara and Niall. "But the quiet is starting to grow loud now. It's filled with the truth that Charles will never break the silence." She sighed. "I would like to go back."

"Then that is what we will do," Niall said. "But first, we have a stop to make."

"Where?" asked Harold eagerly.

"Eyemouth," answered Niall, waving his letter. "I have been meaning to take Kara there, in any case. Now I've had a note from Rob, asking to see me."

"Oh, Rob! We haven't seen him in too long!" The Highlander was a favorite with Harold. The boy's eyes widened. "Can we see his forge? The one you sold to him, way back when you were young? You said it was even smaller than the one we have here."

"It wasn't *that* long ago that I was young," Niall said wryly. "But yes."

"Well, then." Kara winced at Harold's shout of joy. "We'd better start packing."

⟫⟫⟩⟨⟨⟨

"SPILL IT, MAN." Niall watched his oldest friend shift nervously from one foot to another.

"I mean to sell the place, Niall." Rob McRae stilled as he looked for Niall's reaction.

Niall gazed around at the small forge, the very first place he'd owned before he sold it to his friend. "And?"

"And? And I thought you'd be … annoyed. Angry."

"Rob, this place is yours. You must do with it as you wish."

"I want you to know what it meant to me," Rob rushed to say. "You do know. A life of my own, in a place of my own. It's meant everything to me. I don't want you to think I am taking this lightly."

Niall grasped his friend's shoulder and gave a low laugh. "Odin's arse, but we were young then, no? Green lads. But things change, aye? I'm certainly not in the same place."

Rob scoffed. "From a stringy wee gadgie to a duke of the realm? I should say not."

"Exactly," Niall said. "Why would you think I would expect you to remain forever the same?"

Rob straightened. "That's just it. As you said, I don't mean to be in the same place. I'm making a move." He paused. "To London."

Grinning widely, Niall clapped Rob on the back. "Well, why did you not lead with the good news? Saints, but it will be good to see more of you. But what are your plans, man?"

Rob gave a shrug that Niall had seen a thousand times since they were boys—a lift of the shoulder that meant Rob was feeling something strongly, but didn't wish to show it. "It's time for a change, aye? I'm ready for something new. And I cannot shake the feeling that smithing is going to be left in the past. Oh, not the way you do it, to be sure. Your sort of art will always be in fashion. But the hooks, and net weights, and spare parts that I spend my days fashioning? They'll be drummed out by a factory in the Midlands before long."

"I don't think we are there yet, but I do know what you mean. What do you mean to do instead?"

"I still want to forge, but I want to add in my woodworking skills, as well. I've been talking with Sam Grillow. He's a furniture maker, but at the top of the scale. He has contracts to fit out some of the fancier hotel rooms in London and even customized train cars. He means to have me working on some of those projects." Rob shrugged again. "I've some ideas he likes the sound of."

"You'll be brilliant at it." Niall had seen some of the custom pieces Rob had fashioned. "He's lucky to have you. And we will be lucky to get to see you more often."

"I know you have the priory now, and will be spending time there."

"Yes. We'll be splitting our time between London and the priory. The place is shaping up nicely," Niall said with satisfaction. "It's quieter there. The pace is slower." He sobered. "It's what we needed, these past months."

"And Gyda? How is she … recovering?"

"Slowly." He sighed. "It was a great loss she suffered. The peace of the priory was good for her, but we all agreed, it's time to go back to London." Niall smiled. "And now, with the prospect of your being there—it's all the better." He crossed to the door so that he could look out upon Eyemouth's long fishing harbor, feel the sea air in his face, and listen to the cries of the gulls. He'd been so young when he started out here. So full of hopes—and fear that his family secrets would unravel them.

A splash of color caught his eye, and he turned to see his wife strolling toward him, her skirts blowing in the breeze. His heart fluttered too, in joy and gratitude. Back then he never could have imagined the convoluted path he would travel, nor how happy he would be. "Kara's coming," he said, turning back to Rob. "I'm going to take her up to the house."

"What's left of it, you mean," Rob corrected him with a frown. "Is that a good idea?"

"It's fine. It's why we stopped here on our way back. We all wished to see you—and I wanted to show Kara and Harold everything."

"Everything?" asked Rob.

"No need to worry. Malina will never come between us. Kara knows the full story." Niall grinned. "And I want to show her the little forge on the meadow, and the view."

Rob smirked. "It is a good spot. I may have taken a girl or two up there myself."

"We'll be setting out for London tomorrow morning. Will you be ready to travel with us?"

"No, but I won't be far behind you."

"Good. Come straight to Bluefield Park. You can stay with us until you are settled in your new job and comfortable in the city."

Rob nodded. "Thank you, Niall. You are a good friend."

"As are you." Niall clasped Rob's arm. "You shared your

family with me when we were young. I'm more than happy to return the favor now."

He left his friend and walked out to meet his wife. Sweeping her up in his arms, he swung her around and kissed her. "Ready for a walk? I can scarcely wait to show you the place."

Kara beamed up at him. "I can scarcely wait to see it."

"OH, HOW GRAND that will be," Kara said, listening to her husband relate Rob's news. She glanced up at him. "Do you think Beth factored into his decision at all?"

Beth Williams, their young friend who had been writing—and worrying—Gyda, had at one time carried a torch for Rob McRae. Niall's friend had spent some time in London last year, and he and Beth had met in the course of all the adventures that had come with the spilling of Niall's family secrets. They had suspected that Rob might return the girl's interest, but he had returned to Eyemouth without any formal declarations. Beth had asked after him a few times, in a studiedly casual manner that didn't fool anyone.

"He didn't mention her," Niall replied.

"Hmm. She hasn't mentioned him in a while, either."

"Have you had a letter from her?" he asked.

"Not since she took on that position at the charity. I think she's been kept busy, which was what she was hoping for. She and Gyda have corresponded more frequently, however."

"Gyda always was good for the girl."

"Yes. You know how shy Beth is. It was Gyda's idea for her to find a place to volunteer, and I think she writes regularly, asking for Gyda's advice on handling different relationships." Kara paused as they crested a rise, and their destination lay before them. "Ooh," she breathed.

A clearing stretched out before them, grasses and weeds

grown knee high. At the far end sat a shell of a cottage, partially burned out. It was backed by a thick grove of trees that spread out and thickened along the right side of the space. It was lonely and desolate now, but once … "It must have been lovely," she whispered.

"It was." She could hear the sadness and resignation in Niall's voice, and knew he was thinking of his first, disastrous love. She took his hand.

"It's the forge I'd really like to show you," he said, tugging her into the weeds and pulling her toward the line of trees. As they grew closer, she saw a faint path leading in. Kara slowed as they entered the grove. It was cool and sun dappled and lovely. A breeze whispered through the branches above. She tilted her head back to watch them dance as they moved through, but as they reached the end, Niall stepped away so that she could see ahead.

She stopped. "Oh, Niall."

It was a meadow, full of wildflowers, tucked into a depression in the earth. A small building sat to the right. He led her over. Several locks had to be undone before he could slide the door aside to reveal the tiny forge.

"This is where it began—my dream of creating art." He grinned at her. "Where I lit the fire in my belly."

Stepping inside, she ran her hand along the anvil and went to stand before the cold hearth, staring out. "You worked here, looking out across the meadow, to the blue sky and the clouds over the sea." She could hear the crash of the surf.

"Yes. Come and see." He tugged her again, and she let her fingers drift over the blooms as he headed for the edge of the depression on the far side. She climbed the rough path over it with his help. She drew a breath as she reached the top, and the relentless sea breeze hit her, bringing along the smell of brine and tugging at her hair.

They stood atop a wide cliff with the vast expanse of the sea before them. Marveling, Kara clutched her husband's arm. "How could the fire not burn in your belly?"

"Exactly. I practically wore a path from the forge, across the meadow, to the edge of the cliff, lost in thought. It felt like I could pull ideas from the very air."

"The quiet, the beauty, the sea. I can understand it," Kara said. The picture formed vividly in her mind. She could almost see her tall, strong husband in the ratty kilt he liked to work in, pacing back and forth as he worked out an idea in his head.

Niall gestured back toward the meadow. "The forge is small, but there is a cot in there. I had the notion that Gyda might like to stay there, someday soon. I know she is not in a frame of mind to create right now ..."

"No. She's not as recovered as she would like us to believe. She's barely sleeping." Kara pressed her lips together in worry. "She's still slipping out every night. For hours, she just sits, staring at the sky."

"I know she wants to return to London."

"She's looking for something to distract her," Kara guessed.

"And that might be just what she needs right now, but someday she'll be ready to start creating again, and I thought, when the time comes, she might wish to come up here for a few weeks."

"That's a lovely offer." Worry pressed down on her. She shook it off and started for the cliff's edge. "I could sit here for hours."

Niall reached out to grab her wrist. "Tread carefully," he warned. "There are hollows, depressions in the ground that can be difficult to see—especially when your gaze is fixed on that." He gestured toward the deep blue expanse.

"Oh." She frowned at the grass-covered cliff ahead.

Squeezing her wrist, he raised both brows and gave her a suggestive smile. "Couples sometimes come up here to take advantage of them. Find one the right size and you can recline in there, completely hidden."

Kara pursed her lips and lowered her tone. "That's a tradition I wouldn't mind putting to the test."

He laughed. "I had that very thought in mind, but you will have to wait until later. I asked Gyda to meet us up here. I wanted to remind her how lovely it is before I made the offer."

"Later?" she asked, stepping closer and putting a hand on his chest. "The air might be cooler then. What if we grow cold?"

Grabbing her hand, he kissed it. "I'm sure we can think of a way to keep warm." Growing serious, he let out a sigh. "Saints, but I'm glad you are here, Kara. You know there have been some bad memories associated with this place, but seeing you, standing there? I can feel them starting to drift away."

She stared up into his dark gaze. "Let's make some new memories, then."

"Kara! Niall!"

"Here she is," he said. They turned as Gyda climbed up from the meadow.

She waved a paper above her head. "Is there a way to leave tonight, instead of in the morning?"

"What is it?" Kara clutched at Niall, her mind racing. Resentment bloomed in her chest. They were entirely too accustomed to bad news, in her opinion.

"It's nothing drastic," Gyda hurried to assure her.

With relief, Kara let go of Niall.

"I'm worried about Beth," Gyda continued. "It seems there really is some trouble brewing at the charity where she has been working."

Kara frowned, reaching for the memory. "The Waif's Wardrobe, isn't it?"

"That's the one. There is dissension in the ranks, it seems, and Beth is worried it might grow serious."

"Are you feeling up to dealing with that sort of drama?" Niall asked in a careful tone.

Gyda nodded, then tossed him a feral grin. "It might feel good to wade in and set some people straight. Perhaps knock a few heads about." She sighed. "It might be nice to focus on someone else's troubles for a while."

"By all means, then," Niall said briskly. "Let's go back to the village and see if we can round up Turner and Harold."

Gyda looked between them. "Thank you both," she said quietly. "For everything."

Kara rocked back as her friend unexpectedly launched herself at her. "Oh, Gyda," she said as the other woman's arms tightened around her. "You are family. You know we'll always do anything we can for you."

Chapter Two

"Gyda, I don't think we can go in there." Kara grasped her friend's hand as they stood in Bedford Street, staring at the chaos that was spilling out of the Waif's Wardrobe.

They had arrived in London the day before. Gyda had sent Beth a note straight away, and an answer had arrived quickly, inviting them to come for a tour of the charity this morning. Niall had decided to let them go without him, choosing instead to take Harold to visit Lord Stayme in Berkeley Square.

"Of course we can." Gyda started to push through the crowd.

"I'm not sure we should," Kara objected. "Clearly something has happened here."

"That's why we *should* go in," Gyda said, still moving. "Beth was worried something untoward would happen—and it clearly has."

It was hard to argue the point. People gossiped in the street as several crying women stood on the stairs leading into the charity. One woman had descended into hysterics. She screeched and moaned as a group gathered around and tried to comfort her. Gyda moved past without sparing the woman a glance, and Kara, afraid to lose her friend, moved in her wake.

The entry hall lay quieter, but no less crowded. Gyda approached a gentleman standing quietly, listening while another spoke to the gathered volunteers, encouraging calm. "Beth Williams," Gyda said to him. "Can you tell us where to find her?"

The gentleman gestured toward a long, open room to the right. "She was in the back, watching the activity outside, when last I saw her."

"Thank you," Kara told him as Gyda moved off in the direction he'd indicated.

"Beth!" Gyda called, moving past tables, crates, and walls posted with paper schedules and lists.

The girl, tears streaming down her face, turned. Relief flooded her expression when she saw them, then her face crumpled.

Gyda caught the girl in her arms as she started to sob. "Beth! What is it? What's happened?"

Kara smoothed a hand over the girl's pale head. "Are you all right, Beth? Have you been harmed?" Beth's answer was garbled and beyond comprehension, but she shook her head. Kara glanced out the door where she had been standing—and stiffened. "Beth! Is that—?"

"What?" Gyda demanded.

Kara looked again. *A body,* she mouthed to Gyda over Beth's head.

"What? Whose?"

Kara noted the small collection of sober people standing to one side of the figure stretched out on the ground. "A woman," she said. Her skirts were spread out over the lawn.

Beth started to sob again.

A man bent over the fallen figure. He touched the dead woman's hand, then leaned in to examine her head. When he straightened and stood, Kara gasped. "Gyda, it's Sergeant Landover, the man from the coroner's office!"

They had met the coroner's assistant when their friend Josie Lowe, one of London's most famous music hall performers, had been accused of killing her patron.

"Go and speak with him," Gyda urged. "See if you can get some answers while I help Beth calm down."

Kara hesitated. Landover had not understood—or entirely approved of—their involvement in Josie's case. Then, Kara had possessed both the personal connection and an ally in her friend, Inspector Wooten. Now she had neither. Nor was she eager to involve either herself or her makeshift family in another case of murder and mayhem. But Gyda was making shooing motions with one hand, while patting Beth's back with the other. Heaving a sigh, Kara stepped out into the garden.

It must have been a place of tranquility, before being touched by death. A green lawn stretched out, all the way to the back of a church ahead—and Kara realized this must be part of St. Paul's churchyard. She approached gingerly, waiting for the sergeant to notice her. The woman's body lay near a bench and a border of lilies. Oddly, there was a head of cabbage resting nearby. Kara's gaze moved on—and she started when she saw a large, pointed piece of iron lying beyond it, bearing an obvious coat of blood— and other substances she would rather not identify.

As if he'd heard her indrawn breath, Sergeant Landover looked up. "Miss Levett," he said, obviously surprised, but then he flushed. "I mean, Your Grace." He glanced behind her, as if looking for someone. "What are you doing here? Don't tell me you are connected with this victim, too?"

Kara could not help but glance down at the poor woman. "Sergeant Landover," she said with a nod. "No. Nothing like that. Gyda and I are friends with one of the volunteers here. We were invited to tour the place this morning, and found … all of this." She frowned at him. "But what are you doing here alone, Sergeant?" She glanced at the group gathered a short distance away, but they were a mixed bunch that looked like people associated with the charity, not anyone of an official capacity. "I thought the police were meant to summon the coroner? Shouldn't Scotland Yard be here?"

"They are, after a fashion. I am still training with Scotland Yard. It's been thought I would benefit from shifting among departments and working with different levels of officers. I am following Everett Frye at present."

Kara made a face.

"Yes. I gather the detective feels quite the same about you."

"Oh, yes. Me. A woman who had the audacity to discover one of his cronies was working to bring down the monarchy." She rolled her eyes.

"Quite."

"Well, where is the detective? I shall be sure to avoid him."

Landover looked uncomfortable. "A volunteer found the body this morning. The charity summoned a constable, who took stock and reported to Scotland Yard. The case was assigned to Frye."

Suddenly, Kara understood. "And he sent you to act as both police and coroner's assistant. How efficient." She shook her head. "While he, no doubt, enjoys a leisurely breakfast at Carlisle's?" It was a café frequented by the men from the Yard.

Landover's silence told her she was right on all counts.

"I must assume you will be calling an inquest," she said, gesturing toward the heavy iron object. "Foul play seems obvious."

"Yes. I'm not sure where to hold it just yet. I'll need to find a space big enough."

"The Screaming Eagle," she told him. "It's not far, and it's been used for inquests before."

"Thank you."

For a moment, she thought he would ask how she knew that, but she glanced down at the body again. "The poor girl. So young."

"And this is not her first encounter with violence."

At her questioning gaze, he knelt and pulled the woman's hair away from her face. A thick scar ran from her cheekbone and angled to just beneath her ear. "That is no small injury." His gaze moved to the large wound at the back of the girl's head as he stood again. "Nor is this."

Kara's gaze hardened. "I hope you will find justice for her, Sergeant."

"I mean to," he promised. "In any case, it might be an easy enough task, according to the volunteers that work here. Miss Glynn Foulger was her name, and she apparently had an ongoing feud with another of the volunteers at the Waif's Wardrobe. A man who is a cobbler, by trade." He glanced significantly at what Kara assumed was the murder weapon.

She frowned and looked at the iron implement again. It was over a foot long, with a straight, heavy shaft, a base on one end, and a top that curved into a point that reached out to one side. She tilted her head—and then she saw it. "Oh! A cobbler's shoe form? It is hard to recognize when it is not standing up."

"It was definitely used to kill her." Landover sighed and pulled a small notebook from his coat. "I have to ask a few questions of the people who run the place, and I really should not move Miss Foulger until I speak with the woman who found her—but she is inside, trying to gather herself."

"A young girl? Blonde hair?"

"Yes." He looked up, questioning.

"I believe that is Beth Williams. She is a friend. She was the one who invited us to come to tour the charity. I'll see if she is ready to speak with you, if you like."

Landover eyed her, his lips pursed. "You have a varied host of friends, Your Grace."

Kara's mouth twisted. "You have no idea, Sergeant." Turning, she went back to the workroom, where Beth had indeed calmed and was speaking quietly to Gyda.

Kara took her hand. "I'm so sorry about your friend, Beth. The sergeant says that you found the body?"

Blinking back tears, Beth nodded. "I can't believe Glynn is gone. She was a good woman. She really cared about the work we do here." Her voice lowered to a whisper. "She was very kind to me when I started here."

"I remember that you mentioned her in your letters," Gyda said.

"Yes." Beth glanced back. "At first, I just came and did piece work, here in the workrooms. I met many of the volunteers who sew, or craft garments, boots, and gloves—all the things the poorest in the city might be doing without. It was Glynn who encouraged me to apply for a position as a distributor." Beth gave a little curve of a smile. "At first, I thought it was because I was far from the skilled needlewoman she is." Tears welled again. "Was."

"So you applied for a different position in the charity?" Kara asked, hoping that talking would help.

"Yes. Distributors are chosen for different sections of the city, or for different cities, if we have enough donations to send out to them. Glynn convinced me I would be good at it because I live at Lake Nemi. She knew it was close to Covent Garden, and that I meet a lot of women of different stations at the club. And she knew I was friends with some of the flower girls who come to buy their flowers at the Garden." Beth looked anxiously between Kara and Gyda. "Distributors have to be both known and trusted by the poor in their districts."

"Anyone who knows you trusts you, Beth," Gyda said reassuringly. "I'm sure you do a grand job of it."

"I hope so," Beth whispered. "I truly enjoy the work. I like the people who help in the charity, and I feel like I am truly making a difference." Her spine straightened. "You can scarcely credit it, but often I have to convince the needy to accept our offerings. They fear the ties or obligations that might come with accepting help. But they are learning that I—and the Wardrobe— can be trusted."

"Good for you, Beth," Kara said stoutly.

"I'm so proud of you," Gyda said, giving the girl a quick, fierce embrace.

"Glynn sounds like she was a lovely friend," said Kara.

"She ... she was."

"The best thing you can do for her now is to answer Sergeant Landover's questions. Once he has the information you can give him, he can hold his inquest and the police can begin to track down her killer. At the least, we can give her justice."

Beth nodded, blinking back tears again.

"Shall I bring him in here to you?" asked Kara.

"No. He wished to speak with me there, where I found her." Beth gripped both of their hands. "I can do it, with you helping me."

Together, they stepped out into the churchyard. Beth's steps slowed as they approached the spot where Glynn Foulger lay, but Sergeant Landover was busy speaking with one of the men from the nearby group.

Approaching middle age, the other gentleman wore his dark hair cropped close and his beard neatly trimmed. He looked solemn and sorrowful as he answered the sergeant's questions. "Their relationship was definitely contentious," he was telling Landover. "Anyone who worked here in Bedford Street can attest to that."

"He speaks of the cobbler?" Kara whispered to Beth.

The girl nodded. "Yes. That's Mr. Royston talking to the coroner's man. He runs the everyday workings here at Bedford Street. He's talking about John Yardley. Glynn didn't like Yardley at all. She knew him from before, from when she first came to London. She told everyone that he should be run out of the Wardrobe." Beth frowned. "I knew they didn't get along, but I never would have thought that he could—" Shivering, she turned away from the sight of her friend.

"And who is that man?" asked Gyda, gesturing. "The one standing just beyond, watching everyone with that sour, suspicious look on his face?"

Trying to act casual, Kara glanced over to see the man listening to the other two speak. He was of average height, but broad in the chest and in the face. His hair was mostly gone, cut close to his head. His clothes were decent, but not fashionable, and he did indeed wear an unpleasant expression, as if he smelled something that had curdled.

Beth looked over, then quickly away again. "That is Mr.

Jephson. He is one of the board members. He comes sometimes, to check up on how we are doing."

Royston was still speaking with the sergeant. "Miss Foulger lodged a complaint against Mr. Yardley, with the board of directors of the charity."

"You are a member of the board?" asked Sergeant Landover.

"I am. I was there when Miss Foulger accused the man of harassing her."

"Harassing her? In what way?"

"Following her. Threatening her. Leaving nasty notes posted around the building here and in Covent Garden, where she sold flowers during the day. The final straw came when he kicked in her stand at the flower market. Destroyed it utterly." Royston shook his head. "It was a mistake, though, as it was the property of the farmer who employed her. He raised a fuss with the police and they actually investigated it. Constables came around here, even spoke to other members of the board. That was the last straw. I had to revoke Yardley's membership and ask him to leave the charity."

Beth gasped. "I didn't know that. I knew he hadn't been about the last few days, but no one knew he wasn't coming back."

"He was angry when I spoke to him, to be sure," Royston said, "But I never expected … this."

"He hasn't cleared out his spot," Beth said suddenly, loudly enough to be heard by the sergeant. "His leathers, some of his needles and awls and things. He normally left some of his tools and equipment here, at his station."

"Did he leave a shoe form there, among his things?" Landover asked with a glance toward the one lying nearby.

Eyes wide, Beth nodded.

The sergeant turned to Royston. "Is it still there?"

"I don't know, but I'll go look," the man answered grimly.

"I'll go with you," Landover told him. "I want to see his station for myself." He glanced over at Beth. "Can you wait here for me, miss?"

"We'll let her sit over on the bench at the far end of the churchyard," Gyda said.

The sergeant raised a brow. "So, you are here, too, Miss Winther? I should have guessed."

If Landover had been disapproving of Kara when last they had met, he had been utterly flummoxed by Gyda. Kara bit back a smile. Her friend often had that effect on people—and it was only one of many reasons to love her.

"It's your lucky day, Sergeant," Gyda said with a grin.

"Miss Williams is understandably upset," Kara said. "We'll sit with her until you are finished."

The sergeant nodded and set off after Royston. Mr. Jephson followed silently in their wake.

Beth willingly went to settle on the farthest bench. She raised shaking hands to her mouth. "I heard Glynn shouting at John Yardley. I heard her tell him he was not fit to be around vulnerable women and girls."

"Do you know where this Yardley lives, Beth?" asked Gyda.

Beth shook her head. "No. I think he works in a shop on the Strand." She looked between Kara and Gyda. "Will you be in London for a while, do you think? Or do you plan to return to Scotland straight away?"

"We meant to stay in any case, Beth, but we will most definitely stay as long as you need us. Perhaps—" Kara broke off as Sergeant Landover and Mr. Royston returned. She looked, but Jephson had not returned with them. "Was it there? The shoe form?" she asked.

Landover shook his head. "No. We must assume the one that killed the young woman is Yardley's." He bent to speak gently to Beth. "I know it is difficult, miss, but would you come over to have another look at Miss Foulger with me?"

Clutching Gyda's hand, Beth nodded.

"Look carefully, miss," the sergeant said as they looked over the young woman's form. "Is the body situated now as you found it this morning?"

Beth nodded.

"Nothing has been moved? Adjusted?"

"No. I don't think so."

"And the weapon. You saw it just so, early this morning?"

"Yes." Beth gestured. "And the cabbage." She frowned suddenly. "But where is her bag?"

Landover paused. "Bag?"

"Glynn always carried a bag over her shoulder and across." Beth mimicked the fit. "She always had a sewing project going for the charity. Smocks, usually, for the younger girls. Her smocks were prized by those who received them."

"It's true," Royston chimed in. "Miss Foulger was a talented seamstress." He glanced over his shoulder as his name was called. "Excuse me for a moment." He walked back toward the charity building.

"Was Miss Foulger's bag there this morning?" the sergeant asked Beth as Royston headed away.

"I don't think so." Beth frowned. "I'm trying to remember, but it was such a shock, finding her like that. I could scarcely breathe. My ears were buzzing. I went cold all over and nearly fainted."

"It's all right, Beth," Gyda said soothingly. "Just close your eyes and think about what you saw."

Scowling, Beth obeyed. "No. It wasn't there. And it should have been. Glynn would have been coming from there." She pointed at the church.

"How do you know that?" asked Landover.

"Her stall is not far from the front of St. Paul's. It's just outside the flower building. She often closed up for the day, then cut through the church and yard and came in the back over here. She always sewed during the slower times of the day. She had that bag with her nearly always."

"What did the bag look like?" asked the sergeant.

"It was blue and had every sort of flower embroidered along

the edges, like a garland. It was her own work. One of a kind. She would have had it with her," Beth said decisively. "She was working on a special smock, one that I meant to give to one of the girls in my district."

"Special in what way?" asked Kara. She realized she was asking questions that the coroner's assistant should, and sent Landover an apologetic look.

"Glynn always added something special to her smocks. A little surprise. She always put it on the inside, just under the buttonhole for one of the straps that went over the shoulder. Just a little bit of embroidery. It wasn't always the same. A flower. A star. A bird. A boat. A sun. Just a pretty little secret that no one else would know about, to make them smile when they saw it." Beth's lip trembled. "She was making one for me to give to a flower girl who is often hanging about the Garden or in the streets between here and Mayfair. Lily, her name is. Glynn was going to embroider a lush, flowering lily inside the smock for her."

"Did Miss Foulger also have a dedicated spot inside the charity?" asked Landover. "Might the bag be there?"

"She did." Beth's eyes widened. "And I didn't think to look. I only just noticed she didn't have it."

"Will you show me her space?"

"Of course."

They all followed as Beth led them inside. She bypassed the long tables and headed for a corner, where a stuffed chair sat next to a table that held a lamp and several piles of fabric. "Glynn sat here to work. She always said she had enough of an uncomfortable perch at the market. When she came in here in the evenings she wanted to be at ease, both in her friends and in her seat."

"Did she come here every evening?" asked Landover.

"Not every evening, but most, I would say."

"Did you come as well, Beth?" asked Gyda.

"Yes. We both came often. There is always so much work to be done—sewing, pressing, packing. And the company was fun and lively while we worked. Some ladies just came in to socialize while they knitted socks or scarves. But even the older ladies pitched in when we had a shipment to get ready to send out to one of the other towns."

"I don't see a bag like the one you described," the sergeant said, walking around the chair and lifting the folded pieces of fabric to look between them.

"No. It's not here," Beth agreed. "But I don't understand why she didn't have it with her."

"Perhaps the killer took it," Kara suggested.

"But why? She wouldn't have had anything valuable in it."

"Perhaps the killer didn't know that." Landover shut his notebook with a snap. "Is there anything else you can tell me, Miss Williams?" he asked. "Anything that could explain what happened to your friend?"

"No." Beth hesitated. "Do you truly think Mr. Yardley killed her?"

"I think I'd like to speak with him," the sergeant said non-committally.

"I can help with that, I believe," said Mr. Royston as he approached again. "I have addresses on file for most of our volunteers. If you would care to step into my office, sir?"

"Yes. Thank you." Landover turned to Beth. "Thank you, Miss Williams. You have been extremely helpful."

Beth blushed.

"I'd like to send a message to the coroner's office," the sergeant said as he left with Mr. Royston. "I need to arrange for the transport of the body ..."

Beth's shoulders drooped as the men moved out of range.

Kara stepped in to rub her arm. "Perhaps you should come to stay with us at Bluefield for a few days."

"Thank you." Beth sighed. "But I think I just want to go back to Lake Nemi. I want to curl up in my own bed and just—"

"Have a good cry?" asked Gyda softly.

Kara knew that her friend understood exactly what Beth was feeling.

"Yes." The girl squared her shoulders. "And then I'll get back to work. Glynn believed in the work we do here. The best way to honor her is to continue it."

"I'll go with her and spend the night in my rooms at the club, if you don't mind going back alone?" Gyda asked.

"Of course not." Kara smiled at Beth. "Let's meet in a few days. Perhaps we can organize a gathering to honor your friend and bring attention to the charity?"

"Oh, yes." Beth brightened a little. "I would love that."

Kara and Gyda placed Beth between them and walked her through the crowd gathered in the entry and in front of the building. Murmurs of comfort and sorrow followed them. Kara saw Gyda and Beth into a hack, then turned to walk down the street to where her coach waited. She'd nearly reached it when a young girl crossed the street and stopped just before her.

"Miss? I saw ye come from the Wardrobe building. Is it true? Did someone snuff out Glynn Foulger?"

Kara paused, wary. The girl was on the cusp of womanhood, blonde and blue-eyed, and she would have been pretty, had she not been in dire need of a bath, a hairbrush, and clothes that were not too small. Kara understood Beth's urge to help. She felt it herself, but she also had the experience to know just how dangerous street urchins could be. "It is true. Did you know the young woman?"

"Aye. I liked her well enough. The rest o' the flower girls liked her, too." The girl gave a very adult shrug. "Not everyone did, though."

"That's something you could say about nearly anyone," Kara replied carefully.

"I s'pose," the girl said, after a moment's consideration.

"What's your name?" Kara asked her.

"Lily. What's yers?"

"Kara." With a mental sigh, she threw caution to the wind. "Do you need a place to stay, Lily?" Perhaps Lake Nemi had an open room she could let for the girl until they got something permanent sorted out.

"Nah. I got rooms with my sister." Glancing around, the girl leaned in. "Listen, if ye got friends in the Wardrobe, ye should warn 'em ter keep their eyes peeled."

"Why?" Kara asked, startled.

"Word is, they mean to pin it on Yardley, aye? Well, I heard he didn't do it." Lily shrugged again. "So, better to be careful, eh? If a killer is to be left loose."

Kara started to ask more, but the girl glanced around, gave her a nod, and ran off.

For a long moment, Kara stood still on the pavement. She looked back toward the charity building, weighing her options. In the end, she decided to send Landover a note telling him about the girl's warning. She and her little family had experienced enough excitement, suffered their share of losses. The last thing she wanted was to get any of them involved in another murder investigation.

Chapter Three

NIALL AND HAROLD returned to Bluefield before Kara and Gyda. Not so surprising, as they arrived in Berkeley Square to find Lord Stayme was packed and ready to return with them for an extended stay. The viscount was Niall's mentor, and also the closest thing he'd had to a father figure during his formative years.

"He started making preparations as soon as you sent word of your return." Watts, the viscount's butler, had boxes and a portmanteau waiting in the entry hall. "His contacts have all been notified, as well as the couriers. You should likely warn your duchess that there will be a good deal of traffic in and out of Bluefield, what with all the buzzing between the French, the Russians, and the High Porte."

Stayme came down the stairs, shoving files into a bag. "They are all pretending the issues revolve around religious protections, but it's not true. This escalating situation is about British commercial interests and European balances of power." The old man shook his head. "We must prepare. There is a massive amount of work to be done. I might as well do it where I can see the lot of you in between dispatches."

They packed the viscount and his things into the carriage, Harold chattering all the while. The boy asked Stayme's advice on what his next automaton project should be.

"Well, what are you studying right now?" the old man asked.

"Mathematics, mostly," Harold replied. "And while they help with the construction of the designs, they don't exactly serve as inspiration."

"What's been occupying your mind, then, boy?" Stayme actually looked up from his file to watch Harold with interest.

"You mean, besides cherry crumble and beating his young friend Tom at golf?" teased Niall.

"Yes. Besides those. Neither seen likely to make a good automaton."

Harold cocked his head. "Actually, I could create a golfing figure. I hadn't considered that. Wouldn't Tom laugh if I could make it resemble him?" He frowned. "I don't think I've skill enough to manage his likeness. Maybe Kara could, though. Perhaps I'll put that idea aside for a while."

"If I didn't know any better, I'd say you've already found an idea," Stayme remarked. Reaching over, he tapped the boy on the head. "What is brewing in there, eh?"

"Well, I do have an idea, but I don't want to upset Gyda with it."

"What is it, Harold?" Niall asked.

"It's just … there's an owl that rests in the woods at the priory, just past the walled garden. Have you seen it?"

"I know I've heard it," Niall said wryly. "It's not shy, especially during the late hours."

"It's a long-eared owl," Harold said, pointing his fingers above his head "That's what gave me the idea, at first. I would like to make the ears swivel, like it's following a sound."

"An owl could be a complicated project, depending on what you would like it to do," Stayme said. "Extended wings, perhaps?"

"I should like to try. I think the effect would make everyone stare," the boy said eagerly.

"Why would Gyda object?" asked Niall.

Harold's face fell. "Ailsa said owls are spirits of the dead. She thought it might be Lord Charles, hanging about after Gyda."

"That's just superstition," Niall told him.

"You don't think it could be Lord Charles?"

"I would think it highly unlikely. Lord Charles was a curious, intelligent man with a keen interest in creation. Finding himself in the afterlife, I can only imagine he would set out to explore and investigate everything, not hang about the priory."

Harold looked much struck. "You are right. He would. In any case, I spotted the owl several times in the trees over the queen's dig. It was eerie. Like it was watching all the activity."

Harold referred to the Bronze Age burial site that had been discovered deep in the woods on Niall's new estate. He had invited experts from the Hunterian Museum in Glasgow to take over the excavation, but everyone from the priory frequently wandered over to watch the process.

"I thought it might more likely be the spirit of the lady buried at the dig," Harold mused.

"You know, there are other superstitions surrounding owls," Stayme said. "Some people believe they are protectors. When I was a boy, one of the grooms in my father's stables told me that if you walked around the tree an owl was perched in, it would follow you, watching. The bird's head would go around and around until it wrung its own neck."

Harold made a face. "Who would want to do that to an owl? I had heard about them turning their heads full circle, though. That could be an interesting feature." He looked to Niall. "You don't think Gyda would be upset?"

"Not in the least."

"Then I think I will start to design it," Harold said with satisfaction.

"You'll want to do some research into the different types of feathers a long-eared owl possesses." Niall gave a chuckle. "I imagine you will be forging a great many feathers."

"Mr. Blondel might know about that. Or he might know how I can find out." Harold frowned. "It seems like the sort of thing a naturalist would know. Can I come with you to your meeting with him?"

"He would be disappointed if you did not," Niall assured him.

Harold pulled a notebook from his pocket and began to sketch design elements. Stayme went back to his file, but when they reached Bluefield, he offered to help the boy search the library for references.

Niall hung back to direct the servants in the unloading of the carriage. He watched Harold stride into the house, talking fast. Stayme had a hand on the boy's shoulder, and it reminded him of his own youth. He had always been over the moon when the viscount came for a visit. One of his earliest memories was laughing as Stayme bounced him on his knee. He had many other such recollections—kites, fishing, long walks, gruff talks. Stayme had always seemed so mysterious, strong in a completely different way from the Highlanders Niall had grown up with. Elegant, sharp steel versus heavy, thick iron.

But now? Niall watched his mentor slow to climb the steps into Bluefield and found him … not frail, but perhaps fragile. When had he begun to age so quickly?

The thought dredged up an image in his mind. Stayme, grinning, while a dark-haired child with Kara's eyes laughed up at him.

Niall nearly gasped at the resulting swell of visceral longing. Yes, of course he had assumed he and Kara would have children, but this sudden feeling of yearning urgency was entirely new.

He looked to where Turner was giving orders to the footman. The butler was growing older, too. How much joy would it give him to see Kara with a family of her own? To help raise and teach the next generation at Bluefield Park? It would mean everything to Turner—and to Kara, as well.

Niall was seized with a sudden longing for his wife. He wanted to take her upstairs and make tender love to her. He wanted to see her belly grow, wanted to watch her with the curve of an infant's head reflecting the swell of her breast. He wanted to lie in the great bed upstairs with a sleeping child between them, smiling at each other over a slumbering form.

Harold would dote on a baby. Turner would watch over it with care. Stayme would indulge it. Gyda would teach it every manner of mischief.

Oh, how Niall wanted all of it.

He was heading for the stairs inside when he heard the turn of wheels on gravel. Kara's carriage? He spun on his heel and headed back outside.

Now. Now was as good a time as any to begin.

WARMTH SURGED THROUGH Kara as her carriage pulled up before Bluefield Park. She loved the priory and their staff and friends in Scotland, and honestly, she thought she could be happy anywhere, provided Niall was by her side and the friends who had become family surrounded them. But Bluefield Park was where she had grown up, and for some reason, her mother was on her mind today.

She had learned to administer the estate at her mother's knee. With her mother's example, Kara had grown to understand the necessity of fairness and kindness, and the grave responsibility of having staff, tenants, and villagers in the scope of her care. Her mother had taught her the importance of beauty and the beauty in making others feel comfortable and valued. She'd showered her with affection and shared her love of sponge cake and reading. Catriona Levett had taught Kara about grief and bereavement, as well, when she'd grown ill and died when her daughter was just eleven years old.

Kara blinked back sudden tears. She hadn't cried for her mother in years. She let surprise chase such sad thoughts away when Niall came striding out of the house to meet her.

"I thought you would still be in Town," she said, stepping

down, then flushing as he took her up and swung her around. "Did you not find Stayme at home?"

"Oh, we found him—already packed and ready to return here for an extended stay," her husband said with a grin.

"Oh, good." She peered toward the house. "Where is he? Where is everyone, for that matter?"

Niall began to tick off the list. "Stayme and Harold are busy in the library. The footmen are unloading and unpacking. Turner went to warn the kitchen about our unexpected guest." He looked over her shoulder. "But where is Gyda?"

Kara sobered. "There's been an incident—"

He stopped her with a kiss. "No. Shh … No incidents. No worries. Everyone is busy at the moment—and I mean to occupy your time for a while." Taking her hand, he pulled her toward the house.

Kara hesitated. "Niall, I really should write—"

"Let it wait," he urged. Lifting her hand, he kissed it. "How often do we get a free moment together during the day?"

She shivered. The heat of his mouth sent a fire racing through her veins. "You're right." Grinning, she lifted her skirts and hurried toward the stairs at his side.

They made it to her room without spotting a soul, but when he eased open the door, they both heard her maid humming to herself in the dressing room.

Niall closed it again. "My room," he whispered.

It was blessedly empty. Niall let her go long enough to lock the door behind her, then crossed to lock the door that connected to her room. She laughed at his expression as he stalked toward her. "What has got into you?"

"You have," he answered, his tone gone low and rough.

He moved his mouth to her wrist, and she shivered.

"You are in my heart, my mind, my very blood, Kara. You have filled my life with a happiness I never expected to have, and I am so incredibly grateful."

"We've been so lucky," she whispered.

"And I say a prayer of thanks every day. But earlier, I watched Stayme and Harold together, and I realized there is one more thing I want."

Desire, excitement, and worry struck her like forked branches of lightning. "A son," she whispered.

"A child," he corrected her. "Boy or girl, I don't care. Either would be a joy to add to our family." He touched her face. "You will be such a warm and loving mother. So different from my own. I can't wait to see it." He sobered. "Watching Stayme today, after these weeks away, I was struck by the changes in him."

Kara understood. She'd had to face the same realizations about Turner. Both men were growing older. She reached for Niall, trepidation spiking. "I'd thought perhaps, by now ..."

"No, no. I don't want you to worry. You said yourself that it took your parents several years before your mother got with child." He grinned. "I'm just proposing that we work a little harder to put the odds in our favor."

Kara's mouth twisted into a grin. "Perhaps we just need practice."

He laughed. "Now that sounds like a sensible course of action." Niall swung her into his arms and headed for the bed—only to pause as a knock sounded on the door. "Ignore it," he whispered.

But the knocking came again, louder.

"Your Grace," Turner called, "there is a man downstairs. He insists he must see the duchess."

"Tell him to come back another day," Niall said loudly.

"The man *insists* he must speak with her right away," Turner said, the apology clear in his tone.

Niall shot her a quizzical look, but Kara merely shrugged. "Did he give his name, Turner?" she asked.

"He says he is Mr. John Yardley and that the matter is urgent."

Gasping, Kara wiggled out of Niall's arms. Going straight to the door, she threw it open. "Where is he?"

"I put him in the morning room."

"Good. There is only the one door to that room. Post a couple of our men outside it, Turner. Tell the visitor that I'll be down presently. Do *not* allow him to leave that room." She glanced back at Niall. "Send a message to Wooten. Tell him to get out here, right away."

"Kara," Niall said darkly, "who is in the morning room?"

She gave him a sheepish look. "I did try to tell you."

"Who, Kara?"

Her shoulders lifted. "Well, it's just … he might be a killer."

Chapter Four

"WHAT?" NIALL REARED back. "Kara, no! Not again!"

"I know! I certainly did not go to that charity this morning expecting to find a murder victim."

"Who is this man downstairs? How do you know him?"

"I don't know him. I didn't encounter him in person, and I never heard his name before this morning. Listen, let me explain." She looked to Turner. "Set the men outside that door, then come back. I'll explain everything that happened this morning."

Twenty minutes later, both men were staring at her in confusion.

Niall knew his expression held a level of exasperation with it. "But I don't understand. What the devil is he doing *here*?"

Kara lifted her hands. "I have no idea. I cannot explain it. But I think perhaps I should find out."

"Perhaps you should wait for the inspector," Turner ventured.

Kara shrugged. "We will definitely hold him until Wooten can arrive, but he sought me out. I don't know why, but he might speak more freely to me."

"You will not go in there alone," Niall cautioned her.

"I hadn't meant to. But who knows how long it will take for

Wooten to be found? And then he will have to make his way out here."

Niall sighed. "I admit to a raging curiosity. Let's go and see what he has to say for himself." He pointed a warning finger. "But if he is not entirely rational, I will drag you out of there and have him hog-tied."

"Very sensible," Kara agreed. "Let's go."

They stopped outside the morning room. Two footmen waited there. Niall instructed one of them to slip in behind them, so that he might assist at the smallest sign of trouble. His hand on the latch, he raised a brow at his wife.

She nodded.

Niall opened the door and stepped inside. He ran a careful gaze over the man waiting inside. He was thin, and of less-than-average height. In fact, he stood shorter than Kara. He'd been looking out the window, but now he turned, wringing his cap in his hands. He looked nervous, but not agitated. Dark circles underscored pale-gray eyes. His clothes were a bit disheveled. They were not bespoke, but of a decent quality. It was the boots that stood out, though. They were of fine brown leather with an elastic gusset. Yardley was a cobbler with a good deal of skill, it would seem.

The man frowned at Niall, but made no move toward him.

Looking back, Niall gave Kara a nod. She stepped into the room, and the man at once grew animated. Stepping forward, he halted at Niall's warning glare.

"Are you the Duchess of Sedwick?" the man asked, looking between them.

Kara nodded. "I am. This is my husband, the duke. And you are?"

"I'm John Yardley, my lady, but I ain't no killer! You must help me!"

"Help you? How, sir?"

"I heard of you, you see," Yardley said eagerly. "Young Beth spoke of you, back at the Waif's Wardrobe. We would tell tales, of an evening, all of us taking turns. She told us how you helped your friend, the one what was accused of murder—the singer."

"Miss Josie Lowe, you mean," Kara said with a nod.

"Aye! You told 'em it weren't her, *and* you found the black-hearted git what did the deed." His tone became imploring. "My lady, you must do the same for me! I didn't kill Glynn Foulger. Surely you don't want to see an innocent man hang?"

"Of course not," Kara soothed. "But ..." She looked helplessly at Niall.

"Please, my lady!"

"The correct way to address the duchess is 'Your Grace,'" Niall said stonily.

The man paled. "I'm that sorry. Your Grace, of course. It's just, I heard the police mean to pin Glynn's murder on me. I don't think anyone from the Wardrobe will speak up for me." His face twisted and his tone grew bitter. "That is all down to Glynn, herself. She turned them against me. But that don't mean I killed her. I didn't! I need someone to believe me, and you have influence, Your Grace. Power. The police might believe you, the same way they believed you when you helped your friend."

"The situation with Josie was entirely different," Kara began.

"I know! You knew her. You felt safe vouching for her. I want the same, but I don't have no one. I thought, if I could just plead my case to you, you might see your way to helping me."

Kara looked at Niall.

"From everything my wife heard, the victim despised you," Niall said coldly.

"She did." Yardley dropped his gaze. "And not without reason. I made mistakes. I admit it." He looked up, his eyes wide and earnest. "But I am a changed man. I turned myself around. I do good now. I make a difference with people who just need a caring hand. I'm not the same as the man Glynn knew in the past."

"Miss Foulger believed you should not be allowed to work near the vulnerable women the charity helps," Kara stated baldly. "Why? What made her think so?"

"Because of what I did, back when I first met her." Yardley looked miserable.

Kara and Niall waited.

The man sighed. "I'm a cobbler, by trade. I work in a shop just off the Strand. I met Glynn Foulger when she first moved to London. She worked for a seamstress just a few shops down. One of the other girls in the shop—Joan—I was courting her. That's how I met Glynn. We would all go out for a pint or two in the evenings, sometimes."

"What happened?" asked Niall.

"I let myself go too far on the drink," Yardley admitted "I started drinking more than a pint or two. Much more. *Stupid.*" He snorted. "I didn't have the coin for it. And it sharpened my temper. Something fierce, it sharpened it. My girl, Joanie, she tried to tell me to lay off it."

"I imagine you didn't take it well?" Kara asked.

"No. What man ever did? I was a beast about it. One night Joanie tried to stop me ordering another, and I ..." He faltered. His shoulders drooped, but he drew a deep breath and straightened. "I struck her. Hard. Right there in the pub, in front of everyone."

Kara closed her eyes.

"God, the shame of it," Yardley whispered. "It struck me right away. But I was drunk and I wanted to be even more so, and I couldn't back down. So I hit her again. It was Glynn who stopped me. She flew at me and knocked me on my arse. Others backed her up, and I was run out of the pub. Oh, I was furious."

"And embarrassed," Niall interjected.

"Aye." Yardley drew a breath. "I went to Joanie's rooms and waited outside for her. I was still drunk as a lord, but that's no excuse for what I did to that lass." He frowned. "I don't even remember it, to be honest. But I saw Joanie the next day. What I had done." He swallowed. "That's when I knew. I couldn't handle the drink. I hated the man I turned into. I went and sat in a church that day, just praying for the strength to do better. To be better."

He paused a moment. "I don't even remember which church it was. I sat there a long time. Eventually, I realized there was a man in the pew next to me. I looked over and realized he'd been there for some time. He just nodded at me. Said not a word."

Yardley grew quiet again, and Niall thought he had become lost in the memory.

"Finally, I spoke to him," Yardley continued. "I told him I never wanted to hurt anyone, ever again. The stranger nodded, like he believed me. *Turn your attention to helping, instead,* he told me. *Heaven knows there are plenty who need it.*"

Niall heard Kara sigh beside him.

"I thought about that for a while," Yardley said. "Then I realized the man had gone. I stood up, I left the church, and I took his advice. I haven't had a pint since. I started to volunteer to help those who are worse off than I am. I started at a soup kitchen in Bethnal Green, but I made my way to the Waif's Wardrobe, where I became the distributor for Jacob's Island." He stopped and looked between them. "Do you know it?"

"It's a rookery in Bermondsey, is it not?" asked Kara.

"It is. It's one of the poorest spots in London. It's so bad, they've started clearing it. They mean to tear it all down, put up something new and shining, no doubt. But I ask you—where are all the people in that place supposed to go? They've no money. God and his angels know the other rookeries are filled, tooth by jowl. Someone must help them." He sighed. "I've done what I can. I talked with a brewery and a tannery, and found a few family men some jobs. But there's so many more that need help. Just someone to care. To try to point them down a better path. I gained their trust through the Wardrobe. I meet more people in need every time I come through with distributions. I can make a difference—for some of them, at the least. Taking away my position at the Wardrobe hurts them as much as me, don't you see?"

"I understand your dilemma, Mr. Yardley, and I commend

you on the efforts you have made," Kara said warmly. "I own several manufactories, forges, and mills, you know. If you can give me a list of names of men who wouldn't mind relocating for a job, I will make inquiries with my managers."

Yardley's eyes widened. "Will you? Yes, yes! I can give you ten names right now. Thank you, my—Your Grace." He paused. "But my case? Do you think you could see your way to helping me? To intervening with the police?"

Niall spoke before Kara could. His wife had a soft heart, and he knew she would have been affected by Yardley's story. "You do know why the police consider you a primary suspect, don't you, Mr. Yardley?"

The man started to wring his cap again. "I know Glynn and I had our differences—"

Niall interrupted him. "Your shoe form was used to bash her head in, Mr. Yardley."

"No!" The man's eyes widened in shock. Faltering, he grabbed the back of a nearby chair. "Never say such a thing!"

"My wife saw it herself, lying next to the young woman, still covered in blood and brains." It was harshly said. Niall had done it on purpose. He watched the man closely.

Yardley slid into the chair. Bending over, he clutched his middle, and then his head. "No," he moaned. He pressed a hand over his mouth for a moment, then looked up, his eyes wild. "I didn't do it, I tell you! Please, you must believe me!"

Strangely, Niall had begun to believe him. The man had been shocked at that revelation. Niall didn't think the cobbler had been faking his reaction.

Kara spoke up. "Mr. Yardley, Glynn Foulger accused you of harassing her. She said you have been following her, throwing things at her windows and knocking on her door at night, trying to scare her. She said you posted crude statements and drawings in the streets around her rooms, around the charity, and in Covent Garden, near her work."

"She said you smashed her flower stall to pieces, to get back at her," Niall added.

Yardley began to look a little wild. Niall stepped closer to his wife as the cobbler fixed his desperate gaze upon her.

"Your Grace, I never did those things you said. I swear to you! I did approach her a couple of times. I just wanted to talk, to explain how I've changed. I wanted her to know I am different now, that she could trust me. But she wouldn't let me close. She just shouted at me." He dropped his head in his hands. "I did get angry. She was stealing my life away without even giving me a chance to explain. But I never did those things you said."

"Who, then?" asked Niall.

"I don't know! I could not have been Glynn's only enemy. She was … testy. Ill tempered. She hated the river, mistrusted men, and forever complained about how loud and dirty London is." Yardley looked up. "You should ask young Beth. They were thick, the pair of them. She might know of someone else Glynn had trouble with." He paused. "Or the flower girls."

"Flower girls?" Kara asked.

"The flower sellers in the streets. They bought their wares from Glenn and were friendly with her, many of them." He looked pleadingly at Kara. "Will you do it, Your Grace? Will you help me?"

She looked to Niall.

He shrugged. "The shoe form is a damning bit of evidence."

"I never touched it, not in days," Yardley objected. "I left my things at my workstation because I meant to appeal to the board of the Wardrobe, ask to be brought back. I spent the last couple of days in Bermondsey, talking to some of the folks I've helped, asking them to speak for me."

Kara straightened. "Mr. Yardley, we have a friendly relationship with an inspector from Scotland Yard. If you will speak to him, tell him everything you have told us here, tonight, then I will do my best to convince them to look for other suspects, for someone else who might have wished to harm Miss Foulger."

Yardley hesitated. "Won't your inspector want to take me

and throw me in a cell?"

A knock sounded on the door, and the other footman poked his head inside. Niall went to him.

"Your Grace," he whispered, "Inspector Wooten has arrived."

"Thank you," Niall said. He turned to Kara and gave her a nod.

"I don't know," Kara said, answering Yardley's question. "But I believe they will listen more closely if you go to them, instead of making them chase you down."

"If you didn't do this," Niall said, "then do not let them cast you in the role of a fugitive."

Yardley considered for a moment, then nodded. "Very well. If you will help me, I will speak to your inspector."

"Good." Niall nodded at the footman in the room. "Please ask Inspector Wooten to step in."

Yardley looked upset. "You called him already?"

Kara crossed to stand next to him. She patted his hand. "Forgive us, Mr. Yardley, but we had no notion of why you might have come, before we spoke. But you have convinced us. I am sure you can do the same with Wooten."

The inspector entered. Kara made introductions and a brief explanation, then Niall took her by the hand and pulled her from the room, allowing Wooten to conduct his own interview.

They waited, and Niall watched, solemn, as Wooten emerged and asked his constable to escort Mr. Yardley to their carriage. "I'll be just a moment," the inspector said, turning to Niall and Kara.

"Shall I send for tea?" Kara asked.

"No, I should get Yardley in as soon as possible. We have men out looking for him." He tucked his ever-present notebook into a pocket. "You did the right thing, calling for me."

"We had no idea what to expect when he just arrived out of the blue," Kara said, lifting a shoulder.

"Yet, surprisingly enough, we found him convincing in the end," Niall added.

"As did I. But there are a few things I would rather ask him in a more formal setting." The inspector sighed. "It is not my case, as I am sure you are aware. And it won't do him any good in Frye's eyes, that he came to you."

"We certainly did not seek to interfere," Kara said, indignant. "Detective Frye is just going to have to get over his dislike and get on with the case."

"He won't like hearing that Yardley asked for your help," Wooten said. "I've told the man not to mention it."

"Well, I made Mr. Yardley a promise. At the very least, I will speak to Beth and see if she has any insight on someone else who might have held ill will toward Miss Foulger."

"I agree, after talking to him, that other avenues should be explored." Wooten paused. "And if I recall correctly, Miss Williams is a shy sort. You might be the best person to question her, but I will ask that you bring me anything you learn from her. I will pass it along."

"Of course." Kara's eyes widened. "Oh! There is one more thing." She told the inspector about her encounter with the girl, Lily.

Wooten looked to Niall. "You will keep an eye out for your duchess? The urchin is right. If Yardley didn't do it, then the killer is still out there."

"You know I will," Niall said. He grinned. "And I'll let her keep an eye out for me."

Wooten laughed. "Just so. It's served you well, so far."

Chapter Five

"MY DARLINGS! AT last you have returned!" The door to Lake Nemi was thrown open by Emelia Nardonne, the beautiful, fiery founder of the place—a spot that served as both a boardinghouse and a club of sorts. It was a large and rambling home where women could live freely and gather to explore topics they were denied access to elsewhere. The members of the club explored literature, science, history, travel, and other forms of learning, without censure, safe within the welcoming walls.

"Good morning, Emelia," Kara choked out through her friend's enthusiastic embrace.

"You stayed away too long," Emelia scolded her. "It has become quite dull around here without you."

"We know better than to believe that," Niall said, returning her tight hug.

"True. There is always something, is there not? Yesterday we had constables in the kitchen because Cook sent threatening letters to old Lady Pemdale's chef, accusing him of stealing her recipe for seed cake. She threatened him bodily harm if he used it again."

"And had he stolen the recipe?" Niall asked, grinning.

"Of course he had. Not that I blame him. Cook's seedcake is beyond compare. But the trouble has made her crotchety. She is stern at the best of times, but we've lost a kitchen maid and the downstairs maid, too, because of her temper." Emelia waved a dismissive hard. "Ah, well. Domestic squabbles are endless, are they not? In any case, we are glad you are back." She jerked her head toward the stairs and the rooms on the upper levels. "And your extended stay in the north appears to have done our Gyda good. She seems much improved." She raised a brow. "And very concerned about poor Beth."

"Yes. The dear girl has had a shock, and Gyda understands the pain of such a thing." Kara glanced toward the stairs. "Has either come down yet this morning?"

"No. Go on up and rouse them, if you will. Drag them down for breakfast before Cook clears the buffet away." With a last wave, Emelia set off. Kara shot Niall a smile and tugged on his hand, and together they headed upstairs.

They found Gyda's room empty.

"She'll be with Beth, then," Kara said.

She was correct. Knocking, they found Beth still clad in her nightshift and curled up in bed. Gyda stood at her wardrobe, tossing clothes at her. "Time to rise," she commanded. "We are going and I do not wish to hear an argument. It will do you good."

"Where are you going?" Niall asked as he followed Kara in.

"I'm taking Beth to Donnelly House, as my guest," Gyda declared over her shoulder. "A long soak will help her feel better."

Gyda was proud to be, to date, the only female voted into the private, very exclusive bathhouse.

"That's a good idea," Kara said. "But Emelia wants you both to come down to breakfast."

"We'll eat at the baths. They serve the best kedgeree in London."

"Will you spare a moment to speak with us first, Beth? We have questions for you—and a bit of news, too."

"News?" Gyda spun around. "Has Scotland Yard tracked the

cobbler down, then?"

"They did," Niall said, his tone full of irony. "After he showed up at Bluefield begging an audience with Kara."

"What?" Beth sat up, her eyes wide. "Are you all right?"

"Perfectly all right," Kara assured her. "We wanted to tell you all about it and see what you think."

"But what did he say?" Beth asked, pulling on a dressing gown. "Was it an argument gone too far? Did he say what happened?"

"He denied everything," Niall said flatly.

"He would, wouldn't he?" Gyda snorted.

"He not only denied killing Miss Foulger, he vehemently declared it was not him who was harassing her. What are your thoughts on that, Beth?" Kara watched the girl closely.

Beth seemed to seriously consider the matter. "Well, Glynn was convinced it was him. She was furious about it—mostly because she was so frightened. She hated going anywhere alone at night, because she said footsteps followed her and figures darted in the shadows. Even locked up tight in her rooms, she wasn't left in peace. Stones or rubbish would come flying at her window at all hours of the night. There would be pounding at her door—but no one ever saw anyone outside it. Then came the notes and drawings." Her face grew red. "Terrible, they were. Mean and … explicit. We found them everywhere. In the streets outside her home, outside the Wardrobe, in Covent Garden. Everyone knew they depicted her."

"How did they know?" asked Niall.

"The scar on her face?" Kara asked.

"Yes. Glynn has always been self-conscious about it, but when the broadsheets exaggerated it … and they were so vile … she was mortified and furious."

"Did she ever catch a glimpse of Yardley actually at any of it?" Niall asked. "Did she see or know anything that made her so certain it was him?" His brows rose. "What about when her cart was destroyed? Were there any witnesses to it?"

"None that I am aware of, but who else could it have been? They were often tussling with each other, and their arguments were long, loud, and full of temper."

"It must have been a relief for her when Yardley was dismissed," Kara said.

Beth nodded. "It was. It was like a weight rolled off her, especially after the Duchess of Rowledge paid to have her stall rebuilt."

At Kara's questioning look, Gyda spoke up. "The duchess and her friend, the Countess of Canfield, are the founders of the Waif's Wardrobe."

"The farmer had blamed Glynn for it all, but the duchess's kindness fixed everything between them," Beth explained.

Thoughtfully, Kara nodded. She wasn't well acquainted with either of the founding ladies, but she thought she might like to be.

"I know Glynn felt good about Yardley being gone, because she felt that the many women who volunteer there were safer." An odd expression crossed Beth's face and she paused a moment. "But, you know, she had begun to fret again in the last few days. She grumbled about the Wardrobe becoming a hunting ground for unscrupulous gentlemen. I thought she was still talking about Mr. Yardley, but could she have meant someone else?"

"Of course she could," Gyda stated. "There's no shortage of men willing to harm women, should they be given the chance."

"I'm beginning to think that another man might be a possibility," Kara said. "And not just because of Mr. Yardley's denials." She told them about her encounter with Lily. "The girl seemed sure that Yardley was just a convenient answer, and the killer might still be unknown."

"Lily is young, but she's no fool," Beth said. "She knows everyone in the Garden and she watches everything. She sees quite a bit for herself. If she said that much, she likely has a reason to believe it."

"Do you think she would talk with us again? Perhaps share what made her think so?" asked Niall.

Beth made a face. "She's a bit skittish, but she might."

"Would she be more at ease if you made the introductions, Beth?" Kara asked.

"Likely she would—" Beth began.

"But not today," Gyda interrupted. "Today Beth is going for a hot meal and a good soak, then she is to meet some of the ladies from the charity to arrange for a wake for her friend."

"Glynn had no family in London, and we were her closest friends. There is no one else to make preparations for her," Beth explained sadly. "Lily moves about the West End most days, selling her flowers, but I can give you a couple of ideas of where to find her. She has several spots that she considers her territory."

Kara made note of Beth's best guesses and thanked her.

"Get dressed and we'll set off," Gyda said when Beth had finished. She paused, though, in the act of closing the wardrobe. Bending over, she picked up a narrow box. "Beth, is this …"

"Yes," the girl answered calmly. "It's the knife you made me."

"I didn't know you got it back," Gyda said quietly. She opened the lid and gazed down on the lovely, curved blade. Kara knew it—she had helped in the design of the knife Gyda had made specially for Beth, in an effort to make her feel safer and less alone when she was new to London.

"Inspector Wooten was kind enough to return it, after the case of Sally Doughty's murder was resolved." Beth sighed. "But somehow, it just didn't feel right to use it, knowing …"

Knowing that it had been taken and used to kill an innocent girl.

Gyda nodded and set the box carefully back into the wardrobe. "We will wait in my rooms until you are ready."

Obediently, Beth stood. Kara went to squeeze her hand before she filed out after Gyda and Niall.

"Have you told her yet, about Rob coming to London?" Niall asked quietly.

"There's been no time for it," Gyda told him. "I thought I might bring it up after she relaxed in the baths."

"It might lift her spirits," Niall ventured.

"Rob should be so fortunate," Gyda said sourly. "After he left without a real word uttered about his feelings?"

"Now, Gyda," Kara scolded. "Do not color Beth's feelings with your own resentments."

"I won't," Gyda said. "I'll tell her, because I think it will be good for her to have something else to think about besides her friend's death. But I also won't hesitate to tell Rob what I think of his treatment of the poor girl. In my opinion, he gives her just enough encouragement to keep her on the hook."

"Personally, I suspect this move has to do with more than just ambition," Niall said. "I believe the pair of them will find their way."

"I hope so," Kara admitted.

Gyda sighed. "I won't get in the way. You are right. We should let them be while they sort themselves out."

Kara started to speak, but Gyda held up a hand. "I will. I promise." She pointed a finger at Niall. "But you may tell Rob McRae that I'm watching him."

Niall laughed. "If that doesn't scare him into behaving, I don't know what will."

"DO YOU TRULY believe that Rob's move has something to do with Beth?" Kara asked as they set out to look for Lily.

Niall considered. "I've never seen him so restless. And I saw something in his expression when I spoke about you and our marriage."

Kara sighed. "They truly did seem to like each other, back when Rob spent time with us in London. But they danced so tentatively around each other."

"Beth was so timid back then. I think Rob wanted to take his time and not alarm her, but I was surprised when he left with nothing settled at all between them. Perhaps he was testing her feelings?"

Kara thought it over. "Beth definitely still asks after him, although she tries to be nonchalant about it."

Niall sighed. "Ah well. They will find their way to each other, if they are meant to." He nudged his wife and shot her an affectionate grin. "We did a fair bit of dancing about, at the beginning—and here we are."

He was delighted when she hopped over to his bench and snuggled in under his arm. "Yes," she said with a sigh of satisfaction. "Here we are."

Niall was relieved when they found the girl, Lily, at the first spot on Beth's list. She was tucked into a corner between the steps of St. George's at Hanover Square and the railing that lined the street. She looked to be doing a brisk business, selling bunches of lush peonies and some late poppies. They waited while several gentlemen made their selections and moved on, then he hung back a little as Kara approached the girl.

"Hello, Lily," Kara said gently. "We met yesterday, outside of the Waif's Wardrobe, if you recall?"

"Aye." Lily's wary blue eyes watched him over Kara's shoulder.

At the same time, Niall was running an evaluating gaze over her. She was a pretty girl and on the cusp of young womanhood—but he thought she was deliberately trying to hide that fact. She needed a wash, and she wore a loose smock with frilled trimmings and a short tweed coat, and had fashioned her blonde hair into long braids.

It was the thought of why she was making such a deliberate effort to look younger that chilled him. She obviously understood the danger to young women alone on London's streets. They could be preyed upon by unscrupulous men or kidnapped by enterprising bawds. Young women were prized by some men who feared the diseases that ran rampant among London's prostitutes. Those men looked for inexperienced or "clean" girls to dally with—and most of them did not care whether the young woman was willing or not.

It was no wonder Lily wished to look like a child for as long as she could. There were plenty of dangers stalking little girls in London, but not so many as lurked for young and nubile women.

"I was hoping to ask you more about what you said yesterday," Kara was saying to the flower seller. "You said you heard that it was not Mr. Yardley who killed Miss Foulger?"

Lily nodded, still watching Niall over Kara's shoulder.

Kara noticed. "Oh, please. Allow me to introduce my husband. Niall, this is Lily. Lily, my husband, the Duke of Sedwick. I promise, we just wish to speak with you. Neither of us means you any harm."

But the girl's eyes had widened. "Sedwick? Then ye're the pair what cleared that music hall singer's name? Found the man that killed her patron and had her set free?"

"Oh. Ah, yes," Kara said.

"And ye're the ones what took young Pip in? Off the streets and right into your own house?"

"Harold," Kara said firmly. "He is my ward now. But yes."

Lily visibly relaxed. "Well, then. I suppose there can be no harm in telling ye what I heard."

"I'm sorry about the loss of your friend, Lily," Niall said.

The girl's eyes turned down. "Thank ye. She was a nice lady. She was making me a smock special. She said she would include a warm jacket with it, fer when I have to wait outside in the nights."

"Wait outside?" asked Kara, glancing around at the busy street in front of the church. "Do you mean you sell your flowers at night, too?"

Lily shook her head and glanced away. "No. I'm not ready to turn to the nights. Not yet. But my sister, she works nights." She looked up quickly to be sure that they understood what she was saying. "Sometimes she has to bring her customers to our rooms, then I get sent outside. I don't mind so much. I got a spot where I tuck in under some stairs. But I don't like the cold. After being out in the weather all day, I like to hole up inside and keep warm in the evenings."

Kara swallowed. So many things in that short recitation stole her breath.

Niall took a seat on the stairs a bit away from the girl. It was like him to want to put the girl at ease. He gave her a kind look. "What did you hear, Lily? About the night Glynn Foulger was killed?" he asked in an encouraging tone. "And from whom?"

"Well, it come from Soot. We call him that because he was one of the city's best skilled chimney sweeps, back when he was smaller. He's grown too big for it now, but he still has soot in all his creases, aye?"

Kara nodded gamely.

"Soot saw something?" asked Niall.

"So he says. He was tucked up for the night in a doorway on the other side of Bedford Street, down further toward Henrietta. He says he heard a commotion and saw a man leavin' the Waif's Wardrobe in the night. The man was in a hurry. Soot thought he looked spooked, even. The bloke looked over his shoulder and stumbled on the stairs as he left the Wardrobe."

"Did Soot know the man?" asked Kara.

"No. He couldn't see him well enough in the dark. But he knew it weren't Yardley, because the man was tall—too tall and thin to be the cobbler."

"Did Soot say anything about what time it was when he saw the man?"

"I told him someone would ask that very question," Lily said triumphantly. "He didn't recall at first, but when I pressed him, he said it were after dark, but before the chime of midnight—and that's as close as he could remember."

"Well done, Lily," Kara said. "You were right to inquire. Did Soot notice anything else?"

"Nah." The girl shook her head. "He turned over and went back to sleep and might never have thought nothing of it, until he heard Glynn was killed that night."

Kara's manner grew careful. "Lily, I know that you might not think highly of the Metropolitan Police—"

"They are not so bad," Lily interrupted. "Some of the constables are protective of the flower girls. They keep bad 'uns from botherin' us, when they can."

"That's a relief to hear," Kara said. "I have a friend who is an inspector with the police. He is helping to gather information about Glynn's murder. I think he would like to hear about what Soot told you."

The girl waved a hand. "Ye're free to pass it on."

"The thing is, he might want to hear it from you, or even from Soot himself."

Niall saw the girl's sudden loss of color, but Kara had already held up a hand. "You wouldn't have to go down to the Yard. I would be happy to be there with you when you speak to him. In fact, I would love to take you all to Dobb's pie shop. You can have a nice, hot meal while you speak with Inspector Wooten."

Lily blinked at her. "I heard tell that you was close with Maisie and her boy. Is it true that you used to run in these streets, as a girl?"

Niall knew the truth about that was complicated, but Kara merely nodded. "I spent a good amount of time in Covent Garden and the surrounding streets, learning some valuable lessons."

Lily nodded in return. "I heard a bit about yer troubles." She shook her head. "None o' the other lords or ladies understand what life is like here." She paused. "I'll talk to yer inspector, then. I'll see if the promise of a hot pie will tempt Soot, but I make no guarantees for him."

"Understood. Why don't you speak to Soot, then send word of when you would like to meet? If you tell Maisie, she'll see that I get your message."

"Aye, then," the girl agreed.

"Lily, Yardley told us that he was not the one who was harassing Miss Foulger before her death. Did you see any sign of what was happening to her, or who might have done it?" asked Niall.

"I saw the broadsheets. They were nasty. I mean, most are not trying to flatter the poor sod they aim to make fun of, but these were … *hateful*."

"And the stalking, the scare tactics used against her—do you think it was Yardley?"

"Well, Glynn thought so. I sometimes wondered how it could be him, since Yardley spent so much time across the river in Bermondsey." Lily gave a shrug. "I more than once wondered if it were the toff that were doing it."

Niall froze and exchanged glances with Kara. "Toff?" he asked carefully.

"Aye. A young one, he is." Lily shivered. "Now, he has a mean look about him, he has."

"Do you mean it was a gentleman who might have had an acquaintance with Miss Foulger?" Kara asked.

"He did. He must have. I rather thought he might be a customer. Perhaps one of the gentlemen who bought Glynn's specials."

"Specials?" asked Niall.

"Oh, aye. Glynn had a knack for it, didn't she? Arranging a bouquet of flowers up something beyond the ordinary. She could pick just the right mix. And she could sew up a ribbon holder for 'em that spruced it up even further. And she could make these little fabric bees and butterflies to add in." Lily shook her head. "Some of the gentlemen considered Glynn's specials to be good luck. They would order them whenever they *specially* wanted to turn a girl up sweet."

"And you think this young gentleman might have been a customer who bought one of her specials?" asked Kara.

"I didn't see him do it, but I couldn't work out how else he might know her. But he clearly did know her—and he didn't much like her, by the looks of it." Lily grimaced. "I noticed him skulking around the Garden, watching her—and with such a sour, twisted face, and a look of hatred in his eyes. He had that look— ye know it, likely. Washed-out red hair, gone too light, and a complexion gone red—most often with temper." She tilted her head, as if asking if they understood.

Niall nodded. "Did you see this man more than once, Lily?"

"Oh, aye. Several times a week, I would see him, hiding behind a cart here, mixing in with the crowd there. Always watching, always clearly wishing her ill."

"You don't know him by name?" asked Kara.

"No. How should I? He never bought from me, that much I know."

"Would anyone in the Garden know his identity?" Niall asked.

"I don't think—" Lily stopped. "Wait, perhaps Jeanette might."

"Jeanette?" asked Niall.

"She's a flower seller, too. I seem to remember her saying a word to that toff and him scarpering off."

"And where can we find Jeanette?" he asked.

"That one's a night girl," Lily said. "She sells her flowers at night, outside the theatres and music clubs. Look for her at the Canterbury. Ye can't miss her. She's got a shape on her to draw the gentleman's eye and red hair that catches the light. She might talk to ye." The girl paused to run an eye over Niall. "But honestly, yer chances would go higher if you went without yer wife."

Kara opened her mouth, then snapped it shut again. "Thank you, Lily. You have been very helpful." She looked at the bucket of peonies the girl had left to sell that day.

Niall saw her reach for her reticule, but he waved her off and pulled a coin from a pocket. "Thank you, Lily. We'll take the lot of your flowers, if you please."

"Can you deliver them to the Waif's Wardrobe?" asked Kara. "They can likely use them for the wake they are setting up for

Glynn Foulger."

"Aye, but it's too much," the girl said, staring down at the gold sovereign.

"Take it," Niall urged. "And don't forget to talk with Soot and set up a meeting with the inspector."

"I shall be sure to," the girl said. She blinked several times. "Thank ye," she whispered. "This will cover our rent for the month. It will mean my sister can stay in, warm and safe, for nights and nights in a row." She clutched the coin tight, then tucked it away. "I'll take these down to Bedford Street straight away."

"Thank you, Lily," Kara said gently. "We will wait to hear from you."

They set out for their carriage as the girl began to gather her posies into one bucket. "It appears we might need an evening out at the Canterbury," Niall said, handing Kara in. He stepped closer when a constable came striding up.

"Your Grace? Sedwick, is it?" the man asked.

"Yes?"

"A message from Inspector Wooten, sir. He wants you down at Scotland Yard, straight away."

Chapter Six

"GOOD MORNING, YOUR Graces." Inspector Wooten met them, not in his office, but in the section of the ground floor where desks were gathered for the detectives and constables who worked all hours of the day and night, dealing with a dizzying number of cases of burglary, assault, prostitution, muggings, and missing persons.

"Good morning, Inspector Wooten," Kara said. She noticed the man looked uncharacteristically tired, and his waistcoat was wrinkled. It was unusual enough to set her thinking. "I hope your wife is doing well?"

"She is well enough, thank you, ma'am," Wooten said with a grimace. "She's all atwitter, what with our oldest girl soon to be delivered of her first child."

"Oh, how lovely. Congratulations," Kara said warmly.

"Thank you. We are suitably thrilled, but my wife is distracted. She won't truly rest until the babe is safely born."

Kara understood the woman's trepidation. Childbirth was a risky business. The numbers for both maternal and infant mortality were high across the nation, but particularly dreadful in London, where still births, infant death, and puerperal fever were all too common.

"Have you discovered something new in the case of Miss

Foulger's murder?" asked Niall.

"Not discovered, exactly. It's more that we've proved an assumption. I hesitated to mention it before, but, having questioned Mr. Yardley, we know more. If you'll come with me?" Wooten beckoned as he started to move in amongst the crowded desks. "It would be better if we finish before Frye comes back."

Kara did not roll her eyes, but it took effort. Detective Frye was an unpleasant man, to say the least. She'd found him to be a misogynist, and quick to pick the easiest path instead of the one that promised to lead to the truth. She suspected from past experience that the man was easy prey for bribes, as well.

Wooten stopped at a particularly messy desk and began to rifle through the piles of notes, files, and greasy fish wrappings. Kara sighed. Of course this would be Frye's domain.

"Ah, here it is." Wooten pulled a long, white object from beneath a newspaper. He handed it to Niall.

Kara sidled closer, but Niall realized what it was before she did.

"The imprint of a boot?" he asked.

"It is," Wooten said. "The constable who looked into Miss Foulger's wrecked flower stall found a footprint amid the wreckage, left in the mix of water, soil, and general dirt of Covent Garden. He was able to make a plaster cast of it before it could be obliterated."

"I hope you recognized him for his excellent work," Niall said, sounding impressed. He raised the cast to peer at the impression of the heel. "What's this?"

"That, I am afraid, is the proof that Mr. Yardley did indeed destroy Glynn Foulger's flower stall," Wooten said quietly.

Kara frowned down at the mark on the heel. "Are those … initials?" Her heart sank. "JY."

"John Yardley," Wooten said with a sigh. "It seems all of the footwear he crafts is marked in the same way, including the boots he is currently wearing."

Ire rose in Kara's chest. "Where is he?" she asked Wooten.

The inspector gestured. "I've had him placed in our holding area. I suspected you would wish to speak with him—and he has specifically requested to see you, Your Grace."

Kara straightened. "Lead the way."

Wooten led them to a tiny closet of a room. It was fitted in the back with a bench. A chair sat nearby, leaving just enough room for Niall and the inspector to squeeze in after the door closed.

Kara took the chair and scowled at Yardley. The little man was in his stocking feet, but he still had his hat, and once again he twisted it as he gazed at her.

"You lied to me, Mr. Yardley," Kara declared. "Straight to my face, sir."

"I know it seems that way, my—Your Grace, but I didn't. Not exactly."

She raised her brow at the man and waited.

"I … It was your man, the duke, what mentioned the flower stall. *You* asked about the stalking and harassing—and I said I never did any of that. And I never did. Not any of what *you* spoke of, Your Grace."

"That's splitting hairs very finely, Mr. Yardley," Kara replied.

"Indeed," Niall said. "You merely lied to me, not to my wife? *That* is your defense?"

"Well, I could not confess to smashing the stall, not if I wanted you to help me."

"So, now you do admit it?" Niall sounded stern. "You did destroy Glynn Foulger's stall?"

Tears welled in the man's eyes. "So help me, I did. I was so blazing angry at her! She would not listen. She refused to believe that I had changed, that I had worked to become a better man."

Kara merely looked at him.

"I know how it sounds, Your Grace." Yardley's head drooped. "When the board agreed to send me packing, I was that distraught. I wanted to swim in a vat of ale. I never wanted to drown my sorrows so bad in all my life. But I knew that would only lead to bigger troubles. So I set out, walking the streets, trying to stomp and bleed out my anger into the very city itself. I must have walked miles, but eventually I found myself in Covent Garden, late at night." He sighed. "I stood there, grieving like someone had died. It was my life that was gone, and there was just one thought in my head. Glynn had destroyed my livelihood, my chance at a better life, and I was gripped with the need to do the same to her. So yes, I confess. I did smash her flower stall. I took out all that anger on it and ruined it completely." He raised his head to meet Kara's gaze. "But I won't confess to the rest of it, for none of that was me."

"You didn't follow her, try to scare her in the dead of night, or post those broadsheets?" Niall's tone was full of doubt.

"I never did, Your Grace." Yardley turned a pleading look toward Wooten. "You must believe me, sir. I vented my anger and frustration on her stall, but I did not harass Glynn Foulger, nor did I kill her. You must keep looking for the man who did!"

Wooten gazed directly back at the man. "Perhaps I would, Mr. Yardley, if I had a direction to focus on. But every time I ask someone who knew Glynn Foulger, it is your name that comes up."

"There must be someone else, for it wasn't me," Yardley insisted. "Speak with her neighbors, mayhap. Glynn was a sharp-tongued woman. She was bound to clash with someone else. Or ask that toff, the one who loathed her so much."

Kara stilled. "Toff? Who do you mean, Mr. Yardley?"

"Well, I don't know his name, do I? I'm not on speaking terms with the nobility, as a rule," he said sarcastically.

Wooten had drawn out his notebook. "A gentleman, you say? Someone who did not care for Miss Foulger?"

"Well, he looked at her like he despised her, sure enough," Yardley said. "I felt a certain kinship with him when I spotted him, I can tell you."

"Where and when did you spot him?" asked Wooten, his pencil busy.

"At the market. It were last week. Just the day before Glynn took her complaint about me to the board. I went one last time, to try and convince her to stop." He paused, casting back. "I came from the west. The nob stood just north of Glynn's stall. He was lurking behind a stack of baskets, staring at her as she was bent over her sewing." He looked at Kara then. "Say what you will about our disagreements, but Glynn was a fine seamstress and created some excellent garments for young girls who sore needed them."

"What did the gentleman look like?" asked Wooten.

Yardley shrugged. "Rich. Dressed to the nines. Hoby boots, I'd wager."

Kara supposed it was natural the cobbler would notice a man's footwear.

"Young, he was," Yardley continued. "A bit younger than Glynn, I'd say. Still spotty with it, across here." He pointed toward his cheekbone. "He had that sort of light hair, red-gold." He made a face. "And a look of powerful hate directed at Glynn Foulger."

"It's not much to go on," Wooten said, tucking his notebook away. "But I will try."

"Does that mean I am free to go?" the cobbler asked hopefully.

"I'm afraid not. Detective Frye will have to be convinced of your innocence before you are set loose."

Yardley slid deeper into the bench. "That don't seem likely."

"We'll do our best," Wooten said. Standing, he held the door for Kara and Niall. "If you recall anything else, be sure to ask for me."

"I'm sorry, Your Grace," Yardley said as Kara stood. "Please, I hope you'll believe me now."

Kara raised a brow. "Are there any other finely split hairs we need know about, Mr. Yardley?"

"None. I swear it," he said fervently.

"Then as the inspector said, we will do our best."

A constable closed the door behind them. Kara noticed several others furtively watching from their desks.

"My office, I think," Wooten said.

Kara and Niall filed after him. They were all silent for a moment after they entered and the door was closed.

"In general, I hesitate to think that Frye is correct about much," Wooten began.

"I hate the very thought," Kara admitted. "But there is still a chance he is not correct about Mr. Yardley. This is the second time this morning that we have heard of a gentleman who watched Miss Foulger with malice. A wealthy man with reddish hair."

Wooten's interest perked. "Do you know who he is?"

"No, but we know whom to ask."

Nodding, Wooten cast a glance toward the door. "Then you had better go before Frye returns. Any information he thinks comes from you, he might be tempted to disregard. He'll hear of this visit, but he'll be satisfied that you were convinced you were wrong about Mr. Yardley. If you learn something to the contrary, then send word straight to me and I'll find a way to introduce it."

"Thank you, Inspector. We will." Kara smiled at the man. "And if you like, I can ask Dr. Balgate to recommend a first-rate midwife for your daughter?"

Wooten had been through enough excitement with them to know of Kara's physician's expertise. His gratitude showed as he smiled back. "Oh, heavens, yes. Thank you. That might go a long way to setting us all at ease."

"I'll send word later today," Kara said. "And we will see what we can find out about this young gentleman tonight."

LATER THAT EVENING, Niall paced the entry hall at Bluefield, impatiently waiting for Kara to come down. He stopped in his tracks when Harold came running from the back of the house.

"Oh, good," the boy gasped, breathing heavily. "I lost track of time. I was afraid I missed you."

Niall eyed the boy's sweaty brow and reddened palms and fingers. "Been at the rope in the gymnasium, have you?"

Bright-eyed, Harold nodded as he shook out his hands. "I can climb up twice and halfway again now before my arms give out." He sobered. "But don't tell Kara."

Niall chuckled. "Lad, you don't have to hide your triumphs from Kara. Nor from me. She'll be proud as Punch to hear how you have improved. And I'll wager she could do as well or better when she was your age."

Harold nodded. "She would do better now, but she insists on climbing in her skirts, complete with all her extra tools and modifications tucked away. She says if she is ever in a situation where she needs to use those skills, that's likely what she would be wearing."

"See? That's just good strategic planning. It's a wise woman— or man—who knows her limitations."

"She doesn't have many," the boy said ruefully. "I should have started my training younger, as she did. I still haven't managed to best her in a fight, and she would have punctured me a thousand times over had we been fencing with sharp foils instead of blunted tips in our lessons."

"Keep at it. It's the only way to learn," Niall said with sympathy.

But Harold dismissed his training woes as he eyed Niall's evening attire with admiration. "I didn't want to miss Kara's finery, but you will give her a run for her money." The boy's expression turned wistful as he ran his gaze over Niall's tailored coat and fine linen, all topping his formal kilt. "I wish I could wear the kilt one day."

Niall hesitated. This might not be the proper time for a serious discussion, but the boy had given him a clear opening. "Actually, it's serendipitous that you would mention it, as Kara and I have been hoping to discuss—" He stopped as the boy's gaze traveled upward and widened in awe.

Niall spun around. His brows rose and his heart rate ratcheted as his wife descended the stairs. Kara always held his attention. She was intelligent and witty. Her heart was as generous as her mind was quick. Her kindness and creativity were so captivating that he sometimes actually forgot how beautiful she was. And then, suddenly, something would remind him.

Something like the picture she presented now, with her gown of rich blue showing off her creamy-white skin. Her shoulders were bare, framed by a bodice of ruched satin that swept across her collarbones. A bejeweled white satin rose adorned the center of the bodice and two more graced a line of white trim near the bottom of her skirts. Another gleamed in her ebony hair. She wore no other jewelry—but she needed none.

"*Cor*, Kara," Harold breathed.

She laughed as she reached the bottom of the stairs. "That might be one of the loveliest compliments I've ever received, Harold, if only because of the look on your face."

"It's meant as such," the boy assured her. "You look beautiful. I just wish I had better words."

"Your words are lovely. They mean as much to me as you do," Kara said.

Niall stepped forward. Catching his wife's eye, he gave her a significant look. "Kara, Harold just told me that he wishes he could wear the tartan one day." He took her hand. "I know this wasn't how we planned to introduce the subject, but …"

She understood at once and glanced between him and Harold. "Oh, but yes. Perhaps now is the perfect time, then."

Niall reached over and firmly grasped the boy's hand. Kara's eyes began to shine with unshed tears as she took the other. They stood there, all three linked as Harold frowned.

"Kara and I have been wanting to ask you something important," Niall said.

Harold stood, stiffly unsure and waiting.

"When you first came to Bluefield, the courts were wise enough to grant Kara's request to make you her ward."

"And I am so grateful," Harold said quickly. "For everything."

"As are we," Niall assured him. "But now that we are married, and our lives are settling into a steadier pattern, we were hoping that you would agree to allow us to make a formal petition to adopt you."

"Adopt me?" Harold whispered. "You want to …" His words trailed away.

"We want you to be our legal son, as you are already ours in our hearts," Kara said, her voice thick with emotion.

Harold blinked rapidly. "I would be Harold Kier?" he whispered.

"Harold Kier," Niall confirmed. "And once you are legally ours, we'll request the clan laird to recognize you as a member of Clan Kerr."

"And I'll be able to wear the kilt? Like you?" Harold looked between them. "I'll be yours? Truly yours?"

"You are already truly ours," Kara said, her tears flowing at last. "But it would be officially legal. If that is what you want?"

The boy threw himself into Niall's arms. "Yes, yes," he said into Niall's chest. "It's all I want."

Kara moved in and Niall wrapped his arms around them both, swallowing back his own tears.

He'd been alone for so long. Before her death, his mother had been remote and self-absorbed. Everyone in their household had been nervously focused on her whims and moods. Stayme's visits had been essential, but few and far between. He utterly and completely understood Harold's longing for acceptance, belonging, and love. His life with Kara and their collected family filled the same empty spaces in him that they did in the boy.

Standing there, his heart and his arms full, Niall drank in the sort of happiness that he'd never thought to possess. He knew that the greatest honor of his life was the chance to be sure his loved ones never felt that hollow, echoing emptiness ever again.

His eyes were closed and his face pressed into the thickness of Kara's upswept hair, but he heard the faint sniff behind them and knew what it was. "Come on, then, Turner. Get in here where you belong, man," he said thickly.

There came a long moment of hesitation, and Niall thought perhaps the butler's strict sense of propriety would keep him from joining them. But just as Kara's head lifted, Turner moved in at the side, where he could encompass all of them in the long reach of his arms.

Kara's head came back down to rest on Niall's shoulder. She heaved a sigh of relief, joy, and fulfilment—and it was the loveliest sound Niall had ever heard. Right then, he vowed to make her repeat it as regularly as he could possibly contrive.

KARA STEPPED DOWN from the carriage into the lively crowd gathered on the Westminster Bridge Road in Lambeth. Crowds were streaming into the Canterbury and gathered outside the music hall as well. It was quite a mix, with gorgeously dressed patrons ascending at the side of workaday Londoners in their Sunday best. Spectators watched the guests flow in. Putting their heads together, they gossiped about who was there, with whom, and what they were wearing. Groups of laughing young men lingered about. Kara peered among them, but didn't see any young, spotty redheads. Street children zipped through the crowds, seeking to lighten the pockets of the unwary.

Straining to see, Kara saw a vendor selling roasted nuts. "There!" she said, leaning closer to Niall and pointing beyond the man's cart. "A flower seller."

"Dark hair," her husband said with a shake of his head. With his height, he had a better view of the scene. "There's another near the corner, but she's dark too, and quite a bit older. Perhaps

Jeanette might have set up inside?"

"Perhaps. Let's go and see." They entered the flow of people entering the grandly decorated lobby. Thick carpet, rich wallpaper, and bright chandeliers lent an air of sophistication to the place. A grand staircase led up to the gallery seats. A flower seller held an armful of roses at the base of it.

Kara's heart sank when she saw the girl's blonde hair. "Do you see any others?"

"No, but let's see if this one can give us any information, eh?"

Taking Niall's arm, Kara let him lead her to where the girl stood, smiling and offering her blooms to the excited theatregoers.

"A pretty blossom for your pretty lady?" she called to Niall.

"By all means," Niall replied, dropping a coin into her hand.

The girl's eyes widened. "For that you may have two, my lady," she said. Her words were directed to Kara, but she simpered at Niall.

"Thank you." Kara buried her nose in the scarlet roses after Niall bowed and handed them to her. Watching over the soft petals, she noted this girl had made no attempt to hide her age or womanly curves—or her admiration of Niall and his generosity. "We thought we would find Jeanette here tonight," Kara said, drawing the girl's attention back to her.

"And so you would, in normal fashion," the flower seller said. "Jeanette is normally fierce protective of her regular spot here, but the daft widgeon agreed to switch with me. And tonight! The night when Charlie Luster is meant to debut his new set!" The girl's eyes sparkled. "The crowd is fair excited about it—and it's left them in a generous mood, I tell you." Suddenly, her brow furrowed. "Now, don't tell Jeanette I said so, if you please. I don't want her reluctant to make the trade again."

"We won't say a word," Niall promised, his hand to his chest. "But where is your regular spot, young lady?"

The girl fluttered her lashes at him. "I'm outside Drury Lane. You may find me there, if you care to attend a more serious performance." She laughed. "Although I wish Jeanette much luck tonight, as it's just another production of *The Queen of Spades*."

"I've heard lovely things said of the performances," Kara said. "Perhaps we will see you there."

"Come sooner, if you care for dramatics, for the word on the street is that the circus has been invited back," the girl said confidingly. "Either way, you must be sure to look for me, should you come to a performance." She waved as they turned to head back outside. "I shall be sure to save the best blossoms for you!"

It took a while for the carriage to cross the river and make its way through London traffic. Catherine Street lay quiet by the time they arrived. Contrary to what one might assume, the theatre faced here, while its back end lay along Drury Lane. Kara took Niall's hand to descend before the theatre and had no trouble in immediately picking out their quarry.

Jeanette lounged beneath one of the arched entrances, leaning against the pillar, showing off her curves and sharing a smoke with an older man in formal black and white. A couple of large baskets sat at her feet, full of blooms, and her red hair shone in the flickering light of the theatre's lamps. The gentleman straightened as they approached, then melted into the shadows.

The girl tossed the cigarillo and took up an armful of blossoms. "Good evening to you," she called out. Her expression turned scolding as they drew closer. "Sir! Surely you must buy your companion a posy, to ease the shame of bringing such a lady as this so late to the performance! Why, you've denied all the gentlemen their chance to admire her and wish they was you!"

Kara smiled at her. "Thank you for the compliment."

"It's true, though, miss. You look a treat. Ah well. I was just about to move into the lobby, as intermission is nigh. They'll all get their chance to see you, then." The girl extended a lovely white rose. "And truthfully, your gown is just crying out for you to carry this, is it not?"

"The perfect accessory. Thank you." Kara watched the girl closely. "You are Jeanette, are you not?"

The girl's practiced smile faded. "Who is asking?"

"I am the Duchess of Sedwick. This is my husband. We've come to speak with you about the death of Miss Glynn Foulger."

"*You've* come?" Jeanette craned her neck to peer past Kara's shoulder. "But where is the constable?"

Puzzled, Kara paused. "Which constable?"

"Braggs? Briggs? I don't recall his name, exactly!" Jeanette's tone was growing more shrill by the moment.

"You've sent for a constable? Tonight?" Kara glanced around the nearly empty street.

The girl took a step back. "No! Not tonight. I mean the constable I talked to! The one I asked for help—*that* constable!"

Niall stepped forward, his hands spread out, palms down. "Stay calm, miss. We are here to help, if we can. What was it you spoke to a constable about?"

The girl stared at him, her eyes wide. "About Glynn Foulger's murder, as you said! I told him I had information the police needed. He listened and thanked me. I told him what I need is protection. What good are thanks? He said he would report in and return, but that was yesterday mornin', wasn't it? I might have been killed half a dozen times over since then, hadn't I?"

Kara exchanged frowns with her husband. "I'm sorry. We didn't realize that you'd already spoken to the police."

"Why do ye think I'm here tonight, instead of at my prime spot at the Canterbury? I'm waitin' on their help."

Kara gave her a piercing stare. "Jeanette, what exactly are you afraid of?"

The girl glanced around, her gaze darting through the shadows on the street. "*Him,*" she whispered. "I'm afraid of him."

Kara reached for patience. The girl's fear seemed real enough. "Beth Williams is our friend. Do you know her? She volunteers at the Waif's Wardrobe. She was close with Glynn Foulger. She is busy arranging a memorial for Glynn, and she asked us to help look into Glynn's death."

Jeanette listened, but said nothing.

"We spoke with Lily this morning—the girl who sells flowers near St. George's. Do you know who I mean?"

Jeanette nodded stiffly.

"Lily told us there is a man—a gentleman—who might have been Glynn's enemy. A young man with red hair. Is that who you are frightened of?"

Jeanette nodded. "I've every reason to fear him, haven't I?" she asked quietly. "He tortured Glynn—and now he's in a fair way to startin' it up with me!"

"He's harassing you?" Niall asked sharply. "In the way he harassed Glynn?"

The girl glanced about again, shifting nervously. "He's begun. And I saw how bad it got." Her expression grew wild. "And what if it were him who killed Glynn? I don't want to die with my head bashed in!"

"We are not going to let that happen," Kara declared. "Listen, let's get you somewhere safe, where we can talk freely."

"I want to talk to the *police*. How do I know what ye say is true?"

Kara drew a breath. "I don't know for sure, but I will tell you what I suspect, Jeanette. The detective charged with investigating Glynn Foulger's death has a suspect in custody. He believes that it was this suspect, Mr. Yardley, who harassed Miss Foulger. Everyone believes that. Even Glynn believed it."

"But I *told* the constable it weren't him."

Kara pressed her lips together for a moment. "It may be that the detective doesn't want to hear any evidence that might cast doubt on the suspect he has in custody."

"That's wicked, that is!"

"It is. But we have a friendship with another inspector at Scotland Yard. He will want to hear what you have to say. If you come with us, we'll take you to talk to him."

Jeanette began to pace back and forth before her baskets. "No. I'm not daft, am I? I'm not gettin' into a carriage with the pair of ye! Ye're just two more of the fancy, ye are—just like *him*!"

"I'll thank you not to compare us to a possible madman," Niall said.

"Here's what we'll do, then," Kara said. "Why don't we all walk down to the Screaming Eagle? It's not far. There will be plenty of people there at this time of night. We can have a pint in a quiet corner and talk. If we are fortunate, they will still have some of their currant buns available."

Jeanette blinked at her. "Ye know the Eagle?"

"Very well, indeed," Kara assured her. "Let's get you settled there. You can tell us what's worrying you and we will do what we can to be sure you stay safe."

The girl thought it over. "Very well. If we can walk, I'll go."

Niall took up her baskets for her and they set off. It didn't take long to reach the tavern, one of the best-known spots in Covent Garden. The place was filled, as it was most nights. When Kara entered, the barman spotted her. Looking about the taproom, he jerked his head toward the table tucked back by the door to the courtyard. It often went unoccupied, as it could not be seen from the entry.

Kara headed for it, flashing Morris a grateful smile. Jeanette filed after her as Niall brought up the rear. The barman leaned toward them as they passed. "You'll be wanting some o' Bruce's buns?"

"I was afraid they would have been long gone by now," Kara answered.

"He's back in the kitchen, makin' extra, as we went through so many, what with the coroner's inquest held here." Morris grinned at her. "I hear we've you to thank for that."

Kara shrugged. "I just mentioned that you had the space and the experience."

"An inquest is always good for business. We'll send out a fresh batch of buns for your table."

They took their seats as the barmaid brought by three pints, then circled back with a plate of freshly baked buns. Niall set the baskets down in front of the back door. "It's starting on to rain," he said. "No one will be using the courtyard."

Jeanette looked down at the pint and the food, then stared up at Kara. "How does a lady like you chance to be known at the Screaming Eagle?"

Kara shrugged. "The Eagle is famous for welcoming all sorts."

"To business, now," said Niall. "Jeanette, we want to help you, and we are hoping you can help us. We want the truth about Miss Foulger's killer to be discovered. No one wants an innocent man to be convicted and a killer to go free."

Jeanette shivered and took a long drink.

"We've heard from Lily, and from another as well, that a young gentleman might be the one who was frightening Glynn Foulger."

"Lily told us you might know who he is," Kara added.

"And you say he is now frightening you?" Niall asked.

The girl glanced around, but none of the tavern's patrons were paying them any mind. "Yes." Her voice lowered. "I'm afraid. I've stayed away from my own rooms and I switched spots with Helen, hopin' he wouldn't find me."

"Let's start at the beginning," Kara suggested. "You are—were—friends with Glynn Foulger?"

"We were *friendly*, perhaps, more than friends." Jeanette sighed. "She were a good woman and more than good to us night girls. She always kept some of her best blooms back for us, so we weren't always left with the last pick or the wilted blossoms." She shook her head. "And her specials …"

"Lily told us about her special arrangements," Kara told her. "They must have been beautiful."

"Saints, the price I could get from one of her specials," Jeanette said. "I had got one from her the very night she died." She blinked. "I can scarce believe it was the last one." She swallowed and was quiet a moment. "Those specials got quite a reputation amongst the young nobs. Glynn was right smart about it, though. She wouldn't make many, and because they were scarce, it kept the interest high. She would only make them for the girls she liked, too. That put off more than a few of the flower sellers, I tell ye."

"Tell us about the gentleman," Niall said. "Young, red haired, and spotty is all we've heard."

"Aye. That's all true enough. But ye don't have to spend more than a bit of time with him to see that he's dicked in his nob." She shook her head. "He's awkward, that one. Like, he don't quite know how to act. I think he gets fixed on somethin' in his head and he can't let it go. When we ran up against him, I think he had decided that he was of an age and circumstance that what he needed was a mistress."

Kara blinked, but Niall nodded. "Ah, he saw the other young men his age starting to pursue the highflyers and paying to keep them."

"Aye, and he set out to do the same. Except it didn't go so well for him."

"The stars of the demimondaine not being traditionally enamored of spotty, awkward young men," said Niall.

"He got it in his head to woo a certain one o' them. Gave her gifts, wrote her poems, caterwauled beneath her window, like a cat."

"She shunned him?" Kara asked.

"She kept the gifts, and she strung him along for a bit, but then she sent him on his way. Or she tried to."

"He didn't abandon his pursuit?" asked Kara.

"He doubled it, or so I heard. Stopped her in the park, followed her in the street. He heard of Glynn's specials and trooped all through the city, from one flower girl to the next, until he found one who could get him what he wanted."

"Which is where you enter the story, I presume?" asked Niall.

"So help me, it's true," Jeanette said. "He come back to me, after. Said the lightskirt had been impressed he'd managed to get it." She shrugged. "It raised her status, I suppose, getting something rarefied. He wanted another, even grander. But he wanted to go straight to the source. He wanted me to bring him to Glynn."

"He wanted to cut out the middleman—but you were the middleman," Kara said, nodding.

"See? Ye understand. But he wouldn't. I told him I would get him what he wanted, but he wanted to do it his way and he would not stop houndin' me. Relentless, he was, and mean about it. It set my back up, I tell ye, and I dug in. I wouldn't tell him, so he followed me," she said indignantly. "It's sneaky, if ye ask me. But he caught me goin' to Glynn for my flowers and he worked out it were her."

"He approached her directly?" asked Niall.

"Didn't he? He set in to flatterin', wheedlin', and cajolin' her. He wanted her biggest, best, most beautiful creation."

"Did she make it for him?" Kara asked.

"Of course she did—what with the amount of money he offered? She would have been stupid not to do it. It were a beauty, I heard. *A double armful of devotion,* that's what the girls who saw it all happen have called it."

"Saw all *what* happen?" asked Niall. He sounded as if he weren't sure he wished to hear the answer.

"A couple of the flower girls saw him when he come to pick it up his prize one afternoon. It were so big he could scarcely maneuver it through the streets. They followed as he marched it straight through to the park, where he presented it to his light o' love."

"And was it well received?" asked Kara.

"Well enough, at first. The girl were flattered, o' course. Hard not to be, eh? I don't know exactly what happened to shift her reasonin', but she had been strollin' with a few other o' the highflyers. They are a catty bunch. Perhaps one of them said somethin' against him or his offerin', but the girl he'd chased so hard threw his great, glorious special back at his feet. She gave him the sharp side of her tongue, too. Told him to leave her alone, that she had a bigger fish on the hook."

"She humiliated him," Niall said.

"In front o' the whole of Polite Society, all on the stroll during the fashionable hour."

"So, why punish Glynn?" asked Kara.

"He didn't. Not at first. He retreated for a bit, hid away somewhere, licking his wounds—but he was still bound up on setting himself up a mistress. I suppose he thought it would redeem his reputation. He knew that there were flower girls who grow older and switch to peddling themselves, instead of their blossoms. So he decided to look there."

Niall's brows rose. "He looked to you?"

"He might o' done, but I ducked every time I saw him comin'," Jeanette said. "No, he turned to Glynn. I think he thought, because of her scar, she would be sure to accept him. Grateful, even, for the chance. But she didn't. She turned him down flat. Sent him on his way just as roundly as his lightskirt had done."

"Oh, no," Kara breathed.

"Exactly." Jeanette took a long drink of her ale. "It happened in the evenin'. I was comin' into the Garden and I passed him as he stalked out. I shied away from him, he looked so ... furious. White faced and tremblin', and filled with hate and despair."

Kara exchanged pained glances with Niall.

"I could have warned him off, had I known what he meant to do," Jeanette said sadly. "Glynn would never enter into an arrangement like that. She didn't trust no man. Two things about her that anyone who knew her understood—she hated the river and she had no use for men, in general."

"So he took out all his anger and disappointment and frustration on her?" mused Niall.

"He couldn't vent his spleen on his lightskirt. She really did get herself a well-heeled, high-placed protector. His kind never admit their own fault in their own messes. So he threw it all at Glynn."

"But I don't understand. Why did Glynn believe so firmly

that it was Yardley tormenting her?"

"Because this gent is sneaky, as I said before. He didn't confront her out loud and in the open like Yardley did. The cobbler showed her his anger, right to her face. But *him*? He kept to the shadows and the crowds. And Glynn—well, she didn't come from London, did she? I don't think she ever understood the push and pull, the maneuverin' a girl has to do to make her way here. Sometimes I think she believed everyone is as open about what they feel and think as she was. She was so forthcomin' about her own feelings—like not sellin' her specials to the girls she didn't much care for." Jeanette shook her head. "Glynn didn't understand that sort of skulkin'."

The more Kara learned of Glynn Foulger, the more she thought she would have liked her, had they met. "Did you not try to warn her?"

"O' course I did! What do ye take me for? I told her he was lurkin' and starin'. I told her I'd heard from Charlotte and Sue, girls who sell out by St. Paul's and the area 'round there. Those two saw him comin' and goin' from the direction of Paternoster Row, where all the printers keep shop. He was out there arrangin' fer those broadsheets, I'd wager. I warned her that he meant to do her harm. But she thought of him as young and inexperienced. Inept, even. I told her I'd seen him watchin' her— and do you know what she said? She hoped he would run into Yardley and spook him, then perhaps she would have some peace."

Kara sighed. Could the woman's death have been avoided if she had listened to her friend?

Niall narrowed his gaze. "Jeanette, do you think this young man killed Glynn?"

The flower girl looked distraught. "I can't say for sure, can I? Not havin' seen it myself. But I do think he *could* have killed her."

"You still haven't told us the most important thing." Kara leaned toward her. "Who is he, Jeanette? Do you know?"

"I'm afraid to tell you," the girl said, staring down into her ale.

"He should be questioned," Niall said sharply. "No matter who he is. You said he has begun harassing you?"

She nodded. "He came up from behind and caught me unawares. He told me in great detail about the house he means to rent for the woman in his keepin'. I told him it sounded very nice, but that I was not that sort of girl. He left then, but I caught sight o' him in the crowds around the Canterbury, just watchin' me." She shivered. "That's how it started with Glynn."

"His name, Jeanette?" Kara asked.

The girl hesitated, but then she drew a deep breath and slowly let it out. "Arnold," she whispered. "Fred Arnold."

Niall straightened. "Fenton's son?"

"The Earl of Fenton?" asked Kara, dismayed.

"Third son," Jeanette said with a nod.

"No wonder Frye ignored her." Niall sighed.

"Earl's son or not, he must be brought down to Scotland Yard and questioned," Kara declared. "And it might be prudent for you to play least-in-sight until this is all settled."

"How am I to do that?" the girl cried. "I got rent to pay!"

"We'll speak to your landlord," Kara told her. "And perhaps you might come to stay with us—"

"Beggin' yer pardon," Jeanette interrupted, her chin held high. "But I ain't nobody's charity case. I been workin' since I was knee high to a frog, sellin' flowers at my mother's side when I was small, and carryin' on with her tradition once she were gone. I rely on myself. I support myself."

"How about another sort of employment, then?" Kara blinked as Niall nudged her. "Emelia's looking for a downstairs maid, isn't she?"

"A maid? A place in service?" Jeanette straightened, her interest clear. "Out of the weather? With room and board?" Suddenly, her shoulders slumped. "I don't have the sort o' references ye need fer a place like that."

"We'll be your references," Kara told her. "You can try the position on, see if it suits you. If not, you can go back to your spot outside the Canterbury."

"I'll have to talk with Helen, make sure she knows she can have my spot, temporary like, until I make up my mind."

Kara sighed. "It's probably too late in the evening now to take you to Scotland Yard. Let's see you back to your rooms. You can gather your things and then we'll take you to Lake Nemi. Emelia will see you settled for tonight."

Jeanette straightened. "Lake Nemi? The place that used to be a bordello?"

"In the distant past, it was," Kara said, sighing again. "No longer. Now it is—"

"The place where women go to learn about science, and history, and the study of strange plants and animals," Jeanette said quickly. "I know! I always wished I could get inside there. I shouldn't mind learnin' such things, myself."

"Well then, perhaps employment there will suit you well. We'll take you over straight away," Niall said. "Tomorrow we will bring Inspector Wooten by to interview you. Afterward, you and Emelia can discuss terms of a trial employment."

Jeanette glanced over at her baskets. "What of my flowers?"

"Take them as an offering of thanks for your shelter," Kara suggested. "Emelia is as susceptible to a lovely gift as the next woman." She stood. "Let's get you tucked safely away, then."

Chapter Seven

RAIN HAD BEGUN to fall as they left the Eagle. Niall carried the baskets of flowers as they hurried back toward the theatre and their carriage. He saw the women tucked inside and the baskets strapped to the back. A chill wind swept in from the river, making him shiver as it caressed the bits of his legs left bare between stockings and kilt. He gave John Coachman the address provided by Jeanette, and as they set off, he sank down next to Kara with a sigh.

They didn't have to go far through the cramped and narrow streets surrounding Covent Garden. Jeanette said her rooms were in a boardinghouse nearby. Watching out the window, he noticed when they passed by a similar establishment—the house where their friend, Miss Josie Lowe, used to reside. He nudged Kara and nodded toward the place, then gave her a warm, slightly suggestive smile. In that building was the spot where they had shared one of their first kisses, on the night he had finally confessed his secrets to the woman who would become his wife.

Kara returned his grin, but they were distracted as the coach pulled up to a building just around the corner.

"Do you wish to stay here and keep dry while I go in with Jeanette?" Niall asked his wife.

"No, I'll go along and help," Kara said with a glance toward the flower seller.

"I don't want the landlady to get the wrong idea," Jeanette said. "If she saw me taking a toff like you into my rooms alone, she'd likely double my rent."

Niall winced. "Let's go, then. The rain is picking up." He hustled them out of the carriage and through the half gate outside the boardinghouse. They were hurrying toward the steep stairs leading up to the entrance when Jeanette suddenly stopped in her tracks.

"Go on," Niall urged. "The wind is growing colder by the minute."

"Look," she said, gesturing. Her voice was pitched low.

He followed the direction of her gaze. Someone stood before the wide door at the top of the stairs. A man in a greatcoat. He was affixing something to the front of the door.

"It's *him*," Jeanette whispered.

"Back to the carriage," Niall ordered the women. He gave both of them a push back and stepped around in front of them. "*Go,*" he said, before advancing to the first step. "You there," he called up. "What are you doing?"

The figure froze. The man's head turned. Niall just caught the hint of light hair in the glow from the windows before the man turned, grasped the railing, and leapt to the ground, landing and stumbling just a few feet to the side of the stairs.

Niall reached for him, but the man lunged to his feet and ran, jumping over the low fence to the pavement before the next house, then heading into the street.

With a curse, Niall pelted after him. The wind-driven rain stung his eyes as he chased the man along the wet, empty streets. His prey kept his head down as he ran. When he glanced back, he saw that Niall had gained on him, and reached into his coat.

Niall saw the glint of gaslight on the pistol. Cursing again, he ducked, the pavement cold and wet on his bare knee. The shot struck the iron railing to his left, shooting out a shower of sparks and ricocheting into the night.

The man threw the pistol down and took off again. Niall tore after him. They raced through the warren of streets, down a filthy alley and into a wider lane. The fugitive ducked into another dark alley—a mistake, Niall realized as he followed on his heels, for it emerged into a cramped court with no other exit.

Breathing heavily, the man lurched from one side of the space to the other. Niall thought he would dart into one of the buildings facing the court, but instead the man squared his shoulders and came at him on a run, hoping to force his way past.

Reaching out, Niall grasped the man's shoulder and spun him about, shoving him back into the alley wall. He knocked the man's hat off his head, noted the light, strawberry-blond hair, and stared into the man's red, rage-filled face. "Mr. Arnold, I presume?" he asked, his chest heaving. "You saved us the trouble of tracking you down."

The man snarled in response.

From the sporran he wore over his kilt, Niall pulled the set of wrist cuffs Wooten had given him long ago. Honestly, he'd never thought to use them, but now he was glad he'd thought to bring them. The young man resisted, but he was no match against the strength of Niall's forge-trained grip.

"Come along, then," Niall told him. "You've some questions to answer down at Scotland Yard."

KARA, BLESS HER, was quick-witted enough to have left Jeanette inside her rooms when she met him outside. Niall hustled young Fred Arnold into the carriage and set John Coachman to watch him while he took his wife aside. "Listen, the hour is late and there is no one respectable out in this foul weather," he told her. "You'll have a hard time finding a hack, and I don't like the idea of the two of you walking alone to Lake Nemi. Why don't you stay here with Jeanette until morning, then take her to Emelia?"

He jerked his head toward the carriage. "I'll take him to the Yard, wait to see what Wooten can get out of him, then I'll meet you in the morning."

"You'll be all right with him?" she asked, glancing over.

"He's fast, I'll give you that, but he poses no threat now."

"Fine, then," she agreed reluctantly. "But take these." She handed over a stack of broadsheets.

He moved so that he could see them in the misty light of a streetlamp, then sighed. It showed a voluptuous, red-haired girl with a flower between her teeth importuning gentlemen in the street. "Accusing her—disparaging her, really—for the exact behavior she refused to engage in," Niall said in disgust. "And how much of his father's money do you think he spent, commissioning this image and having it printed?"

"There's my thrifty Scot," Kara said, placing a hand on his cheek and standing on tiptoe to kiss him. "Do be careful," she whispered.

He gave her his promise and another smacking kiss before he climbed into the coach and they set off, but it was several hours before he sorted the confusion at Scotland Yard, succeeded in convincing a sergeant to summon Wooten, explained the situation, and ended up sitting in an interview room with the inspector and the sullen young nobleman.

"Why is *he* here?" Arnold sneered. "And where is my father? I don't want to say anything until he arrives."

"I'm representing the interests of the man who was accused of the crimes that *you* actually committed," Niall said dryly.

"We've sent for your father," Wooten added. "But do you truly wish for him to hear all the details of your recent behavior? Do you want him to hear us discussing the possibility that you killed Miss Glynn Foulger?"

Arnold straightened right out of his slouch. "Wait! What? You think I *killed* that girl? You cannot! I didn't!"

"Why should we believe you?" Wooten asked. "We know you were harassing her."

The young man scowled and crossed his arms. "I don't know what you mean."

"I think you do." Wooten spoke calmly as he ticked items off his fingers. "We have multiple witnesses who saw you skulking about after Miss Foulger. We have others who saw you coming and going from Paternoster Row, where you had some very nasty broadsheets printed, all featuring the young lady."

"I did no such thing," Arnold said loftily.

"Tsk, tsk. where is your honor, man?" Niall slapped down one of the broadsheets that Kara had collected at Jeanette's boardinghouse. He shook his head. "Getting caught in an outright lie? Bad enough. But besmirching the names and reputations of innocent young women?" He tapped the broadsheet. "And while this one is vile enough, I've seen the investigator's collection of the ones you posted featuring Miss Foulger. Vulgar, indeed." He shook his head. "No one loves a bully, Mr. Arnold."

"The artist incorporated his signature into this one and a couple of the others. One of my constables is right now knocking on his door," Wooten said. "We'll have his statement within the hour, stating who paid him to create such disgraceful images."

Suddenly Arnold slammed his hands down onto the table between them. "She should have taken me up on my offer, then, shouldn't she? It was the height of stupidity for her to refuse me. A lowly Covent Garden merchant? And with that scar? She's lucky I made the offer at all!" Neither Niall nor Wooten responded, but the young man continued, his lip curled. "It was ludicrous that she should turn me down."

"Making such an offer to an innocent woman strains the tenets of gentlemanly behavior," Niall said. "Refusing to accept her rejection with any sort of grace breaks them absolutely. But the way you have behaved?" He allowed his disgust to show. "Beyond the pale, sir."

"It was her own fault, in any case," the young man said sullenly. "She led me on."

"How so?" asked Wooten, his brow raised.

"She made a showpiece of a custom arrangement for me. She asked all sorts of questions about the woman I intended it for and about our relationship."

"Did Miss Foulger proposition you?" asked Wooten.

Arnold frowned. "No."

"Did she suggest that she should take the place of the young woman you spoke to her about?"

"No."

"Did you ever see Miss Foulger flirting with other men? Or accepting illicit proposals from them?"

Arnold shifted in his seat.

"Did you?" demanded Wooten.

"No!"

The inspector gave a snort.

"She spoke kindly to me," Arnold said.

"So, Miss Foulger did business with you, sir. She did a thorough job of it. And she *spoke to you kindly*? And somehow, in your mind, this translated to her *owing* you?" Wooten sounded incredulous.

"God save the good women of England, if this is how you treat every one of them that spares you a kind word," Niall said on a sigh.

"And what, exactly, did you think this young Jeanette owed you?" Wooten asked, pointing to the image of the redhead in the newest broadsheet.

The young man pursed his lips and said nothing.

"You were at Jeanette's home posting this on her door and presumably throughout her neighborhood. How did you know where she lived?" asked Niall. He paused, and when the boy said nothing, he continued. "You followed her home, didn't you?"

"You might as well answer, given that you were apprehended at her door," Wooten said.

Arnold merely gave a curt nod.

"And Glynn Foulger? You followed her home, too?"

At that question, the boy looked up. "No. I tried, but that one was cagey. Somehow she always knew when I was on her trail."

"She was a challenge," Niall said.

"More than that one, I'll tell you," Arnold said, glancing at Jeanette's image.

"What did Miss Foulger do when she suspected you were following her?" asked Wooten.

"She would duck in a pub or just go and spend the evening at her charity work. She was always canny enough to leave with a friend or a group, then."

"And you didn't want to chance getting spotted or caught, eh?" Niall said wryly. "Not so much risk when you are stalking a woman alone."

Arnold scowled and folded his arms in front of him again.

But Wooten had leaned in. "But you outsmarted her. You found out where she lived. How?"

The young man lifted a shoulder, but there was pride in his tone when he answered. "She kept taking refuge in that charity, so I used it against her. I waited outside and chatted up the bloke that runs the place. I told him I came from her employer, the farmer who hires her to sell his blooms. I said I needed to discuss a business matter. He was in a hurry and wanted to be off, but I persisted. He didn't want to go back inside and look at his records, so he gave me the general direction. I went to the spot and asked after the woman with the scar, and it didn't take long to find her."

"So very clever." Niall leaned forward too. "You discovered her home, so you spent the next weeks pounding on her door in the middle of the night and throwing rocks and garbage at her windows. It wasn't a bad bit of investigating. I can't help but imagine what positive things you could do with your opportunities and skills, instead of getting your excitement from terrorizing helpless women."

"Very well," Wooten said. "We have established that you stalked Miss Foulger. You frightened her at her home. You commissioned, printed, and posted foul images of her. Now, let's discuss your whereabouts two nights ago." He took up his notebook again. "Where were you between sunset, which would have been around half-eight, until midnight?"

Arnold's eyes widened. "When? Do you mean the night she was killed? I told you, I didn't kill the girl!"

"I'm afraid you will have to convince us," Wooten said coldly. "Where were you?"

"I … I …" The young man cast his gaze about wildly. "Two nights ago?" He straightened. "My mother hosted a dinner party! Yes, I was trapped there all evening. She had a card room set up for entertainment after dinner and the guests stayed until well after midnight. Until half past one, at the least! Speak with them all, if you like. They can all tell you. I was there the entire evening."

Wooten finished writing in his notebook. Standing, he gestured to Niall and turned toward the door.

"Wait! Where are you going?" Arnold cried. "What about me?"

"You will stay here," Wooten told him. "Unless you decide to give any trouble, in which case, you will be carted off to a cell. *I am going to speak with your father to confirm what you have told us.*" He glanced back. "Then I might, perhaps, stop by the nearest parish church and give thanks that I do not have a son such as you."

Niall watched the young man put his head down on the table, then followed the inspector out.

"We need that artist's statement to lock this up tightly," Wooten said. "Let's see if he has returned."

As they headed toward his office, they heard signs of a commotion coming near. "That will be his father, the earl, I predict," Wooten said, sounding tired.

A gentleman turned into the passage, snarling threats. A phalanx of constables followed him, clearly trying to placate the irate man. Wooten made a gesture of dismissal and the constables melted away, but not before one stepped forward to hand over a file.

"Good morning." Wooten tucked the file under his arm as he approached the gentleman. "Lord Fenton, I must assume? I am Inspector Wooten. I have just interviewed your son. We had questions for him regarding his relations with—"

"With a street seller?" the earl interrupted. "A strumpet who stands outside, selling wares to the public?"

"With two innocent young women, one of whom has been murdered."

The earl's jaw dropped. "Never say you are accusing my son of murder. Impertinence! Slander! I'll have your guts for garters. I'll speak to the commissioner myself—"

Wooten cut him off. "Lord Fenton, did your wife host an evening of dinner and cards two nights ago?"

The earl blinked. "Yes. Yes, she did."

"Did you attend?"

Fenton barked out a short laugh. "Did I attend? Of course I did!" Comprehension dawned in his face. "And so did my son, for that matter! If that was when your sly little street seller was killed, then we have an entire houseful of witnesses who can vouch for Fred's innocence."

"Excellent. We will require a list of those guests. We will question them, but I must assume, if you speak the truth, that your son did not kill Glynn Foulger. There is, however, the matter of the very distasteful harassment he subjected her to." The inspector raised a hand as the earl began to object. "And now we know he's begun the same pattern with another young woman."

"Ridiculous. You can have no proof of such a thing."

Niall bristled. "I saw him in the act tonight, with my very own eyes."

The earl looked him up and down, sneering at his kilt—and likely at his dirty knees. "And who the devil are *you*, sir?"

"You are understandably distraught, sir," Wooten said. "It is no surprise that you do not recognize the gentleman." He turned to Niall. "Your Grace, if you will permit me to present the Earl of Fenton?"

"Your Grace?" The other man's eyes nearly bugged out of his head. "Who the hell *are* you?"

"As I said, you are perhaps too upset to recognize the Duke of Sedwick? I believe he is known by most of Society as a favorite of the queen. Were you, perhaps, present at Her Majesty's soiree a couple of months past, where she presented him with an award for courageous service to the nation?"

The earl gaped.

"Shall we step into my office to discuss the matter?"

Fenton's belligerence returned. "No. I want to see my son. If I hear he has been treated with anything but the utmost respect—"

Wooten sighed. "We have multiple witnesses of your son's disgraceful behavior." He pulled out the file and flipped it open to read what was inside. "And physical evidence, as well, it seems." He looked up. "In addition, your son confirmed his transgressions in his discussion with us this morning."

"He was likely intimidated," the earl blustered.

"You cannot excuse his misdeeds, my lord. Nor should you." The inspector pursed his lips. "Here is the thing. This sort of violent emotional reaction doesn't just come from nowhere, does it?"

He waited, but the earl did not respond.

"Here is what I am going to do, my lord," Wooten continued. "If you continue to bluster and discount our very convincing evidence, then I am going to speak with your neighbors at your country estate. To the villagers nearby. To your servants. To the servants who have been dismissed from your household. Then I will go to the very fine school I am sure your son attended, where I will interview his professors and fellow students."

Fenton had grown noticeably paler.

"Yes, you know exactly the sort of stories I will hear about your son, do you not? I shall collect them all into a file."

"And do what with your file? My wife is a cousin to the commissioner's wife," Fenton declared with quiet triumph.

Wooten nodded. "Ah. Then perhaps you will be successful in keeping his misdeeds quiet—for a while. But every constable, detective, and inspector in the Metropolitan Police will hear the whispers. And they will be watching. Please, I beg you to do your best to turn your son to more honorable pursuits, for if you do nothing to curb his abusive behavior toward those less fortunate than him—those it should be his duty to care for—and he engages in this ugly sort of harassment again—"

"Then you will do what?" Fenton demanded.

Wooten shrugged. "I am an inspector. I have newspapermen dogging my heels day and night looking for a story—the more sensational, the better. I think a young nobleman allowed to indulge his cruel urges would make for some very clever headlines, don't you?"

The earl glared, but did not respond.

"Good, we understand each other, then." The inspector waved a hand to indicate the officer standing guard outside the interview room at the end of the passage. "The constable will allow you inside to see your son, but he may not yet leave."

"When?" Fenton asked.

"Not for a little while longer. We will let you know when it is time."

Fenton stalked past them without a further word.

"That was well done," Niall said when he and Wooten finally reached the inspector's office.

"Frye should be in soon," Wooten said, dropping into his chair. "He will have to let go of the harassment charges against Mr. Yardley."

"He won't like that," Niall said. "He will like it less if he spots me and knows I have something to do with the bad news. I should go before he sees me."

"Thank you, Your Grace. That was a good catch. You may have stopped the young man's cruelty from growing even more dangerous."

"Let's hope so," Niall said. "I think we should advise young Jeanette to stay hidden until we know how the boy has been dealt with, though." He paused in the doorway. "Good luck with Frye, Wooten."

"Send your lady my thanks, as well."

"So I will. She'll be champing at the bit, waiting for news."

Wooten laughed. "Best hurry, then."

"So I shall," Niall replied as he left. He did not tell the inspector that he was just as eager to see Kara. He grinned. Doubtless, he didn't have to.

Chapter Eight

KARA SPENT THE night sharing Jeanette's narrow bed. She didn't sleep much. This was the first night she'd spent away from Niall since their marriage. She missed the warmth of his big body and the comfort of knowing he was always there—in every way.

The two of them rose at the crack of dawn. Kara took Jeanette to Dobb's Pie Shop, where they indulged in warm pastries and sound, practical advice.

"Service ain't for everyone," Maisie said. "Just like bakin' ain't for lots of folks. Both have early starts, long hours, and hard, hands-on work."

"Ye think sellin' flowers ain't work?" Jeanette demanded. "Up before the sun to try to catch the best blooms at the lowest prices, before they are all gone? Sittin' out in every sort of weather? Runnin' out into the street, dodging traffic for those who just beckon ye from their carriage? Fightin' off the blighters who think ye must be sellin' yer body along with yer roses?"

"I feel yer pain, young lady," said Maisie. "Took me years of selling my pies in the streets before I saved enough to get the shop."

Jeanette sighed. "I know it's hard work to be done in service, but at least ye ain't fightin' alone. I always thought the belowstairs folk must be like a sort of family, workin' together to get things done and to make things nice for everyone, upstairs and down."

Maisie paused in her work. "Aye, I have heard o' households where there's such unity, but there's others that are more akin to a battlefield. Take care not to end up in such a place, now."

"Emelia is fairly fond of drama in her own relationships," Kara said around a mouthful of apple pastry, "but I cannot see her allowing such animosities to interfere with the domestic running of the club."

"Good, then. It might be a fair choice, if that's so," Maisie said, pouring Jeanette another cup of tea. "But take my advice and agree to a trial, before you decide outright."

"That's exactly what Niall suggested," Kara told her.

"Ah, well then. There you are," Maisie said with a grin. "Great minds," she added, tapping her head. "I always did like that big, hulking husband of yours."

"He likes you, too," Kara said, leaning into her friend's sturdy frame. "But not as much as I do."

"Ah, sweet girl," Maisie said fondly. "You know you are in my heart." She started to gather up dishes as Kara savored the last of her pastry. "And I miss Harold, too, I do. Tell him to come by and visit old Maisie."

"So I will. And send my love to Davey." With a satisfied sigh, Kara stood. "Thank you, Maisie." She paused. "Perhaps we might all meet for a picnic in the park? Just take a day of relaxation together?"

"Don't that sound nice?" Maisie said. "Let's do it."

"You are not to cook," Kara warned.

Maisie's eyes widened. "And won't that be a treat."

"I'll have Turner compare everyone's schedules and set up a date." Kara hugged the woman close. "Thank you, Maisie. I can always count on you for a bit of peace." With a deep breath, Kara stepped away. "Come, Jeanette," she said. "Let's go and find you a safe hiding spot—and possibly a bit of family feeling."

They went straight to Emelia when they arrived at Lake Nemi. The club's proprietress looked doubtful at first, and warned about the hard work the position required.

"Why does everyone assume sellin' flowers is all sunshine and daisies?" Jeanette said, exasperated. "I got to deal with cost and profit, worry about making my rent, lug my wares through the loud, busy, smelly streets, swelter in the summer, and freeze in the winter. I have to smile and cajole, even when I feel like cursin' or cryin'." She gave Emelia a frank look. "Frankly, if you give me a bucket, a mop, a rag, a quiet room, and tell me to set it to sparklin'? It sounds like heaven."

In the end, it was Jeanette's wish for a place with a feeling of community that won Emelia over. "Yes!" she exclaimed. "That is exactly the view we should be striving for at Lake Nemi. Staff, residents, members—we are all in this together. We live, work, learn, and grow together." Finally, she looked at Jeanette with approval. "If you understand this from the first, you could do very well with us."

Kara left them to hash out their agreement. She went to peer out the parlor windows, looking for a sign of Niall. Her vigilance was rewarded, for he arrived just after Emelia and Jeanette finished their negotiations. Kara ran to meet him, but stopped, drawing up short at the sight of him. "Oh dear. You do look tired, my darling."

"I am tired," Niall admitted. "Tired in my soul, after spending so many hours in that horrid stripling's company."

She went to him and burrowed into his embrace. He held her for a long moment before heaving a sigh. "Is Gyda still here?" he asked.

"I believe so. I haven't seen anyone but Emelia, but the good news is that she has agreed to take Jeanette on. I believe they are currently bonding over the fact that they both love primroses and also that neither believes that a room is truly clean unless the baseboards have been dusted."

"A match made in heaven," Niall said. "Let's call Gyda and

Beth down. I only want to tell this story once."

They all gathered in the parlor, and Niall told them everything he and Wooten had learned. "I do believe that Jeanette should stay hidden away here for a time, though," he said as he finished. "I very much doubt there will be any official charges brought against young Fred Arnold. Until we see if his father can keep him in line, you'll be safer here," he told the girl.

"I've already sent word to Helen about taking my spot at the Canterbury for a few weeks," Jeanette said. "I want my shot here, in any case, to see if we suit."

Emelia invited them all in to breakfast, but Jeanette asked to be introduced to the staff instead. "Best to start off like I mean to go on. Better not to have any confusion."

Emelia saw the wisdom of that. Jeanette hugged Kara before she left and dipped a curtsy to Niall. "Thank you both. I don't think anyone has ever been so nice to me, not since my mother passed."

"Keep yourself safe," Kara whispered.

Niall turned as the women headed belowstairs, lifting his nose and inhaling deeply. "I smell rashers of bacon." He glanced at Kara. "I want breakfast and my bed, in that order."

She laughed. "Let's go. Emelia won't mind if we begin, I'm sure."

"If you eat quickly, you can make the next train out," Gyda said with a glance at the clock.

"After you, then," Niall said.

Beth fell in beside Kara as they trooped into the dining room. "I wanted to thank you for the flowers. One of the volunteers is a skilled artist—we hung his sketch of Glynn at her workspace and placed the flowers beneath them."

"That sounds like a lovely tribute. How are plans going for the memorial? Has the charity agreed to allow you to hold it there?"

"Yes. It's starting to come together. Mr. Royston has been surprisingly supportive. He's approached me several times, asking all about our plans."

"I spoke with our cook about a possible menu. Just trays of finger foods, she thinks, if that is fine with you." Kara put a hand to her head. "Oh, saints! I was just with Maisie this morning! I should have put in an order for her little tartlets."

"There is still time. We've been discussing ways to present the work that Glynn did, to best showcase the charity. I think it would be best to wait a few weeks for the memorial, so that everyone's emotions are not so raw."

"That's likely wise," Kara agreed.

"The coroner has signed the burial form, so now Glynn can be laid to rest." Beth bit her lip. "We took up a collection to pay for the expenses. The burial is to be tomorrow." Her eyes glistered with unshed tears, and Kara's heart wrenched. "Mr. Royston has agreed to attend. He may be the only one to be at the graveside."

"Oh dear. That is sad." Kara looked to the buffet, where her husband was piling food onto a plate. "I'll have a word with Niall, shall I? We might persuade him to attend."

"Do you think he would?" Beth asked hopefully. "I hate to think of Glynn being buried without a friendly face to see her put to her rest."

"Mr. Royston is not friendly?" asked Kara.

"He's … efficient. He likes things done a certain way. As long as his secretary keeps things smooth, he is easygoing enough. But friendly? I wouldn't have said so before, but he's been attentive lately." Beth looked doubtful.

"I'm sure Niall will agree to go to the cemetery, but why don't we have a small gathering to offer up prayers for Miss Foulger at the charity building? Since the women cannot attend the burial, we can gather to say our own goodbyes?"

"Oh! Yes. That is the perfect idea." Beth grasped her hand. "Will you come?"

"Indeed, I will. It will be an honor." Kara looked over to find Niall happily piling bacon between slices of toast. "Let Niall eat, then I'll take him home to get a few hours of sleep. *Then* I will bring up our plans for tomorrow."

"Thank you so much, Kara." Beth hesitated a moment longer. "I hope you won't mind if I mention it, but Gyda isn't sleeping well. Emelia and some of the women here have mentioned finding her outside in the garden in the middle of the night."

Kara pursed her lips and gave the girl a nod. "She was doing the same in Scotland. Sitting outside for hours, staring up at the sky. I think she finds it easier to think of Charles out there."

"She cared for him, very much."

"She did. She does. They grew very close, very quickly. They made plans. Now she has to find a way to go on without him." Kara could not imagine trying to adjust if she lost Niall. Her heart and mind shied away, refusing to contemplate such a thing.

Beth swallowed. "Gyda mentioned that Rob McRae is coming to stay with you?" she asked with forced casualness.

"Indeed he is. We expect him any day now. He stayed behind to see to the final details of selling his forge, but he meant to follow us fairly quickly."

"Gyda said he means to stay in London?"

"Yes. He has work with a man who customizes high-end hotel rooms and train cars. He'll be able to use his creativity in new ways."

"And he's coming … on his own?" Beth asked carefully.

"Oh, yes. Quite on his own. But he'll stay with us for a bit. It will be grand, having a chance to be all together again, won't it?"

Beth colored. "Yes. Yes, it will."

"Maisie and I were just discussing setting up a picnic. You must join us, when we finally manage to sort out all the schedules."

"Thank you. I would love to."

"Excellent," Kara said, trying to appear as nonchalant as Beth was striving to be. "Look, I think the maid has brought out a platter of your cook's famous seed cake. Let's go get some before Niall eats it all."

NIALL MADE IT home, collapsed into bed, and slept hard for several hours. He woke up feeling refreshed and thinking of Kara's agreement that they should "practice" to increase their chances at parenthood. Luckily, his wife peeked in to see if he was awake. He lured her close with a sleepy smile, grabbed her, pulled her in, and nuzzled her until she was persuaded to set aside the letters she was writing.

All of this put him in a very fine mood, of course, but it wasn't the reason he agreed to Kara's proposal that he attend Glynn Foulger's internment. They were discussing it over dinner and Niall nodded obligingly. "I will do it for the lass, of course, but also because I wouldn't mind a word with Royston, either. It doesn't sit well with me, knowing that the girl successfully evaded young Arnold until Royston practically led the man to her home."

"I was there when Royston gave Sergeant Landover Mr. Yardley's address," Kara said, clearly looking back in her mind's eye. "But that is a far cry from giving a young woman's information to anyone who asks you in the street."

"I'd like to be sure he understands the distinction," Niall said darkly. He turned to Stayme. "Do you know anything about the man?"

"Royston, you said?" The viscount looked up from his salmon. "I don't believe so. Would you like me to have a poke around in my files?"

"I might," Niall answered. "Let's see how he responds to my warning."

"Excuse me, Your Grace." Turner cleared his throat from the doorway. "Inspector Wooten is here."

Niall stood as Turner moved aside to allow the inspector to enter. "Come in, come in, sir. Have you dined? Join us."

"I have. My wife packed a sack of sandwiches for the train,

but I thank you." The inspector took the offered seat and thanked Turner as the butler poured him a glass of wine.

"You can have dessert with us, then," Kara told him. "Harold requested Cook's jam roly-poly, and she made enough for everyone in the house."

"Well, now." Wooten looked pleased. "Who would turn down jam roly-poly?"

"Peasant food," Stayme said with a sniff. He caught Kara's look and raised a hand. "But I am not turning it down! No, indeed."

Wooten took a sip of wine. "Was it Royston you were discussing as I came in?"

"Indeed," said Niall. "He is to attend Glynn Foulger's burial tomorrow."

"He was going to be the only attendee," Kara added. "That is, until Niall kindly agreed to go."

"Perhaps I shall accompany you," Wooten said. "Where is she to be buried?"

"At All Saints, in South Bermondsey," Kara said. "The charity volunteers took up a collection to pay for it. Beth said there was some discussion on which cemetery would be acceptable, but All Saints was judged to be close, but also far enough away from the river." She lifted a shoulder at Niall's questioning gaze. "You'll recall that Miss Foulger's loathing of the river was mentioned several times?"

"Yes, along with her general loathing of men," Niall agreed.

"Well, Beth told me the reason for her hatred of the river. Any river, it would seem. Apparently the scar on Glynn's face came from an accident when she was a very young woman. It was a bridge disaster that occurred in Yarmouth, where she grew up. Glynn told the story to her friends at the charity. A large group of children had gathered on a bridge over the river. It must have been a festival of some sort, because they had all gone out to watch a clown in a barrel being pulled downriver by a flotilla of geese. As he passed under the bridge, the weight shifted, which caused the chains on one side to snap. The bridge deck flipped over, dumping the children into the river. Seventy-nine of them died, including Glynn's younger sister. Beth said that the special smocks she made for the charity were in memory of the girl."

"Good heavens," said Niall.

"I recall the story in the papers, when it happened," Stayme said. "Dreadful."

"I remember it as well," Wooten said. "That poor woman saw a great deal of tragedy in her young life—and it may continue on after her." The inspector met Niall's gaze. "When we see Mr. Royston tomorrow, I will tell him that the harassment charges against Mr. Yardley have been repealed."

Niall heard what Wooten did not say. "But he hasn't been released?"

"No. He's the only suspect Frye has for the murder."

"Is he even looking for another?" asked Kara.

"Not that I can see," Wooten said.

They all sat in silence for a moment.

"Well, perhaps Mr. Royston will have an idea on where to point us," Niall said. "But for now, there will be tragedy here if we do not do justice to Cook's special dessert. Let's bring on the roly-poly."

Chapter Nine

MORNING MISTS STILL hung in the air when Niall and Wooten made their way into All Saints Cemetery. Niall eyed the cast-iron decorations on the gates, examining the closest one—an hourglass in relief—with a critical eye. A bit on the nose, in his opinion.

Covering fifty-two acres, the place stretched out, quiet and green before them. The paths appeared to be weed-free and looked after, and the lush foliage of late spring gave the place a pretty, restful air. They passed the white obelisk dedicated to five men who had been transported for campaigning for parliamentary reform and headed into the narrow avenues between the graves. They varied from imposing monuments to important men to small, simple headstones that marked the resting places of the common dead and more modest burials.

Niall spotted a clergyman and two gentlemen standing at a fresh gravesite ahead. A couple of cemetery employees with shovels stood nearby. They withdrew as Niall and Wooten arrived.

Royston gave Niall a nod and stood stiffly straight as the vicar began to speak. The service was short, but the charity manager's attention seemed to wander. The gentleman next to him merely stared ahead, frowning. The man of the cloth also apparently had other things on his mind, or perhaps demands on his time, for he consigned Miss Foulger's soul to her heavenly father, gave the men a nod, then strode away.

"Not much of a service," Wooten whispered as the groundsmen came forward to begin the filling of the grave. He and Niall moved away. They went slowly, though, allowing Royston to catch them up.

The manager obviously knew who Niall was, although they hadn't yet met. He hailed them and spoke as he came abreast. "I am Royston, manager at the Waif's Wardrobe. It was good of you to come, Your Grace. And I understand your lady wife is helping with the memorial that the volunteers at the charity are planning. Please, extend our thanks to her."

"I will do so, sir."

"Perhaps you will allow me to introduce Mr. Stephen Jephson? He is one of the board of directors of the Wardrobe. He was kind enough to accompany me to the burial today."

"Sir." Niall gave the other man a nod.

"Sedwick," the man said slowly. "Ah, yes. Sedwick. The artist." It wasn't said with a sneer, but it skated on the edge of it. "And the duke. Although that is rather a late development, isn't it?"

"The title is," Niall agreed easily. "Not the art. That is of long standing."

"As is the steadfast character and brave service to his country that led to the grant of a ducal title," Wooten said loyally.

"Please, you'll put me to the blush," Niall said with a laugh. He opened his mouth to introduce the inspector, but Jephson shot him a narrow look.

"Why are you here at this girl's burial, Sedwick?"

"Because the women at the charity feared there would be no one to see Miss Foulger interred," Niall answered. "That would be a sad, lonely shame, for a good woman to be so abandoned. My wife asked me to make sure that was not the case, and so here I am."

"Very good of you," Royston said.

"Thank you." Niall turned to the newcomer. "And you, Mr. Jephson? Why are you here?"

"Because Royston insisted," the man said.

"I always find it very interesting to see who turns up at the graveside of a murder victim," Wooten said mildly.

Niall bit back a grin. "Gentlemen, allow me to introduce you both to Inspector Wooten, from Scotland Yard."

Obviously surprised, Royston gave Wooten a nod. "Wooten? You are the one who apprehended Yardley, I heard. Well done."

"He needed to be questioned," Wooten said. "But I'm sure you know he denies the charges."

"Well, he would, wouldn't he?"

"I assume you lot will be able to make the charges stick?" Jephson asked. This time the condescension was clear.

"We will if we find that he did indeed commit the crime," Wooten replied, unperturbed. "We have proved that he most definitely was the person responsible for the destruction of Miss Foulger's market stall." Royston nodded again, but Wooten continued. "We also have definitely proved that he was *not* the person who had been harassing her."

Royston stopped walking, shock written all over his face. "He was not?" he said in disbelief. "But Glynn … She was so sure! We dismissed Yardley because of it."

"Erroneously, it would seem," Niall said wryly.

Royston still looked flabbergasted, but Jephson's scowl had deepened.

"But who *was* harassing her?" asked Royston. "She told some chilling tales."

"It's ironic that you should ask that," said Niall. "It seems the perpetrator was a young man who had propositioned Miss Foulger and been rejected. A young man she had managed to avoid, until you gave him the information he needed to find her at home."

Royston blinked. "Surely you are jesting?"

"Indeed, we are not," Wooten told him. "The guilty party said as much during our formal interview with him at Scotland Yard."

Royston still looked shocked. He gave Jephson a nervous glance. "I don't know what you mean. I have not the slightest notion of which you speak."

"It was a young man who approached you in Bedford Street as you left the charity. He asked for Glynn Foulger's direction."

Royston started walking again, moving slowly. They all moved with him. "Yes," he said. "Now that you say so, I think I do recall him. Several weeks ago, it was. I turned him away at first, but he was annoyingly persistent." His head lifted. "Yes. I do remember! He said he worked for the farmer who employed Glynn in the market."

"Did it not occur to you that her employer should likely already know where she lived?"

Royston stopped again, closed his eyes for a moment, and breathed deeply. "No. It did not, but I suppose it should have."

"You could have saved Glynn Foulger a lot of misery, perhaps, had you thought about it," Niall said.

"But not her life, surely?" Royston asked. "Yardley did destroy her market stall, you said. He must have killed her as well. His shoe form—there can be no denying it was the murder weapon. We all saw it." He looked to Jephson for confirmation.

The board member did not give it. Instead, he swept a cold look over all three of them. "If you will all excuse me, I have other business to attend to. Good day to you." He strode off, heading for the cemetery gate.

Royston looked as if he wished to hurry after the man, but he looked back to the inspector instead. "Surely Yardley did kill her?"

"The murder is still under investigation, sir," Wooten reminded him. "But I suggest if anyone else asks for personal information about the volunteers at your charity, you should please refrain from giving it."

"Well, it's not *my* charity, is it?" Royston asked irritably. "I am the manager, but the Waif's Wardrobe is not my primary business."

"What is your primary business, then?" Wooten took out his notebook and pencil.

"I am a mill owner," Royston said proudly. "The owner of several mills, as a matter of fact. I have a bobbin mill in Cumbria." He raised a brow. "Do you know how many bobbins the cotton-spinning mills in Lancashire alone use? Business was going very well indeed, so I opened a second mill here in London. The city has both a large workforce and the ports to recommend it. The Isle of Dogs is becoming a manufacturing center at the moment, and its position means I can easily send my bobbins to Yorkshire, Derbyshire, Nottinghamshire, and even to the mills sprouting up in the colonies."

"If business is so good, why bother with the Waif's Wardrobe?" asked Wooten.

"I took the position on as a favor to a friend," Royston said. He shrugged and started walking again. "The work is easy enough. I do not have to be present every day. I have a secretary installed there to handle most of the day-to-day organization." He rolled his eyes. "To be honest, I wouldn't even be needed, if most of the volunteer force did not consist of women."

Niall halted. "What would make you say that?"

Royston stopped too, and looked back over his shoulder. "I'm sure you know what I mean. Women are emotional. Volatile, even. They require direction and instruction."

Niall snorted. "Based on that pronouncement, I will venture that you are not married, sir."

Wooten interrupted. "Hold a moment. I had thought that the charity was begun by women. Do I have that right?" He consulted his notebook. "The Duchess of Rowledge and the Countess of Canfield?"

"Well, yes." Royston started moving again.

"And several of the board members are prominent, charita-ble-minded ladies?"

"Yes. And they are intelligent enough to allow themselves to be guided by the gentlemen." He cocked his head. "And to hand over the organizational reins to someone like me."

"Definitely not married," said Niall.

"Mr. Royston," said Wooten, "consider for a moment that Yardley is telling the truth. If he did not kill Miss Foulger, then who do you think might have done it?"

The man looked taken aback at the question. "How could I know, Inspector? Look, I have learned, since her death, that the girl was quite popular among the other volunteers, but I did not have much interaction with her, myself. In the normal course of things, I might never have encountered her. But once she discovered Yardley had been made a distributor, she raised a fuss. *Quite* a fuss." He glanced at Niall. "I was forced to step in, meet with her, and hear her tale of his past misdeeds. I thought it prudent to bring her complaints to the board—and now you tell me that at least part of her list of accusations was false? Perhaps you will understand why I use the word *volatile*?" He turned to Wooten. "And frankly, sir, I am surprised that you would ask me such a question. Finding Glynn Foulger's killer is *your* job. And now, I must return to mine. Good day, gentlemen."

Niall drew to a halt and watched the man stride through the cemetery gate.

"I think he was genuinely shocked to hear that Miss Foulger had been wrong about Yardley harassing her. Don't you?" asked Wooten.

"Yes," Niall agreed.

"He suffered a moment's twinge abut carrying a false tale to the board of directors, but he didn't let it bother him long." The inspector stared after the man. "What do you think?"

"I think he's a genuine ass," Niall said with a sigh.

"I rather think Jephson is worse," Wooten mused.

"Just because he disparaged me to my face?" Niall asked with amusement. "Believe me, I've heard far worse."

"No, that was foolish, but it's not why." Wooten pressed his lips together a moment. "I've been with the police for a long while now. I've learned much about people, and I've recognized some patterns. Someone who doesn't understand kindness often is unkind themselves. And someone who is often suspicious of those around them nearly always has something to hide." The inspector stood a moment, rocking on his heels. "Yes. I think I shall part from you here, Your Grace. I believe I will do a little digging into the background of Mr. Jephson."

Niall shrugged. "I think that we'd better hope that Kara had more luck with the ladies. We'll speak again soon, then." He started toward the gate. "I'll go and see if they have learned anything useful."

KARA SAT WITH Gyda in the parlor at the charity building, holding her hand throughout the simple, touching gathering of Glynn Foulger's friends. There were tears aplenty, tales of Glynn's impressive sewing skills and of her willingness to teach others, tales of her humor, of her forthright wit, but mostly of her kindness.

"I know this cannot be easy for you," Kara whispered to her friend. Witnessing the loss these women felt must bring Gyda's own bereavement bubbling to the surface.

Gyda lifted her chin. "Actually, this is good. I need to be reminded that I am not the first or only person to lose a loved one. It's a good, swift kick to show me that our job is to go on, remembering and carrying on with what was important to them."

"Are you thinking of the museum?" Kara asked. Lord Charles Osbourne had achieved his long-held goal of opening a museum dedicated to the idea of human creativity. Unfortunately, he had been killed during the opening-night celebration.

"Yes. Ansel has been managing on his own, but I need to get

back into the thick of it and make sure Charles's dream lives on."

"You know we will help in whatever way we can."

"I do know." Gyda sat quietly for a moment, listening to another volunteer share a memory of Glynn. When the woman finished, Gyda turned and clutched Kara's arm. "Kara, this is all setting my brain on fire. I can't stop thinking."

"Of what, dear?"

Gyda glanced around. "This is a lovely way to bid goodbye to someone, isn't it?"

Kara followed her gaze. The women and men of the Wardrobe had laughed and cried together this morning. She thought it must be healing, as well as a fine tribute to their friend. "Yes."

"It seems to represent all that was best of Beth's friend, but I cannot help but compare it to the somber, sad gathering that Charles's mother held for him."

Remembering, Kara nodded.

"Everyone followed his mother's lead, of course, to respect her grief. They had to, I know—but Kara, there was *nothing* of Charles in that sad room! None of his passion, of his love of life and the human potential for beauty and creation."

"You are right, of course," Kara gave her friend a small smile. "But he has you to make sure his bright-eyed wonder, his curiosity, and his remarkable ability to find beauty in even small things lives on."

"And so I will, you may be sure of it. But I should have done something like this." Gyda's grip on her arm tightened. "Kara, I want you to make me a promise, right here and now. When I die, I want you to throw a party. To hell with black mourning and quiet grief. I want you to throw a crush of a party with glorious food and endless drink. Let everyone get drunk as lords and tell their most outrageous stories about me. Scream it to the heavens, so everyone knows I lived, and lived well." She paused, her eyes wide. "Then put me in a boat, set it ablaze, and shove it out into the river, like a Viking warrior of old. Promise me!"

"I'll promise, if you vow to do the same for me—except for

the boat," Kara said with a laugh. "We'll have to tell Niall about it, of course. He has the fortitude to go against societal expectations in such a matter."

"We need to tell *Harold* about it," Gyda corrected her. "I don't expect any one of us to pass on to our glory until we are of a ridiculously advanced age. We'll have to rely on him to see it through."

"I have no doubts on the matter of Harold's fortitude."

"Nor I. Still, he *is* male. I think we will have to remind him regularly."

Kara thought about it. "I think we must document all of our wishes, so there is no question."

"It sounds dark, doesn't it, when you think of writing it all out?" asked Gyda. She grinned. "But it also sounds bizarrely fun. We can make outrageous requests. I'll want fire breathers and a demonstration of swordplay by Viking shield-maidens."

"I'll ask for the party to be decorated with hundreds of bluebells," Kara said decisively.

"What if they are out of season?"

"Then someone with a greenhouse had better be planning ahead."

Gyda bit back a laugh, but she gave Kara's arm a last squeeze before letting her go. She seemed to be in an easier frame of mind, and was everything gracious as Beth brought over a few of the volunteers to make their acquaintance. Some of them were eager to discuss the upcoming memorial and the chance to present their organization to the women of money and influence who might be persuaded to aid their cause.

Kara and Gyda were listening to a couple of eager young women hoping to recruit some of the families who had been helped by the charity. "I think it will be moving to hear them share what our work has meant to them," one of the ladies was saying, when Beth sidled over and touched Kara's arm.

"Would you mind coming over to be introduced to Mr. Royston's secretary?" she asked quietly.

"Of course not." Kara looked about.

"He asked if he could speak with you in the garden." Beth hesitated. "Would you mind if I don't accompany you? I haven't been out there since ..." Her words trailed away and her lip quivered.

"Don't worry a bit," Kara assured her. "I shall introduce myself. What is the secretary's name?"

"It's Mr. Chambers. He's a very nice young man. I'm just not ready to step out there."

"Nor should you, then. If Gyda asks, be sure to tell her where I've gone, would you?" With a last pat of the girl's hand, Kara ventured outside. She couldn't say she blamed Beth. The image of Glynn Foulger spread out across the grass rose in her mind's eye, even as she turned away from the spot.

A young man had been sitting on a bench near the Wardrobe's building. Dressed as relentlessly unobtrusive as any clerk in London, he stood as Kara stepped outside.

"Mr. Chambers?"

"Yes. Thank you for meeting me. I thought it wise to speak to you here, as most everyone has been avoiding the garden." He indicated that she should take the bench, then perched at the other end.

Kara paused. "You don't wish to be seen speaking with me?"

The young man hesitated. "It's just that, with my position here, I try to remain ... impartial."

Kara considered that.

"There are a lot of different sorts of people working with us," Mr. Chambers explained. "Though we all work toward a common goal, there are inevitable conflicts. It's best if I maintain a neutral stance."

"I imagine that was difficult, in the conflict between Miss Foulger and Mr. Yardley."

The young man sighed. "It was, indeed. Glynn was adamant in her wish to protect the women and children who work with us, as well as those who benefit from our work. I found her feelings laudable, of course. But Mr. Yardley was equally convincing about his changed ways."

"Miss Foulger did not find him convincing in the least, from all I have heard," Kara said, watching for his reaction.

He gave her a pained look. "That's true enough, but I suspect Glynn's inflexibility was due to her own experiences."

"I've heard a bit about some of the things that happened to her. It's understandable."

Mr. Chambers nodded. "She was betrothed at one time, you know," he said sadly.

Startled, Kara blinked. "No. I did not know."

"I only heard it because I was in attendance during the meeting she had with my employer, Mr. Royston. I was taking notes." He paused. "Mr. Royston naturally wished to see if their conflict could be resolved before he had to bring it up to the board. Glynn was resistant. I'm afraid Mr. Royston grew a bit condescending. She became rattled, then angry. She raged about the men in her life who had not acted as they ought and vowed that she would not allow him to be another. One of the men she mentioned was a fiancé who abandoned her after her unfortunate accident, it seemed." Mr. Chambers glanced at her. "You heard about the bridge accident, I presume?"

"Yes. The poor girl," Kara breathed.

"Indeed. I'm afraid she endured rather a lot of misfortune in her life, and in the end, she suffered the ultimate betrayal." Mr. Chambers looked disturbed at his own pronouncement. "It's why I asked to speak with you, Your Grace."

Kara waited.

"I heard that Mr. Yardley asked you to help him prove his innocence?"

"He did."

"I also heard that you have improved his case, somewhat, but have not yet absolved him of Glyn's murder."

"You are remarkably well informed," Kara said curtly.

"I am, and for several reasons."

"Which are?"

"Well, first, because everyone here at the Wardrobe is naturally invested in seeing Glynn's murder solved and the killer brought to justice. That means every bit of news is brought back here, shared, and picked apart. I manage to hear most of it, I believe." Drawing a deep breath, Mr. Chambers stood. Walking a few paces away, he stopped and stared at the spot where Miss Foulger's body had been stretched out. "I liked Glynn, Your Grace. She had undeniable skill, and she shared it generously. She had an organized mind, and made several suggestions about our processes that I actually used. She could tell a good story." He glanced back. "But I liked Mr. Yardley, too. He genuinely wanted to help people. I heard his praises from several people in Jacob's Island, people he helped with their displacements. He went far above and beyond his duties for us in that matter. So I was relieved and not entirely surprised to hear that Glynn was mistaken about Yardley terrorizing her. And I have reason to think the police may be wrong in thinking he is the only suspect in her murder."

"What reason?" Kara asked bluntly.

Mr. Chambers turned. His expression showed more than a bit of discomfort. "I happen to know that Miss Foulger had requested a meeting with the Duchess of Rowledge. Apparently she believed that there was another man possibly ... behaving inappropriately with the females associated with the Waif's Wardrobe." He dropped his gaze. "She made the request directly to the duchess, without going through me or Mr. Royston."

"Then how could you know about it?" Kara raised a brow.

Mr. Chambers cleared his throat. "I know because my sister is the Duchess of Rowledge's private secretary, and she brought it up to me."

"I see."

The young man rushed to speak again. "It is because of my sister and her closeness with the duchess that I was appointed to this position, but that is a fact that I do not wish to become common knowledge."

Kara could imagine several reasons why that might be so. Pride, for one. But she did wonder if Royston knew. "I will not share your secret, Mr. Chambers, but tell me, did Miss Foulger meet with the duchess before she died?"

"She did not. Family matters kept the duchess out of London for a few weeks. She had just returned and their meeting was set to happen the morning … the morning after Glynn died."

"You mean Glynn was killed the night before she was to meet with the duchess?"

"Yes, and the thought of it has haunted me. If Mr. Yardley did not harass Glynn, he might not be the killer, either."

"Or he very well could be," Kara said, thinking of the ruined market stall.

"But if he is not? What if Glynn was silenced? What if someone else might be lurking about with an eye to violence?"

"If Miss Foulger was going to the duchess about it, she must have believed the man to be associated with the charity." Kara paused. "I assume that you are the one who actually handles the organizational matters here, sir. Do you know how many male volunteers are associated with the Waif's Wardrobe?"

Mr. Chambers paused to think. "If I count the merchants who donate fabrics, others who donate notions, crates, and other supplies, and add in the volunteers who help us with packing and transportation …" He cast his gate skyward. "There must be more than a dozen."

"Does that include the members of the board of directors?" asked Kara.

Mr. Chambers looked startled. "Surely you do not think …?"

"I think if we mean to consider this theory, then we must consider everyone. Can you get me a list of all of those men—*all* of them?"

"Yes. Yes, of course."

Kara stood and met the man's gaze directly. "Mr. Chambers, do you have any idea who it was that Glynn Foulger might have suspected?"

"No. I'm sorry. I wish I did."

"Do you think any of the volunteers might have a suspicion? Might Glynn have told any of them?"

"She and Beth Williams were close friends. Perhaps her?"

"No," Kara said firmly. "If Beth knew, I would already know."

"Then perhaps one of the other volunteers who regularly spend evenings here, sewing, ironing, folding—and socializing? Several of them are older women. Solid, respectable widows, or those without family to occupy their evenings. She might have confided in one of them."

Kara nodded. "I will make enquiries."

"And I will keep my ear to the ground. If I learn anything more, I will, of course, contact you."

"Thank you, Mr. Chambers. You have been extremely helpful."

The young man bowed. "And, Your Grace, I don't mean to be rude—"

"Please, do not worry," Kara interrupted. "I will keep your secret, sir."

"Thank you." His relief was evident. "Good day, Your Grace."

Kara left him and went to search out Beth and Gyda. The gathering in the parlor was breaking up. Some of the volunteers were leaving, while others rolled up their sleeves and went to pursue their endeavors in the long workroom. Kara found her friends and invited them both to come back to Bluefield Park. "We will all want to hear Niall's report on the burial," she reminded them. She gave Gyda a significant look. "And I think we all need to sit down to review everything we've learned and think about what to do next. If indeed there is anything more to be done."

Beth took a bit of persuasion, but Kara insisted. "Besides talk of the enquiries, it's been too long since we had the chance to simply enjoy everyone's company. Please. Do come," she wheedled.

Beth finally agreed, and with a sign of relief, and before any-one else could detain them, Kara dragged them both to the street, where they could get a hack to the train station.

Chapter Ten

NIALL ARRIVED BACK at Bluefield on the heels of the women. There was a flurry of greetings in the drive before they all trooped in to find that Turner, with his uncanny instincts, had asked Cook to prepare a lavish tea. They called Stayme down, pulled Turner in, and gathered in the parlor, where a table was set with both egg and cucumber-and-cress sandwiches, scones with plenty of clotted cream and Kara's favorite blackberry jam, and lovely, delicate pastries.

Thrilled, Niall reached for the sandwiches, only to have his hand knocked away by his wife.

"Not yet," Kara told him. "We talk first. It won't take Harold long to sniff out a spread like this, and I would like to finish our discussion before he finds us."

She was right, but that didn't keep Niall from eyeing the cream-filled puffs while Kara started at the beginning and summarized everything they had learned. Dutifully, he filled them in on the burial and listened with interest as Kara shared what Royston's secretary had told her.

"So that's where we stand," Kara said as she finished. "We've done as Mr. Yardley asked. We have even lightened his burden a bit, freeing him of the charge of harassment, but it still appears that Frye intends to see him tried for Glynn Foulger's murder.

Now we must decide on *our* next course of action. Or if, indeed, we should pursue the matter any further at all."

Stayme shrugged. "I think your decision hinges on whether you believe Yardley killed the girl or not. Kara?" he asked, eyeing her closely. "What do you think?"

She drew a deep breath and sat quietly for a moment. Niall knew her well enough to know that she was searching her feelings as well as reviewing the facts. At last, she shook her head. "I believe him. I don't think he did it."

"Niall?" asked the viscount.

Niall followed Kara's example and searched his gut. "It was a desperate move for him to come to us for help," he began.

"Or a strategic one," Stayme interrupted.

Niall shook his head. "I considered that. But I believe his story."

"I want to hear what Beth thinks," Kara said before the viscount could speak again.

Beth started, clearly not expecting to be asked.

"Do you think Mr. Yardley killed Glynn?" Kara asked gently. "Please, you knew them both. Tell us what you feel about it."

Beth frowned, thinking, before she glanced uncertainly about.

"Tell them what you think," Gyda urged.

"I just …" Beth sucked in a breath and surged on. "Glynn was my friend, but I never felt easy about how she accused Mr. Yardley. I only met him a few times, but he seemed kind. Sincere in his desire to help. We all heard that the people in his district appreciated him. Some of them even wrote to the board, thanking them and Mr. Yardley in particular." She paused. "I asked her once if she was sure. She told me I just didn't understand the sort of man Yardley was." Her shoulder lifted. "But I think he wasn't that man. Not any longer."

"Then there isn't really a choice, is there?" asked Gyda. "If you are all right in your assessments and Yardley didn't do it, then Beth and the other people associated with the Wardrobe still have a killer in their midst. What if something else happens?"

Niall sighed, facing the inevitable. "Then it is agreed? We continue looking for another suspect in Glynn Foulger's murder?"

"Yes, but how?" asked Gyda. "Where do we go from here?"

"We can start with that list of male volunteers with the charity," Kara said. "Mr. Chambers promised to get it for me."

"Wooten is ahead of you," Niall informed her. "He's even now looking into Mr. Jephson."

"Why?" asked Kara.

Niall made a face. "I told you he was at the burial. Wooten didn't like the cut of his jib."

Gyda snorted, but Kara nodded. "The inspector has good instincts." She looked to Beth. "What of Royston? What is your feeling about him?"

Beth winced. "I really couldn't say. I have not had much contact with him, until lately. He comes in at all sorts of odd hours. Early and late, but that's because he has other responsibilities, or so I've heard."

"And what of the oh-so-helpful Mr. Chambers?" asked Gyda.

"Oh no, it couldn't be him," Beth said at once.

"Why not?" Gyda demanded. "He could have been looking to put Kara off his scent."

"No, no. Mr. Chambers is genuinely kind. You know, the sort of kind that sends you home when you feel ill. He arranged for a temporary replacement for Mr. Martin when his son had an accident, so that he could see to him. He remembered that Mrs. Nolan loves eels and brought her a pie on her birthday."

"Well. Fine, yes. That would seem to be a stretch," Gyda grumbled.

"We can divvy up the list when it comes," Turner said. "I can investigate the merchants, under the guise of looking for supplies or contracts for Bluefield."

"Get me a copy of it when it arrives," said Stayme. "I'll check all the names against my files."

Niall's mind was turning. "I think I will go down to Scotland Yard to speak with John Yardley again. He's had plenty of time to think these last days. Maybe he's recalled something useful."

Before anyone else could say anything, they all heard the overly loud voice of Tom, the underbutler, beyond the parlor door.

"Yes, indeed, Master Harold." His voice was coming closer. "It is indeed teatime. I believe everyone is gathering in the parlor. Let me get the door for you."

The latch was fumbled a bit before the door swung open and Harold came through.

Thank you, Niall mouthed to Tom.

Harold stopped, looking surprised to see all the faces staring back at him.

"Harold, there you are, at last!" Gyda said without a trace of guile. "We were waiting for you to come before we started."

The boy's face lit up at the sight of the food. "Good! I'm hungry. I only had two ham sandwiches and a bowl of soup for lunch."

They all dug in then, and the talk turned general and a good deal lighter. Niall did serious damage to the pile of chicken salad sandwiches and the cream puffs. He watched everyone eating, laughing, teasing each other, and felt the tension ease from his shoulders. *This.* These moments. These people, who returned his care and regard wholeheartedly—they were what had him waking every morning with anticipation and excitement. His art used to be the only way he could cover the holes inside of him, but this … this filled them in. And they felt it, too. He was overwhelmed with love, and pride, and again with the desire to widen their circle.

Beth asked Harold to show her the laboratory, and they all decided to accompany them, except for Stayme, who went back to his rooms, and Turner, who went to see to the wines for dinner.

They all praised Harold's sketches for the design of his owl. Niall stepped in to wrap an arm around his wife as everyone marveled over Kara's latest automaton project. It was a princess in a tower who emerged onto a balcony, waved down at her would-be knight rescuer, and rolled her long hair down for him to climb.

"Never say he's going to climb it?" gasped Beth.

"No, I haven't figured out how to make that look natural," Kara told her with a sigh. "But the client didn't ask for that, in any case. I will have to add a few more movement details, though." She gestured toward the ivy covering one side of the tower. "I was thinking of some flowers opening into a bloom along the ivy."

"Or perhaps a cat sunning on the terrace?" suggested Beth.

"Excellent idea," Kara said thoughtfully.

They stayed a little while longer before all heading back to the main house. Niall eyed his closed, cold forge as they passed. "I need to choose my next project," he began, but Harold interrupted him with a shout.

"Look! Someone is coming!" The boy started to run as a carriage swept up the drive and pulled to a stop before the house. As the door opened, Harold shouted again. "Rob! It's Rob!" he called back with glee. "Rob McRae!"

Beth, who had been walking before Niall and Kara, faltered.

Niall met Kara's gaze. They let go of each other and moved to flank Beth, each taking an arm.

"Chin up, Beth," Niall said.

"Come," Kara whispered. "Let's go and greet him. I know Rob will be thrilled to see you."

The girl looked at them both, then stiffened her spine and stepped forward.

"Well done," Niall said, low.

Together, they went to welcome his best friend.

Rob had Gyda wrapped in a bear hug. As they drew near, he let Gyda go and came striding toward them. "Beth!" Rob cried happily. "You are here, too?"

Niall and Kara let her go as Rob picked Beth up and swung her around in a circle. The girl's face flushed as red as fire, but she laughed and greeted Rob, then stepped back close to Kara when he set her down and turned to shake Niall's hand.

"Here I am, landed on your doorstep, as promised!" Rob said with a grin.

"Thank goodness—we were beginning to wonder if you'd got lost," Kara scolded, then smiled. "Your rooms are all ready for you. We are so glad to have you staying with us. Dinner might be a little later than usual this evening, as we all just stuffed ourselves at tea, but Cook will be delighted to hear you've arrived. You know she loves a man with an appetite."

"And I love her apple tarts!" Rob said appreciatively.

"Let's get your things moved inside," Niall said, stepping forward.

Beth cleared her throat. "Perhaps I'll take this opportunity to head back home, then." She met Rob's gaze. "Will your hired coach be heading back into London? Perhaps the coachman will agree to drop me off at the train station?"

"What? No!" Rob looked alarmed. "Surely you will stay for dinner as well?" He looked to Niall for support.

"Of course she should," Kara said, before Niall could answer. "And you should spend the night with us as well, Beth. We'll get you back to Lake Nemi in the morning." She looked to Rob. "Your driver and his horses must be tired from the long journey, too. Tell them they are welcome to spend the night in the stables. There are plenty of stalls and an empty room with a bed over the tack room."

Beth tried to object, but Kara would brook no resistance.

Surprisingly, Gyda supported her. "Come, Beth. You know you want to hear all of Rob's plans just as much as the rest of us do." Niall hid a grin as Gyda pointed a finger at his friend. "We'll let you unpack, Rob McRae, but then we will wish to hear a full report of what has dragged you from the hills of Scotland."

"Oh, aye, and ye'll have it, ma'am," Rob returned in his thickest brogue.

Gyda began to drag Beth toward the house. "I'll have Turner

put her in the blue guest room?" she called back to Kara.

"Certainly."

Footmen began to file out of the house. Harold picked up a bag and started toward them. "Come on, Rob. I'll help you unpack."

Rob laughed helplessly back at Niall as he followed. "I'll see you at dinner, then?"

"At dinner," Niall confirmed with a nod. He looked down as Kara took his hand.

"Here we are, left all alone." She blinked up at him with innocent eyes. "Whatever shall we do?"

"I have an idea or two," Niall said, drawing her close.

"Yes. Let's practice," she whispered.

"Come on," Niall said, pulling her toward the side of the house. "Let's go around and enter through the terrace so no one will stop us."

NIALL WOKE LONG before the sun the next morning. He lay still a moment, watching Kara sleep, loath to get out of bed. They had all had a lovely evening. Harold had seized the chance to tell everyone about his pending adoption and reveled in both the resulting congratulations and the teasing. Rob had been gracious, answering all of their questions. He seemed both nervous and excited about his new direction in life. Niall had seen how smug Kara had looked, watching the way Rob and Beth surreptitiously watched each other when they believed the other wasn't looking.

Niall heaved a sigh. He wanted more days like that. He wanted to stay here, to wake his wife with soft kisses and exploring fingers before he slept late, ate well, then went to his forge. But after a few moments, he rolled out of bed instead. The sooner they found Glynn Foulger's killer, the sooner he could focus on his family and his art. He crept to his own room, dressed, and went out the front without waking anyone.

John Coachman was ready and waiting at the stables. He would drop Niall off at the train station in Hammersmith. Niall wanted to approach Scotland Yard as early and unobtrusively as possible. If he were lucky, he could get his business done without alerting Detective Frye or attracting the attention of the man's cronies. His odds of success would increase if he didn't arrive in the ducal coach-and-four.

The coach rumbled its way down the dark, empty lanes and into the local village of Ambleburrow. The streets lay quiet, but as they passed the river quay, Niall sat forward and rapped on the ceiling. "Can we stop here a moment?"

He hopped out when the carriage slowed. "Good morning," he said as he approached the quay.

George Armstrong, a local farmer, looked up from his work, loading crates from his wagon to a sturdy little boat. "Your Grace, good morning to you. I'm surprised to see you out so early." He glanced eastward, where the sky was just beginning to lighten.

"I'm heading into Town. You must be going to one of the markets?"

"Aye. Hungerford." Armstrong slapped a crate as he added it to the stack on the boat. "Sweet cherries are in early this year."

"I'll be happy to help you transfer your load, if you'll allow me to sail along with you? You can drop me at the Whitehall Stairs, if it is no trouble. I'll send the coach back for the duchess to make use of."

"Well, I am running a tad late. I won't mind the help getting loaded." The farmer grinned. "Fancy a dawn on the water, do you?"

"Hard to imagine a prettier start to the day," Niall agreed. "But I also wouldn't have to wait for the train."

Armstrong grimaced. "Noisy, detestable, smoky things." He shrugged. "Aye, then. Grab a crate, Your Grace, and we will both get in earlier than planned."

It was true. Predawn on the quiet river was a thing of beauty.

Niall put his head back and breathed in the cool mists—until they sailed into the heart of the city and the river traffic grew heavier. The eastern sky was turning pink when he shook Armstrong's hand, wished him luck at the market, and climbed the slick Whitehall Stairs. He turned into the mazelike precincts of Whitehall and weaved his way through the mix of old and new buildings and alleys, making his way to the roadway that had become synonymous with the Metropolitan Police.

Turning right into Great Scotland Yard, he headed for the archway that led from the street into the station. He was still twenty feet away when he came to an abrupt halt. *Is that—?* Yes. Surely that was Stephen Jephson emerging from the police building's public entrance. The man looked furious, his jaw set as he stalked away, his hands curled into fists.

Niall took a step behind a couple of constables who had paused to appreciate the smell of bacon wafting from a pub. Watching Jephson head for his carriage, he almost missed seeing Wooten slink out of the arch, his gaze fixed on the man. As the first scowling gentleman barked an order to his coachman, Wooten snapped his fingers at a hack driver. Running to climb inside the hack, he gestured after the departing coach, and both carriages lumbered off in the direction of Northumberland House.

Before Niall, the pair of constables finally decided to step inside the pub for breakfast, leaving him standing, indecisive, in the street alone. What had that been about? Should he follow as well? But no, Wooten knew what he was doing. Niall would do better to get inside and speak to Yardley before Detective Frye got wind of his presence. He started forward again, only to duck into a doorway as another figure appeared in the archway.

Niall's mouth dropped open. John Yardley? It was *Yardley* now moving at a clip away from the police office. *Odin's arse!* What did this mean? Had he been released? Had Jephson had something to do with it?

But no. Yardley was walking away at a steady pace, but he

had just looked over his shoulder for the second time. Had Yardley *escaped* from Scotland Yard? Absurd! What in hell was going on in there?

Niall couldn't go in to find out now. If Yardley was free when he should not be, then Niall had to follow him. He kept to the far side of the street and a good distance behind as Yardley moved quickly away. The cobbler passed the first street to the right, but took the second—and set off at a run as soon as he was out of the line of sight from the police office.

The wharf. He was heading to the river. Cursing, Niall started after him. Yardley was already aboard a waterman's boat when Niall drew up at the wharf. They were heading downriver. The man didn't bother to look back, now that he had made his escape.

Niall hailed another waterman from a group gathered around the quay. "Head toward Westminster," he told him. Niall thought he knew where Yardley would go. Surely the man would make his way through Lambeth and Southwark to Bermondsey, where he had friends he had helped—and who would likely help him in return. He kept his eye on the cobbler's boat, and sure enough, Yardley quickly headed for the other side of the river.

"To the stairs," Niall told his waterman. The water traffic was heavy near the bridge. They weaved through it slowly. Niall could see Yardley disembarking as they drew closer. He paid the waterman and hurried after the cobbler. As he'd expected, the man headed east on the Bridge Road. Niall stepped quickly to shorten the distance between them. Yardley would likely continue to Borough Road, but if he were heading to the rookery of Jacob's Island, then he could cut north and east at any number of spots. Niall didn't want to lose him.

It was a long walk, but Yardley didn't falter. Niall stayed back as he headed east on White Street, but inched closer when the cobbler turned north on Bermondsey Street. He had a vague notion of where the rookery lay and expected Yardley to make another turn to the east.

A stink began to grow in the air as they headed toward the

river again. A tannery lay ahead. A large pub sat on Russell Street, across from the tanning yard. Yardley made to hurry past, but several men stepped away from the door to intercept him. Smiling, jesting, looking surprised, the men shook his hand and clapped him on the back. Yardley bit his lip and glanced around, his manner nervous. The men, still laughing and lighthearted, surrounded him and hustled him into the pub.

Niall slowed as he approached. Stopping, he stared up at the sign. The Black Swan. He traced the elegantly carved image with one eye while watching the street with the other, debating with himself. If he went in, he risked exposing himself. If he waited outside, Yardley might sneak out another way.

Niall waited several long, agonizing minutes before deciding to go inside. He wasn't a constable. He could approach the man in a quiet, calm manner. Yardley's friends would not be spooked if he made it clear that he was on the cobbler's side. They could talk. He could ask the questions that had dragged him out of bed this morning.

Throwing his shoulders back, Niall entered the pub. He paused, letting his eyes adjust from the bright morning light to the dim interior. A few tired-looking workers sat about, perhaps stragglers from the night hours at the tannery. His gaze swept on.

Ah. There. Yardley sat at a table in the back, watching him with large eyes and a worried expression. Niall started forward, then slowed and looked down. A large hide had been spread across the pub floor. His brain made the connection instantly. His head snapped up—and something struck him hard. He toppled forward and everything went black.

Chapter Eleven

"**I**S HE STIRRING?"

"I can douse him," someone offered eagerly. "Gotta bucket right here. Shall I douse him, then?"

"Naw. Give him a minute. He'll wake. His own stink will do the job."

Niall rolled his head. It was true. As he came awake, he realized he reeked of fermented fat. The smell of decay clung to him. With a groan, he tried to lift his head. It throbbed like the very devil and his stomach rolled with nausea. At last he managed to lift his head and keep it up—though he was instantly tempted to sink back into unconsciousness.

Blinking, he took in the situation. His hands were tied behind him. He was sitting with his back propped against something soft. A tanned hide, he guessed, as he realized he was in a boat—a lighter used to carry goods on the river. They were heading out from a dock, toward the middle of the Thames. Two men at the stern stood and worked the long oars. The sunken middle contained piles of tanned hides, several strangers grinning at him, and John Yardley, who gazed at him with a glum expression. The stinking, badly tanned hide that Niall had obviously been rolled up and carried in lay at his feet. The smell had him suppressing a gag.

"At the least, you could have used one of the good hides," he said sourly.

"Where's the fun in that?" one of the men answered with a grin.

Niall looked to Yardley. "I suppose you were not set free, then?"

The cobbler shook his head.

"How did you do it?" Niall was genuinely curious.

"Yeah, tell us," one of the men urged.

"Broke yerself right out o' Scotland Yard," another marveled. "Who would o' thunk ye had it in ye, Yardley?"

Niall merely watched the man and waited.

"If only I had removed my equipment from that workroom," Yardley said mournfully. "That is the thought that haunted me all these days locked in there. Someone used my shoe form. It's the only real evidence they have. If I had only taken it home, my life would not have turned into this disaster."

"Yeah, but how did you get *out*, man?" one of the oarsman called.

Yardley cleared his throat. "Someone came in this morning and caused a big ruckus."

"Stephen Jephson?" asked Niall.

"I don't know. I didn't see him. But I heard it. A lot of shouting. It sounded like Detective Frye was involved." The man's mouth twisted in distaste. "That bastard is determined to see me hang, Sedwick, and I will tell you again—I didn't kill that girl."

"I believe you," Niall said quietly. "*We* believe you. I was coming to speak with you this morning, to see if you had any new thoughts on who we might look into."

"I appreciate that, I do, but you don't know what it's like in there. They shouldn't even be keeping me in that holding cell, do you know? I should have been sent off to the Millbank prison or even Newgate while they worked their case. But Frye likes to bring me to a room every day and taunt me. He wants me to confess and thinks he can bully or trick me into it."

"I'm not sure prison would be an improvement," Niall said.

"Why? Because I'd be abused? Browbeaten? What do you think Frye is doing? He likes to tell me about the interviews he's done. He's only talked to the people who knew me when I was imbibing too much. He tells me how they describe me as mean, arrogant, and violent, how the grand jury will get to know the real John Yardley and the charges will reflect it." He sighed. "I heard someone say he'd never get away with it, had the commissioner not been called out of town."

"You do have an ally in there, but Inspector Wooten is trying not to draw attention to his work on your behalf."

Yardley shook his head. "Frye badgers me, needles me, threatens me. One of his cronies comes around at all hours, waking me from sleep, taunting me, drinking my water rations, putting my meals just out of reach and leaving them there for hours."

"That ain't right," one of the men said.

"This morning he came and said the great row that I could hear was about me, but that Frye wouldn't be fooled. He said that I was going to hang for sure and laughed as he said I would piss myself and lose my bowels in front of the crowd gathered to watch me die."

The man in front of Niall made a sound of protest.

"But I'd been waiting on my chance," Yardley continued. "I had the slip from my pillow all ready, folded into a strip, with a long-handled spoon tied into one end. When that damned pest of a constable mocked me, I shouted back. I came right up to the bars and cursed him soundly—and he pressed right up on his side too, spitting at me. I just … reached out and grabbed him. I grabbed his jacket collar and leaned back, pulling him tight and hard against the bars, while I stuck my foot out and hooked it behind his to keep him off balance and unable to pull away." He looked pale, but went on. "Then I wound that slip around his neck with my other hand. I twisted it tighter and tighter while he fought and grunted and his eyes bulged out—and he eventually went down."

"Damn, Yardley," someone said, low.

Yardley shrugged. "Once his lights went out, I grabbed his keys, let myself out, and dragged him inside before I locked it back up again." He sneered. "Let him yell until his voice goes rough, with everyone ignoring *him* for a change."

Niall shook his head, then winced at the stab of pain. "This won't help your case. Every policeman in London will be out for your blood."

"They were already out for my neck!" Yardley cried.

"We won't let them hang you, John," one of the men assured him. "We'll get you out."

The cobbler shot Niall an anguished look. "I cannot stay here and wait for them to hang me for a murder I did not commit."

Niall knew then there was no changing Yardley's mind. He could see it in the man's eyes. He nodded. "We've found that Glynn believed that a man inside the Waif's Wardrobe is preying on women and girls associated with the charity. Think, man. Do you have an inkling who it could be?"

Yardley shook his head. "I don't know. I'm sorry."

Niall sighed in disappointment.

"I'm leaving. Getting out," Yardley said. "I'll start over somewhere."

"Which is more than you'll be doing, mate," someone said to Niall.

"No," Yardley said sternly. "You will not harm him. You cannot. He's a duke."

"What? Him?" the closest man scoffed.

"Him. And more than that, he and his lady wife came to my aid when I asked it of them. They cleared me of what charges they could." Yardley met Niall's gaze. "And he showed up today, trying to do more."

"We cannot play nursemaid to a duke," the same man objected. "We have to move fast, John, if you are to set sail—"

One of the men hissed and the man stopped talking.

"It's your decision, Yardley. I won't try to stop you. And there's a part of me that might do the same, in your shoes," Niall said, still nauseated and trying not to breathe deeply.

"Well, what do we do with him?" someone asked.

"Toss him over," one of the oarsmen called.

They all looked to Yardley, who hesitated a long moment before nodding.

Niall was hauled to his feet and boosted up from the hollow interior to the flat, narrow platform at the bow.

"You can swim, can't you, Your Grace?" Yardley called.

Niall looked at the bank, which seemed very far away. "Not with my hands tied."

"Cut him loose," the cobbler said.

Niall was spun around. He felt the blade go through the rope holding his hands. In one smooth motion, someone stripped the rope away and pushed him overboard.

He came up sputtering, but since his hands were free, he did come up. The lighter eased past him, and as the stern came abreast, the mouthy oarsman tried to strike him with the long oar.

Niall dodged it, but in a fit of temper he surged forward, grabbed it, and held on, arresting the long sweep of movement. The sudden cessation surprised the oarsman, and he nearly lost his balance. The man teetered on the narrow stern and almost went into the water himself.

Niall saluted him as hoots of laughter rang out, but the lighter continued on and he turned and struck out for shore.

KARA WOKE LATER than usual. She was surprised she hadn't roused when Niall left, but he had meant to leave before dawn, and she must have been deeply asleep. Yawning, she dragged herself out of bed and rang for her maid.

"Miss Winther and Miss Williams waited for you to go down for breakfast," Elsie told her.

"Oh goodness, then we had better move quickly," Kara said with a laugh. "You know how Gyda gets if she doesn't eat in the morning."

The speed at which Elsie fetched her gown was answer enough. It wasn't long before Kara was heading downstairs.

"Thank goodness," Gyda called from the parlor. "I'm starving!"

"Apologies! I must have been more tired than I thought," Kara said. "And now I'm hungry, too. Has Harold eaten?" She knew Rob had meant to head into Town early as well, with his hired coach.

"Long since. He and Stayme are in the library, where Harold is attending his lessons and the viscount his correspondence."

"Good." Kara took Beth's arm. "Then it will be just us ladies, and we can have a nice talk."

"Yes, please," Gyda said as they entered the dining room, where footmen were bringing hot trays of food to the sideboard. "Beth wants to head straight home after breakfast, but I was debating the wisdom of having her stay on here." She waited until the footmen finished and left the room before raising her brow at Kara. "You know, due to the situation with ..." She mouthed the last word—*Rob.*

Kara considered as she chose salty bacon, paused, then added a bit more to her plate. "You know I would normally encourage you to stay, given any excuse at all, Beth, just for the pleasure of your company," she told the girl. "But in this case, I do wonder ..."

"What?" Gyda asked. Then she stopped and blinked. "Odin's arse. Yes. I think you might be right." She looked at Beth. "Men do like the chase. And Rob is not just a man—he's a *Highlander.*"

Beth flushed as she took her plate of eggs and toast to the table. "Please. You mustn't think—I don't know—I don't expect—"

Kara set her plate down at the next seat and laid a hand on the girl's shoulder. "Do not be shy about it, Beth. Not with us. You know we wish only the best for you." She paused, struck by a thought. "Unless we have it all wrong and you are not interested in Rob at all, or perhaps not any longer?"

"No!" Beth said, growing even more scarlet. "I do. I mean, I am interested. It's just … he's so …" She sighed. "Why would he be interested in *me*?"

"Oh, he's *interested*," Gyda said knowingly. "I saw him sneaking peeks at you all evening long."

"Of course he's interested," Kara said. "Look at you. Gorgeous, pale skin, lovely blue eyes, and with that fair hair? You are the perfect English blossom. But more than that, you are thoughtful, kind, and courageous."

Beth's hands lay in her lap, with her gaze fastened upon them. "No." She shook her head. "I'm not courageous. Not like Gyda." She glanced over at Kara. "Not like you."

"Horsefeathers," Kara declared.

"Don't talk nonsense," Gyda said at the same time. She shook a finger from across the table. "You forget. I know the situation you escaped from when your parents died. I know how brave you were, standing up to your sodding family, claiming what was yours, leaving all that you knew to start again in London."

"That's not the same," Beth objected. "You and Kara, you *fight*. You stand up to villains. You defend yourselves and others, too."

"Just as you do, Beth," Kara said. "You fight against poverty. You help those in need." She shot the girl a frank look. "We've spent time at your charity. We've spoken to the other volunteers."

"We know you do more than distribute clothes," Gyda said, setting down her fork.

"Beth, we've heard what the other volunteers know of you. You see the humanity in the people you are working with. You are not looking down, you are standing at their side. You give of yourself—and what is braver than that?"

"Quiet courage is still courage," Gyda declared.

Beth blinked back tears. Kara gave her a moment while she took several bites of toast, then pointed the end of it at the girl. "Rob McRae is not a stupid man. I am sure he admires your pretty face, but I know he is surely more enamored of your big heart."

Beth drew a long breath. "I hope you are right."

"She is," Gyda said. "But Rob is still a man. He's bound to act like a fool and make a mess of your courtship, at least once. By Freya's cats, Niall did take forever and blunder about, but he finally got there with Kara. You are going to have to be patient, but hopefully not as patient as our duchess here."

Kara laughed. "She has a point. There is an art to it all, and honestly, I don't think it will hurt your case at all for Rob to come back here tonight to find you gone and busy with your own occupations."

Beth blinked. "I think it's a good thing that I will have the pair of you to guide me in this, but yes, I'm happy to head back to Lake Nemi this morning. I'm anxious to see how Jeanette is faring."

"As am I," Kara said.

"And I think I'll find Lily and check on her," Beth continued. "I know she acts tough as nails, but she and Glynn were friends, of a sort. She must be missing her. Also, Lily should know how helpful she has been."

"Let's finish our breakfast first," Kara said. "Afterward, we will see you into Town. Perhaps Mr. Chambers will have that list ready for me." She turned to look at the sideboard. "Is there more bacon?"

They were just finishing up when the door opened and Prudence, the downstairs maid, rushed in. "Oh, miss! I mean, Your Grace! You have a visitor!"

Kara exchanged glances with Gyda. "I wasn't expecting anyone. Were you?"

Gyda shook her head.

"Who is it, Prudence?" asked Kara.

"Oh, but that's just it, Your Grace! It's a duchess! A *real* duchess!"

Gyda let out a bark of laughter. "A real duchess, Prudence? Who do you think you are *Your Grace*-ing?"

"Oh, I do beg your pardon, ma'am, but I daresay you will know what I mean when you see her! We've known our own duchess from when she was a girl with oil under her nails. But this one? She looks like she was born to it! She's got fur trim on her cloak and little jewels dangling from her pelerine! Turner is showing her to the ivory sitting room and sent me to fetch you."

Kara cleared her throat. "Prudence, do you know, by chance, *which* duchess is being shown to my private sitting room?"

"Oh, yes. Apologies, ma'am. It's the Duchess of Rowledge, and she says she needs a private word with you."

They all three straightened at the name of the woman who had started the Waif's Wardrobe charity.

"What do you think she wants with you?" asked Gyda.

"I haven't the faintest notion." Kara felt quite at a loss. "I believe I met her once, at the Crystal Palace, but I don't know much about her. All I recall is that she is a bit older than me. Perhaps a decade? And she has several daughters, but no sons."

Gyda was frowning now, too. "Do you think she wants to tell us to stop mucking about in her charity's business?"

Beth gasped.

"No. Certainly not," Kara said with conviction. She stood. "There is no use speculating. I'll go and see her."

"I should go." Beth stood too. "There is a late morning train into Town, isn't there?"

"Don't let the woman run you off," Gyda said. "You are a volunteer, not an employee."

"Yes, I know, it's just … I don't know. I don't want to be seen as thinking I am above myself." Beth raised a hand as Gyda started to object. "And I truly do wish to check on the other girls.

Let them know they are not going through this alone."

Gyda sighed. "Very well. I'll take you to the station in Hammersmith." She gave Kara a stern look. "Then I'll be back to hear what all of this is about."

With a nod for Gyda and a goodbye hug for Beth, Kara saw them off. Her curiosity growing, she turned and headed for the room that was usually marked as her private retreat.

The Duchess of Rowledge looked up as Kara entered. To give Prudence credit, the woman *did* make an intimidating impression at first glance. Her gown was a rich pumpkin color and the pelerine atop it was a work of art, covered in jet and jewels in the pattern of orange and black butterflies. A matching pin anchored her heavy chestnut hair, where just a few grays could be seen mixed in.

Kara suppressed a sigh, though, as the woman straightened. She'd been bending over Kara's drafting desk, examining the designs for the project she was working on in the lab.

"Your Grace," the woman said with a nod. "Do forgive me. I'm afraid you've caught me snooping." It was said stiffly, as if the duchess was not used to apologizing. "Thank you for seeing me," she continued. "We have met, if you recall?"

Kara nodded. "At the Crystal Palace. Yes. I do remember."

"The clocks and automatons you had on exhibit there were fascinating," the other woman said. "I was impressed and quite encouraged to see you presenting something that mixed both beauty and science."

"Thank you."

"I returned to the Great Exhibition with my daughters, specifically because I wished for them to see you and the few other women exhibitors." She smiled. "You were their favorite by far."

"I am flattered."

"They did enjoy the bubbling water, though. And the bears and elephants and such. But *this* ..." The Duchess of Rowledge gestured toward the new plans. "Oh, my youngest would delight in this."

"The client who commissioned it has a fascination with the old folk tales."

"I imagine you meet a great many interesting people in your work as an artist. Again, I am impressed. We have read about some of your exploits in the papers, of course. I am very thankful to be able to point to you as an example to my girls."

Kara made a sound of protest.

"No. It's true. You are a woman of intelligence and taste. You have managed to live a life far beyond the high walls that Society has tried so hard to place around most gentlewomen. And you have done it while maintaining the grace and decorum of a true lady."

Kara laughed. "I hate to disappoint you, Your Grace, but there are more than a few people about who would disagree with that."

"Pssh." The duchess waved a hand. "Jealous, the lot of them. And perhaps their greatest envy comes from your choice of husband."

Kara let a smile curve across her face. "I cannot blame them, there."

"There are more than a few rumors that you knew about the duke's bloodlines before they were revealed."

"They may say what they like in order to make themselves feel better," Kara told her. "But I did not know." She made a face. "Not until it was too late." She indicated a pair of chairs next to a small table at the unlit hearth. "I had already fallen in love. Honestly, I wasn't happy at all when he was asked to take up his title, but it has all worked out well enough, I suppose."

The other woman looked thoughtful as she took the seat. She looked around the room. "This is your private study?" She glanced around at the collection of books, an assortment of Kara's early automatons, the comfortable furniture and colorful art. "I knew your mother, you know. She was a leader of the *ton* when I made my debut. She was kind to me. I always hoped to see Bluefield Park. It's even more beautiful than I imagined."

"In large part due to her," Kara said. "My mother worked hard to improve the estate. I have made a few changes, but mostly I just perform upkeep on her work."

The duchess raised a brow. "And what would your mother think of your bonny, braw duke of a husband?"

The unexpected question brought sudden tears to Kara's eyes. She refused to let them fall. "She would love him, as he would adore her."

"From what I know of him, I believe you are right." The duchess leaned forward. "Your marriage is another thing I point out to my girls as something to emulate, for you have done what so few of us have. You have found yourself a husband who supports you in your art, and in your independent ways when it comes to handling your family businesses and fortune." Her mouth twitched. "As well as in your *other* endeavors."

A chuckle bubbled up and out of Kara. "Our adventures are not all due to me and my pursuits, no matter what whispers you might hear."

"I believe you," the duchess said. "I also know that you are very fortunate in having such a supportive husband."

Kara heard the stark truth behind the words—a sad truth about the lady's own husband. "I see."

"It is very easy to see. I am a duchess with four daughters and no sons. I am a failure."

"Surely not," Kara objected, a shiver running up and down her spine.

"In my husband's eyes, at least," the duchess said calmly. "Our nephew is my husband's heir. He's a perfectly charming young man, but the duke despises him, nonetheless. Almost as much as he despises me, and he becomes more furious with me with each passing year."

"I'm sorry," Kara whispered.

"You understand, then, why I hope my girls will look around with clear eyes and not allow themselves to be dazzled by rank and fortunes." The duchess nodded. "Fortunately, I think they will. They see how resentful and vindictive their father is. How he hates everything I do that is not dedicated solely to his comfort or ambitions."

"He does not approve of your work with the Waif's Wardrobe, then?"

"He rails against it. Or he used to."

Kara stilled at the ominous tone the other lady used, but Turner came in with a tea tray at that moment. She poured, and once Turner had gone, she looked to the other woman over the rim of her cup. "Something changed in your husband's attitude about the charity?"

"It did. It was last year that we grew large enough to purchase the building on Bedford. Once we settled in, we attracted more attention, more volunteers. We began to grow again, and quickly. It became clear we needed a manager to see to the overall organization, to keep it all moving smoothly so that we may help the largest number of the needy."

"Is that when you hired Mr. Royston?"

"It is. That period also marks the first time that my husband became interested in the charity. He vowed to help us find just the right person for the position."

"So your husband recommended Mr. Royston?"

"My husband *insisted* that we engage him. Royston was newly arrived in London. He had experience as a factory manager. He was presented to us as a *fait accompli*, already hired and eager to begin."

They sat silently for a moment.

"We heard no complaints about the manager in our dealings with the charity in the last few days," Kara offered.

"Nor have I heard any, and believe me, I have listened."

Ah. The reason for Mr. Chambers's appointment as secretary became even clearer.

The duchess lowered her voice. "And yet, my dear, I cannot shake the feeling of suspense. I await the dropping of the other shoe in a sea of anxious anticipation."

"You think your husband placed Mr. Royston into the charity to cause trouble?"

"I have no evidence to think so, and yet I absolutely believe it with everything in me. The duke wants the Wardrobe to fail. He wants *me* to fail. It would be his greatest pleasure to rub my nose in it forever, just as he does my more personal failures." The duchess set down her cup and met Kara's gaze directly. "When I heard from my secretary about Miss Foulger's wish for a meeting, and when I heard about what she believed might be happening to the women associated with us, Royston was the first thought in my head."

"Do you have any information on his background?"

"No."

"Your husband didn't give you any specifics as to his past employment?"

"None."

"So you would like someone to dig around a bit, to see what might be uncovered about Mr. Royston's past?"

"Yes, exactly,"

Kara nodded. "I am persuaded. I will take on the mission, for all of our sakes."

The Duchess of Rowledge did not do anything so plebian as to slouch in relief. But it was there in her eyes, just as her gratitude sounded clear in her voice. "Thank you, my dear. I look forward to hearing what you discover, but we must be careful."

"I will report only to you."

"Or to Mr. Chambers, as long as Royston does not see it. The young man may be trusted."

"Understood."

The duchess stood. "Thank you, once again. I should not linger." She paused in the doorway and looked around at the room once more. "Your mother would be very proud of you, for so many reasons."

Kara only nodded, but as the duchess disappeared, she slumped back into her chair, suddenly overcome with myriad emotions. A fresh wave of grief for her mother chased gratitude, pity, and determination around her chest. It took her several minutes to gather her composure and dry her tears, but she managed at last, and stood to head upstairs. By the time she had changed into one of her modified skirts and matching bodice, full of hidden pockets and useful objects, Gyda had returned.

Her friend's eyes lit up when she saw her. "Why are you wearing—"

"Gyda, listen," Kara interrupted. "Do you recall what Niall said about Mr. Royston owning a mill? Did he say where?"

"No. It was only that he had opened a second mill here in London somewhere."

"Drat. That's all I remember, too. Come on." Kara grabbed her friend's hand and started pulling her toward her room. "Let's get you into something plain and sturdy. I'll wager Stayme knows where to find that mill. I want to go and check it out. We'll pose as a workers' aide society or something similar and see what we can find."

"Niall …" Gyda started.

"Who knows when he will return? I don't want to wait. Do you?" Kara already knew the answer.

"No. You go ask Stayme while I change."

"We'll take my gig," Kara said, smiling as she headed down the stairs. "Just two sober, charitable young women, looking to help."

Chapter Twelve

IT TOOK NIALL an unexpectedly long time to reach the shore. The water was cold and his boots were heavy. His arms felt leaden by the time he waded out onto an empty stretch of shore. Falling into the muck, he rolled onto his back, his chest heaving. For a long time, he lay there, staring at the sky, trying to catch his breath, and wondering what he was going to tell Wooten.

Perhaps he'd fallen asleep, even as cold and mud covered as he was. In any event, his eyes were closed when he felt the first poke. He opened them and stared into the filthy visage of a young mud lark.

"Argh!" The boy jumped back, his face falling. "Alive, then."

"Sorry to disappoint." Groaning, Niall rolled over and got to his feet. His boots squelched as he covered his eyes and squinted, trying to figure out where he'd landed. Wapping, he'd wager.

"It's jest … ye woulda been my first dead 'un."

"I came a mite too close to it for comfort, lad," Niall said with sympathy. Mud larks were often very young or very old, and among the most destitute in London. Scavenging the riverside was a difficult, foul-smelling occupation, and the bits of coal, iron, and bone they could find and sell barely kept their bellies full. Niall felt in his pockets, but either Yardley's friends or the river had emptied them. Shaking his head, he looked west. "Isn't the

Red Lion near here?"

"Aye." The boy still looked forlorn at his loss of a corpse.

"Show me the quickest route there and I'll spot you a warm meal."

The lad lit up. "With a sweet at the end?"

"As much as you can hold," Niall agreed.

"The deal's struck, then. Follow me."

Niall did as he was bidden, dripping river water and mud through several alleys he would have missed, and arriving far quicker than he expected. He stood in the courtyard with the mud lark lingering just out of reach and sent one of the grooms inside to fetch the innkeeper.

After several minutes a tall man came out, wiping his hands on a towel tucked at his waist. When he caught a glimpse of Niall, he frowned.

"Edvin," Niall called, raising a hand.

The innkeeper stepped closer. "Niall?" he asked in astonishment. "What in seven hells happened to you?" He stopped suddenly. "Wait! I thought you were a duke now?"

"It seems even a duke can get tossed into the Thames, if he runs afoul of the wrong people."

"That's the Niall Kier I know, always making friends." Edvin made a face. "Well, I suppose you will be wanting a bath? Just try not to leave a path of filth behind you, eh?"

"No, no. I wouldn't ask it of you. However, if you would, I'd like you to feed this young whelp a feast of a meal." He indicated the mud lark. "And if you could have one of your grooms find me a hack that won't object to the smell? I'll send payment as soon as I'm … back to myself."

Edvin raised a hand. "Yes, yes. I know you are good for it." He eyed the boy. "You. I'll take you around to the kitchens. You smell near as bad as him, but you can eat your fill in the scullery. And you." He looked back to Niall. "Any cab willing to take you is already going to stink like hell."

"I figured as much, but needs must."

He had to wait a bit, but eventually Niall found himself stretched out in a cab, heading for Marylebone. Gyda had been right—when one was disheveled or distraught, Donnelly House was the place to go to begin to get your equilibrium restored.

He entered the private bathhouse through the back, leaving dirty, everyday London behind to enter a world of elegance— even at the back entrance. "Good day, Jones." All the porters were called Jones.

"Good day, Your Grace." The man made no comment regarding the state Niall was in. "Not the public baths today, I imagine. Shall I prepare a private bathing chamber for you?"

"Yes, thank you," Niall said with longing. "Hot and scented, if you please. And I'm afraid I will need that change of clothes." After he had taken his title, he'd paid the extra fee to store a complete change of clothes here, including boots. "I'm afraid all of this is past even Donnelly House's extraordinary skills."

"We'll see what can be salvaged, sir. If you will follow me?"

Mere minutes later, the sturdy, carved door was closing behind the porter and Niall was crawling into a sunken tub. The heat eased his aching limbs, and he just soaked for a few minutes before sitting up to scrub himself top to bottom. He rang for the tub to be emptied, rinsed, and filled again before he stretched out once more in the blessedly hot water. His mind whirled, going over the morning's adventures.

He could scarcely wait to tell Kara everything, but he would go to Scotland Yard first. Wooten needed to know about Yardley's plans to leave England. Also, Niall was beyond curious to know what had happened with Jephson this morning.

Once the water cooled, Niall climbed out, dried, and dressed. When he finally left the private chamber, he found Jones waiting in the passage. "I was just coming to tell you, Your Grace, that we may be able to save your boots."

"Thank you, Jones. Your efforts are hugely appreciated." Thanks to his foresight of leaving a purse with his extra clothes, Niall was able to tip the porter handsomely. And now, restored to his ducal splendor, he exited out the front and had no problem finding a hack to take him to Scotland Yard.

He was striding toward the arched entrance when he pulled up short, for the second time that day. Had he heard someone call his name?

"Niall! Niall!"

He turned about, searching—and finally saw the small figure pushing her way toward him.

"Beth! What is it?" Tears streaked the girl's reddened face. She looked like she'd run all the way from Covent Garden.

"Oh, Niall! I'm so glad you are still here!"

He didn't bother to correct her.

"I'm so glad I caught you! I need help!"

"Yes, of course. What is it, Beth?"

"It's Lily! She … She …" Choking on a sob, Beth couldn't seem to get the words out.

Niall took both of her hands in his own. "Breathe, Beth. Yes. That's it. Now, tell me."

"Lily! She's … clean!" The girl broke down into a spate of sobbing again.

"It's fine. You are fine." Niall pulled the girl in and wrapped her in a hug. He glanced ahead. The Carlisle lay just beyond them. It was a respectable café frequented by the men of the police force. "Let's take you inside and get you some tea."

Beth grew calmer as he arranged for a table. She was quiet as the waiter brought them mugs of tea. "I'm sorry. I'm so sorry," she said quietly. "It's just … I don't know if I can explain."

But Niall had been thinking of what she had said. "When Kara and I talked with Lily the other morning, I noticed the way she looked," he told Beth. "She needed a bath. She wore childish clothes and her hair in pigtails. I had the thought that she was making an effort to appear younger, perhaps, than she is."

"Yes. Yes, that is it, exactly. Most gentlemen don't see beyond the smock and the dirt. She hasn't said as much to me, but I think she felt safer, appearing younger. Her sister, you know …" Beth paused, and her face went scarlet. "As Lily's sister grew older, she began to sell her flowers at night, in an attempt to earn more. But then, as some of the night flower sellers do, she turned to …" Her voice trailed away.

"Prostitution. I gathered as much from something Lily said."

"Lily told me once that she wasn't ready to make such a change, but her sister expected it of her."

"It probably earns more, but …" Now Niall was the one to let his sentence fall away. Rage filled his heart at the thought of that young girl being forced into such a life.

"Yes, quite," said Beth. "Lily used her disguise as a delaying tactic as much as protection. When I arrived in Town from Bluefield this morning, I went looking for her. I wanted to tell her that her help had been particularly useful. I thought it might make her feel a little better, after losing Glynn. She wasn't at her usual spots. When I finally found her …"

"She had bathed," Niall said, understanding. "You took it at a sign that she is considering making that transition into … something darker than flower selling."

Her eyes filled again. "Yes. And do you know, I think she had been right all along? She knew which were the good spots for sales and had a good rapport with the men who always seem to be buying a nosegay for their sweethearts, mothers, or mistresses. Lily always did a decent trade, but today … she was scrubbed clean and smiling, with her hair washed and flowing down her back, and she had the usual crowd of gentlemen around her, but they were lingering. Eyeing her differently." She shuddered. "But that's not the worst—"

"Take a sip of tea," Niall urged. "Good. Now you can tell me."

Beth leaned forward and lowered her voice. "Lily was wearing a new smock. She wasn't shy about it. She gave a twirl and told the gentleman she'd just been made a gift of it last evening. Niall—the new smock, I recognized it at once! It was the garment that Glynn had been making for her."

A chill went down Niall's spine. "Are you sure?"

"Yes! But I made a mistake. I reacted badly. I was just so shocked! I grabbed her. I demanded to see the embroidery, the special embroidery that Glynn put in all her garments. That one was meant to be a lily, especially for her. But she pulled away. She refused to show me! And then she said ..." Beth breathed deeply. "Lily said it was time. Time for her to grow up. Since it was coming in any case, she was making her own choice, choosing her own time and her own gentleman."

Niall scowled. He was thinking back to what Kara had told him after her first day at the charity. "The bag with the smock inside went missing after the murder, correct?"

"Yes!"

"It wasn't found?"

"No. The coroner's man looked for it, all through the charity house."

A dark thought wiggled its way into his head. "You don't think that Lily—"

"Killed Glynn?" Beth's mouth dropped open. "No! Absolutely not! When I reached for her and tried to see the embroidery under the strap, Lily grew fierce. She said it was hers. It had been meant for her. She said that her gentleman had given it to her as a gift, because she'd wanted to wear it before ... before she stopped selling flowers."

"But that could only mean—"

The tears fell. "Who else could have had that garment? It means that whoever gave her that smock is likely the killer!"

"Did she tell you who it is? Who the gentleman is, the one she is choosing?"

"No! She pushed me away. She ran away, Niall. She knows the streets. I couldn't catch her. But we have to find her!"

"Yes we do—and quickly." He stood. "That smock is evidence. Wooten will want to know. He can help, get his men looking. Come on, Beth. Let's go get them started."

"OF COURSE I looked into him," Stayme said, grabbing Kara by the arm and ushering her and Gyda out of the library. "Quiet now!" He glanced back at Harold, sitting at a table, surrounded by books. "The boy is knee deep into the restoration of the monarchy. Let him think, will you?"

"You looked into Royston?" Kara asked as they all crossed into the parlor, only a little surprised, but extremely grateful.

"Well, this is not my first go-round with the lot of you, is it? I started examining the major figures surrounding the charity right after you agreed to get embroiled in the matter, but Niall asked me to look into Royston after the funeral, if you will recall. The Countess of Canfield seems to be exactly what one would expect. Her friend the Duchess of Rowledge, though? The poor woman is weighed down by her ass of a husband, who is no better than a boulder strung around her neck. Still, she manages to stand tall. I've no worries about her."

"She was only just here." Kara explained about the woman's request.

The viscount appeared to be thinking. "Hmm. Well, I only just started in on Royston after Niall mentioned their discussion at the burial. It doesn't make much sense for a man claiming to own multiple mills to also be employed managing a charity, does it?"

"He did tell Niall that he took the position as a favor to a friend. And now the duchess says that her husband hired him."

"An association with the Duke of Rowledge is not the feather in his cap one might think," Stayme said with a sniff. "The duke is mostly known for his gambling habits, his cruelty to his wife, and the unseemly amount of time he spends at certain specialty fleshpots in Southwark."

"Which specialty?" asked Gyda.

"Those that peddle in young girls and boys," Stayme said darkly.

Nausea roiled Kara's stomach and she suddenly regretted that extra bacon. "Do you think Royston frequents such places?"

"I don't know, but I can send my people to find out. I do know that I could not find his name associated with any bobbin mill in the Isle of Dogs. As far as I can tell, there is only one such mill in that area, and it seems to be a side business established by the Brown and Long Timber Works."

"Then that is where we will go," Kara declared.

"Slow down, young lady. Neither of you are going anywhere without me."

"What?" Kara gaped. "But—"

"No *buts*," Stayme interrupted. "You need me. If Royston is there, he'll recognize the two of you. You will need me to distract him. Even if he is not there, you'll get further as two workers' rights advocates with a wealthy investor looking to sink his funds into businesses that protect and care for their employees."

Gyda shrugged. "He's right."

"Don't sound so surprised," the viscount snapped. "Did you think I developed an information network the likes of mine without being able to ferret things out myself?" Rubbing his hands together, he grinned. "I'm old, not dead, and it has been far too long since I indulged in a bit of fieldwork."

Kara just looked at him, helpless to protest.

"Don't worry so, girl," Stayme said. "You've got Gyda for muscle and me for brains. All will be well." He headed for the door. "Just give me a moment to prepare. This calls for a gaudy waistcoat and a jeweled walking stick." The viscount laughed. "Oh, this will be fun."

Not so much later, Kara was facing into the breeze as they moved at full speed on the river, heading east in a steam-powered wherry.

"It will take you near all the day to drive," Stayme had said, dismissing the idea of the gig. "We have to get all the way to the farthest side of the peninsula. There's a mast yard with a private dockyard just north of the timber works. We'll try to land there.

If they object, we'll go further up to the Blackwell Stairs."

Fortunately, the workers at the dockyard did not object to two women and an older gentleman disembarking. They assisted Kara and Gyda from their wherry with exaggerated politeness, and only a few suggestive calls came from men perched high on a crane. The three of them made their way out of the mast yard to the main road and headed south.

"It is not far, according to my reports," Stayme said, moving jauntily along. There was not much traffic, apart from the rumbling of wagons. A few clerks rushed to and fro, but for the most part, all the activity was occurring in the businesses they passed. Kara noted a cement works and a seed oil mill. She was staring at the long, open-air lane of a rope walk across the way when Stayme gave a satisfied grunt. "There is the timber works," he said, gesturing. "Keep your eyes peeled for the bobbin mill."

The road veered inland slightly, giving way to a large, shallow timber pond. The smell of freshly cut wood filled the air. They kept their distance as they traveled the long way past the large barns, warehouses, and stacks of lumber, until at last they reached a short, graveled drive. It led to a bricked, two-story cottage. It was a mishmash of a building, with multiple roof levels, three chimneys, and the addition of several small attached rooms. A tiny sign at the end of the drive labeled it the Bobbin Mill.

"The first, single-story section looks to be the offices," Stayme said. "We'll start there and see if Royston is about. Keep your heads down."

A door and a window faced the road. Approaching, Stayme knocked. Kara inched closer to the window and leaned so that she could see inside. It was indeed an office, with several stacks of file drawers and a desk that sat empty. A man stood in a corner, looking over a stack of papers spread over a small table and consulting what looked like a schedule on the wall.

Stayme knocked, and the man looked over his shoulder. Kara leaned away to keep from being spotted. She stepped back in place behind the viscount and lowered her head.

They waited. Stayme knocked again.

"I'm not ready," the man inside called.

Gyda snickered, and Stayme tossed a grin back at her before knocking again. This time the door was yanked open.

"I told you, I don't have—" The man, tall and ginger haired, stopped speaking. "Oh. You're not Henderson."

"No," Stayme agreed amiably.

"Who are you, then, and what is it you want?" The man was the very picture of exasperation.

"I am Mr. Hervey. Are you Mr. Royston?"

"I am not," the man replied sharply. "Although I do seem to be saddled with most of his work."

"I was told Royston was the owner of this mill," Stayme said.

"Is that what he's saying now?" the man asked with a snort. "I suppose he thinks that sounds better than 'partner in management,' which was already a stretch."

"I am misinformed, then?" asked Stayme.

"Brown and Long own this mill," the man said shortly. "It's an arm of the timber works." He shot a glance at Kara and Gyda before turning away and going back to the table.

"I expected to find Mr. Royston here," Stayme said, still pleasant.

"Yes, he is expected daily, but rarely shows his face, so you will just have to join all of us here in our disappointment."

"May I ask *your* name, sir?" asked Stayme. "And your position here?"

"I am Lowell. Supervisor."

"Well, then. It's a pleasure, Mr. Lowell. It sounds as if you are the man I should speak to, in any case."

"You will pardon me, sir. But I must complete the work of two men and have no time to talk."

"Perhaps you will indulge an old man, then, and just listen for a moment?" When Lowell began to object again, Stayme chuckled. "Indulge a very *rich* old man, would you?"

Startled, Lowell looked back.

"It's true," Stayme said. "I am an old man with a fortune, but no wife or children." He gestured behind him. "My two nieces will inherit. They are very good girls, Mr. Lowell. They have big hearts and a great deal of passion for a specific cause. They advocate tirelessly for workers' rights to better conditions."

Mr. Lowell glanced at them again, this time with respect. "That is a cause I support as well."

"When I am gone, their income will derive from the investments I make now. My nieces have pleaded with me to use my money to support companies who make a real effort to support their employees instead of treating them as replaceable chattel. I had heard that this mill might be such a place. It was suggested that it might be thanks to Mr. Royston's efforts?"

Mr. Lowell's expression went through a curious transition, his face coloring with a potent mix of both pleasure and fury. "You are partly correct, sir. We do make efforts to improve safety for our workers, but Royston would not know an improvement if it rose up and bit him on the arse. I do not believe he has ever even set foot beyond these offices." He flushed again. "I do beg your pardon for my language, ladies."

"Yes, well," Stayme said stiffly, his disapproval clear, "clearly you feel strongly about the subject. I would love to hear your views, but perhaps we can speak about your efforts while my nieces wait outside? I saw some tables and chairs in the shade near the back of the mill."

"Yes, of course. I know Mr. Brown and Mr. Long would be thrilled to hear of your interest in investing."

"And it wouldn't do you any harm if I chose the mill due to your care for your workers, would it?" asked Stayme knowingly. He turned to face Kara and Gyda and raised both brows. "Why don't you allow us to talk a bit of business, my dears? You may have a stroll outside for a bit."

"I must ask that you do not enter the workroom," Mr. Lowell said over Stayme's shoulder. "It's not safe for visitors to wander in there. I have already had to enforce the rule forbidding outsiders once today."

Keeping her shoulders hunched and her form small, Kara nodded. She and Gyda waited until Stayme entered the office with Lowell before they turned to go.

Laughing, Gyda pulled Kara along by the hand. "Does he really believe that *two passionate advocates for workers* would stay out of his workroom?"

Kara lifted a shoulder. "Well, he can rightly say that he warned us."

They headed for the longest, tallest section of the building, which stretched out with two doors below and a long gallery of windows up high. Even from outside they could hear the racket. When Gyda pulled open the door, it was all Kara could do not to cover her ears.

They stepped inside. It was all one long room, with white-washed walls and bright light coming from the windows. The floor was covered in a thick layer of wood chips and wide shavings. To the left, a long table ran along one wall, its surface covered with scattered metal tools and great, wide, shallow baskets filled with square-sided, long wooden bars. Overhead, a shaft drive stretched out across most of the room. It circled ceaselessly, powering belted drives that angled downward in several spots to run lathes and horizontal drills. More wide baskets sat around the machines, holding bobbins in various states of manufacture.

Men worked at the machines, sending sawdust and noise into the air. They all wore curious hats with wide brims. In the front, fine mesh was attached, descending to curve out and then down under the wearer's chin.

Gyda gave Kara a nudge. "Look!" she said loudly in her ear, gesturing to a gathering of women at a back corner.

Kara saw that several men were working at the machines, but noted that one driller was empty, as well as a few other stations that appeared to be meant for hand tools. "All of the women are back there. What do you think they are doing?"

"I don't know, but we need to find out." Gyda started down the right side of the room, where there were fewer buzzing machines at work.

Kara followed. As they drew near, the entire group of women all turned to look at them.

One of them gripped one of the hats with the mesh veil at her side. She glanced back at the woman near the back of the group, next to the door. "They came with you?"

The woman at the back shook her head. Her expression was … serious. In fact, Kara realized they all watched them with wary, solemn faces.

"Good day to you," she said with a nod. "We've come to view your mill with an eye to workers' conditions and safety." She gestured toward the woman's hat with its mesh veil. "It seems you have made some strides in that area."

The woman holding the hat snorted. "Well, there's safe, and then there's *safe*, isn't there?"

"Come now, Louisa!" another woman chided. "Give poor Lowell his due. Our supervisor does look out for us, miss," she said to Kara. "Why, we lost two good men to shards of wood in the eye last year. Mr. Lowell were that mad! It were him who came up with the wearin' of the veils to block the shards." She tilted her head to take both Kara and Gyda in. "Are the two of ye writing an article? A report? Ye should include it, if ye are. We are ever so grateful not to have to worry about losin' an eye."

"And Lowell hired an extra lad to come around with fresh water from the well, to keep us cool, and keep us from faintin' from the heat," another woman said.

"He hired young Paul to fetch and deliver our full baskets," the woman called Louisa corrected her.

"Aye, but he bade the boy to bring fresh water in exchange, didn't he?"

"Is that what ye're doin', then?" Louisa asked Kara. "Writing an article?"

"Not exactly," Kara hedged. "It's more that we are making observations on behalf of some manufactory owners." It wasn't a lie. Not truly. She did own a half a dozen or so such places—and she was always looking for ways to keep her employees both safe and contented.

"We got it better than some," Louisa grudgingly admitted. "Lowell does look out for us. The floors is usually swept clearer than this, but Fiona, the girl who sweeps, had to go up to the timber works today to help out with some staining."

"And recall the time Lowell horsewhipped that delivery driver for lighting his pipe too near?" the other woman said. "The man fair lives in fear of a fire in here."

"It's only sensible," Gyda agreed. "This place would go up in a flash."

"Fire's a quick, honest death, at the least," the woman by the door said darkly. "Better than what some women get from the mill owners and their ilk."

"Now, Mary," Louisa said.

"Don't *Now, Mary* me," the woman spat. "I came down here in search of my sister, and I'm doin' you all the favor of givin' you fair warning about the wolf in your midst. So do you think I'd pass up the chance to tell my fears for Maggie to someone who might spread the word out to places I cannot reach?"

"Let her say her piece," someone called out. "If those two want to know about the dangers workers face, they should hear all of it."

"Perhaps we might talk outside?" Kara suggested. "It would be easier to hear and perhaps a bit cooler."

They all exchanged glances. "I want to hear what she has to say," someone said. "She's come all this way."

Kara realized the woman, Mary, clearly not a part of the usual crew, must be the visitor Mr. Lowell had mentioned.

Louisa nodded. "Just for a bit, mind. We don't want to fall behind."

They all shuffled outside and gathered in the shade of a couple of small trees. Louisa gestured to the woman who had been lingering by the door. "Tell us, then," she said, sounding resigned. "And I noticed you only asked to talk to the women, didn't you? We do get the worst of it." She sighed. "Why should it be any different here than in the rest of our lives?"

Gyda's face had set into a hard expression. "You said something about dangers?"

Mary drew herself up. "It's the usual poppycock, ain't it? Women who must work for their bread must also be of loose morals, no better than they ought to be, eh? At least, that's the way some owners and overlookers think."

"Not Mr. Lowell," someone said loyally.

"Yes, well, he ain't the one I come to warn ye about, is he?" Mary snapped.

"Where is it you've come from?" Kara asked gently.

"Manchester," Mary answered. "And my story ain't the usual poppycock, neither—and all of ye need to hear it."

"Tell it, then," said Louisa.

Mary leaned in, her face earnest. "Me and my sister worked in a cotton mill up north. Dreadful work it is, hunched at the machines and breathin' in the fluff until it fair fills yer lungs. The hours are long and sometimes we was so tired at the end of the day we could barely lift our feet to walk home. But we had no trouble of the other kind, not at first. Not until *he* come."

"Who?" asked Gyda.

"Mr. Selby Royston," Mary said darkly. "Devil's spawn, he is. He was hired by the mill owners. It was whispered he knew how to make the mill run better. More profit, less expense. But all I ever saw him do was make things worse for us, the workers."

"How?" Gyda demanded.

"He gave every overlooker a strap and told them he expected it to be bloodied at least twice a shift. He docked the wages of those who didn't spend enough of their pay at the company store." She sighed. "It were the little 'uns that got hurt the most. The scavengers crawl underneath the machines to clear it of stray wool, leaky oil, or trash. They get their hair ripped out by the looms, or sometimes their arms broke or their fingers cut off. If they got stuck down there, their heads could be crushed or their little bodies mangled."

One of the women gasped.

"The piercers are the bigger kids who put together any breaks in the threads. They almost always end up with their knee joints givin' way. It was never good when anyone got hurt, but Royston started docking all of us when any injury happened."

Mary stopped, her lips pressed together. The women all stood quietly, waiting.

After a moment, she spoke again. "Royston was one of the men who felt free to chase the workin' women for … improper purposes."

Kara and Gyda exchanged dark glances.

"It started with young Amy White. Everyone teased her and called her Amy Bright, because they said the sun bouncin' off her yellow hair blinded them. She had finally growed old enough to be set to work at the looms. That's when Royston noticed her."

"What did he do?" someone asked, sounding nervous about the answer.

"He started by praising her work and her manner. He would pull her aside to speak with her when they closed the mill for our half-hour lunch break. She would linger to talk to him when we all shuffled out at the end of our shift. There was rumors he was seen in her street at night. One Sunday, she showed up to church wearin' a new, fancy silver bracelet."

"What of her family?" Gyda asked. "Did no one object?"

"Amy only had her younger sister. The girl works as a drudge in one of the mill kitchens. Ye cannot truly blame the lass. What was she to do? How could she refuse him, when he could make her life even more of a misery? When he likely made her promises he never meant to keep? People muttered, but no one felt able to do anything to stop it. Then one day, Amy showed up with her eyes red and her face blotchy from cryin'. The next day she came in with a blackened eye. And the next day, she didn't come in at all."

Louisa let out a long sigh.

"When she didn't come to the mill on the second day, the overlooker went lookin' for her. He found only the wee sister, who hadn't seen Amy in days."

"Were the police notified?" Kara asked.

"Oh, aye. They said they'd look, but by then, the rumors were flyin'. Folks were sayin' she'd got herself with child and gone lookin' for a way to get rid of it. They said she ran off with a tramp. They said all manner of things."

"What did Royston say?" asked Gyda.

"Nary a thing. He told the police he hadn't seen her since her last shift."

"Of course, they believed him," Louisa muttered.

"Amy was pulled out of the river several days later."

"Was she with child?" Kara asked.

"We could not know," Mary said with a shrug. "She was laid in a pauper's grave with no real service. Just us what cared for her, stoppin' by with a token bloom to lay on her grave."

Everyone kept quiet for a moment, until Mary's expression darkened and her brows lowered into a ferocious expression. "And then Royston started whisperin' in my sister Maggie's ear."

Someone moaned.

"There's just the two of us. No brother or father for protection. But I wasn't goin' to let that foul blighter touch my sister— not without a fight."

"Good for you," Louisa said.

Mary's shoulders slumped. "People joked about it at first. Said 'cause she had blonde hair, old Royston had to give it a go at her. But they all expected Maggie to send him packin', with his ears ringin' for his trouble." Her voice lowered. "But she didn't."

There came a chorus of objection and calls of "Why not?"

"I don't know!" Mary cried. "I told him off, let me tell you! I called him every name I'd ever heard and threatened to cut his bollocks off. He just laughed and called me a vixen, at the first. Then he got tired of me harassin' him, and he started to make threats. *Horrible* threats about what could happen to Maggie if I didn't back away. I went to her, then. I pleaded with her, but she just shook her head, her face set like a stone. She didn't seem like a girl with a beau. She didn't act like she was in love. She seemed … determined."

"Maybe she thought she could bring him up to scratch?" Louisa ventured.

"Maybe he was making threats to Maggie, too? Threats against you," Gyda said.

"That's what I was afraid of. Maggie came home with a necklace one night. A simple thing, twisted leather and a green stone pendant, but it gave me the shivers. Amy had disappeared soon after she started wearin' that bracelet." Mary shook her head. "That was the last straw. I was too frightened *not* to do anything, so I decided I was goin' to end it. End Royston. No matter what happened to me, I would finish him. I went to bed and lay there all night, makin' plans." She let out a sob. "But when I woke, Maggie was gone."

A communal groan went around.

"I lost my wits," Mary confessed. "I ran into that mill, grabbed the strap off Royston's belt, and started to beat him with it. I raised a few welts on him, too, before they dragged me off him."

"What happened?" Louisa asked.

"They threw me into a cell. But everyone in the mill made a big fuss over it and it couldn't be ignored—not a second time. The police truly looked for Maggie. The mill owners got wind of it all, and they were not best pleased. They released me, but I lost my position at the mill. I didn't care. I just wanted to find my sister. I looked everywhere I could think of, for weeks. Friends helped, for a while."

"She wasn't found?" Kara asked quietly.

"No. Royston was let go from the mill, too. He quickly disappeared. I bribed my way into the offices and found some correspondence that told me he'd been sent here, as Mr. Brown is a relation to one of the owners."

"They just dropped him into our midst, without even a warning?" Louisa sounded outraged. "That explains why Lowell has not got on with him, not from the start. Perhaps he tried to make the same sort of changes here as he did in Manchester?"

"I did hear the two of them having a grand row, just after Royston arrived," a woman volunteered. "It sounded like he wanted to lengthen the hours in our shifts, and Lowell was insisting it could not be done without adding to our pay."

"Yes, but have you seen any sign that Royston did not come here alone?" Mary asked a little desperately. "Could he have brought Maggie with him, perhaps posing as his wife?"

"He wouldn't bring his wife to the mill," someone said.

"He scarcely shows his own face around here," Louisa said.

"Do you know where he is living?" asked Mary.

The women glanced around at each other, shaking their heads.

"You won't find that sort of information here," Louisa told her. "Perhaps in the office of the timber works, where such files are kept?"

"Well, that's where I will look, then," Mary vowed. "I will do what I have to."

Gyda sent Kara a questioning look. She took a moment to consider, then gave a slight shake of her head.

"We might be able to help," Kara told Mary. "We have a friend who is very good at ferreting out that sort of information. We will consult him. Is there a way we may contact you?"

Looking vastly relieved at the offer, Mary rattled off an address. "It's a boardinghouse in Wapping, so do be careful if you come looking for me. It's all I can afford."

"We will be in touch," Gyda assured her.

Mary turned to the gathered mill workers. "You lot look out for each other. Don't fall for that man's evil ways."

"We ought to go and warn Fiona," said Louisa. "She's the only blonde, of all of us."

"Tell her now," Mary urged. "Before he can sink his claws in."

She might have continued, but a call came from the front of the building. "Nieces!"

"That's us, then," Gyda said.

"Thank you for sharing your stories," Kara told them all. "Would you mind if we checked in on you again, perhaps in a few months' time? To be sure that you are still being treated properly?"

"Come and visit us then," Louisa said, settling her hat over her head. "We'll be here, with good luck and the Lord willing."

"Amen," Kara said as Stayme called again and Gyda turned to go. "Amen."

Chapter Thirteen

NIALL TOOK BETH straight to Wooten's office, sat her down, and let her explain about Lily and the smock, chiming in with his own observations when she looked to him for reinforcement.

Wooten was effusive in his praise for the girl. "Very good observational attention, Miss Williams. You have given us a lead just when we most needed one. Thank you."

"A lead that does not include your lost suspect," Niall said. "There is no way that Yardley could have gifted Lily that smock. He has been in custody. She was wearing the thing this morning, before the cobbler made his run for it."

Wooten blinked at him. "How do you know about that, Your Grace? And *what* precisely do you know of it?"

Niall recounted his morning's adventure. Beth gasped at all the appropriate moments, but the inspector merely pulled at his notebook and began to write.

"Good heavens," Wooten muttered, once Niall had finished. "Well, I suppose his escape is not so critical now, with this new thread to follow, but the entire thing is a disaster for our reputation." He gave Niall a wry glance. "Which you know is unstable at the best of times."

"Yardley was not quiet about the unusual treatment he's been subjected to."

"Frye." Wooten sighed. "He never would have been able to pull such a stunt had the commissioner not been busy with a family issue. I tried to alleviate the worst of it, but we are of an equal standing in the detective's division. There was only so much I could do."

Niall raised a brow. "Now it is your turn, Inspector. I saw Mr. Stephen Jephson stalk out of here this morning with you slipping silently into his wake. What was all of that about?"

"Yes. In a moment, please." Wooten finished writing, then stood and went to open the door and poke his head out. "Poulter? Poulter? Ah, there you are," he said as a constable came in response to his call. "Poulter, are you familiar with a flower seller named Lily?" He glanced at his notes. "Young, usually in want of a bath, pigtails, works several spots in the West End?"

Poulter nodded. "Yes, sir. I think I know the girl you mean. She's a bright one. Funny. Makes change faster than a seasoned merchant."

"Excellent. Listen, Constable, we've got a bit of a situation. The girl has gone missing, and *after* she was spotted wearing the missing garment from Miss Glynn Foulger's missing bag."

The constable straightened, understanding the implications at once.

"Quietly, and without attracting attention, search out a few others who would know the girl on sight. Head out, split up, and see if you can locate her. Be advised that she has recently cleaned up a bit. And go gently, Poulter," the inspector warned. "The girl has done nothing wrong. We need to keep her from becoming another victim. If you find her, bring her in, but be sure to tell her we will make sure one of her friends will meet her here."

Wooten glanced back, and Niall nodded agreement at the same time as Beth.

"Yes, sir. Understood, sir."

"Thank you, Poulter. Keep me updated." Wooten closed the door and came back to his desk.

Beth leaned forward. "Lily has an older sister, Inspector. Perhaps she might know something?"

Wooten's interest perked. "A good thought. Do you know where we might find her?"

Beth's face fell. "Not during the day. I know they share rooms, but I don't know where. Lily can be ... reluctant to share personal information. She doesn't trust easily."

"Well, we can scarcely blame her," Niall said. "At the very least, we might be able to find the sister out on the streets tonight." He looked to Wooten. "But first, Jephson?"

Wooten leaned back in his chair with a sigh. "Yes. Jephson. He came in this morning, asking to speak to the officer in charge of Glynn Foulger's murder. He was taken to Frye."

"What did he want?"

"He suggested that someone investigating the murder should look into Mr. Royston. It seems he heard some gossip about the man becoming embroiled in trouble in his previous positions."

"Plural?" asked Niall. "Meaning more than one position?"

"It seems so. Jephson mentioned Cumbria and Manchester." The inspector shook his head. "He said it was the sort of trouble involving women employed under his authority. Frye didn't want to hear it. He told the man he already had the murderer in custody. He was rather rude about it, in fact, and Jephson didn't take it well."

"You followed him to learn more?" Niall asked.

"I did. It took a bit of effort to thaw the man enough to speak with me, but it seems he'd noticed that Royston doesn't treat the women on the charity's board of directors with the same respect as the men. He wondered if the same prejudices were carrying over into his supervision of the volunteers. Jephson started stopping in at the charity to gauge the man's performance."

"Did he discover anything?"

"Nothing substantial, although he did speak to Royston's assistant, who had to advocate very directly to keep Royston from dismissing Miss Foulger's complaints. Jephson also found it odd that Royston was insistent that he should attend the burial. He said it felt manipulative. He wondered if he had been singled out due to the attention he'd been paying to the charity, and because he had arrived at the Waif's Wardrobe on the morning that Glynn Foulger's body had been discovered."

Niall thought about that. "Manipulated? As in, perhaps placed in the frame as a possible suspect?"

"That is what Jephson thought Royston might be up to."

"Isn't that something that might be said by a man who is worried he might *become* a suspect?" asked Beth.

"That would be deep play," Niall mused.

"The simpler explanation is usually true," Wooten said. "And it is simpler to believe that Royston might be setting the man up to be investigated—something a guilty man might do. Especially if the rumors about Royston prove to be true."

"Either way, it seems you now have two suspects to investigate, which puts you ahead of where you were when Yardley escaped," Niall said wryly.

They all paused when a shout echoed down the corridor. "Wooten!"

The inspector straightened as the door shoved open. A red-faced, irate man strode in.

Niall suppressed a grimace at the sight of Detective Frye. The older man looked furious, his brown hair sticking up every which way as he slammed a hand on Wooten's desk.

"What's this I hear about you sending men out to look for a flower seller? Are you interfering in my case?"

"It would appear that I am the only one making any progress in your case, Frye," Wooten said calmly. "Here is a witness who has spotted evidence that was noted as missing from the murder victim." He explained Beth's discovery. "It makes sense that the girl might have been given the smock by the man who was suggested to you as one who has previously interfered with females in his employ."

"Or it might just as easily have been given by the man who

came in to accuse another," Frye snapped.

"Either way, it could not have been given to her by Yardley. But now, instead of empty hands, you have a lead on missing evidence and two suspects to investigate." Wooten tilted his head at the man. "You are welcome."

Frye cursed under his breath. He gave Niall a dark look. "I'll send men over to Bedford Street. Either of them might be there. Their home addresses should be available there, if they are not." Turning on his heel, he stalked out.

Wooten stood. "I should make sure a couple of my men go along."

"Could you spare one of your messengers?" asked Niall. "I know you must have several trusted men or boys around. I should send a message to Kara."

"I'll send a man in," Wooten said. He paused in the doorway. Looking back, he gave a nod that included them both. "Thank you."

Niall helped himself to a bit of paper and ink from the desk. "Let's have the others meet us at Lake Nemi. Do you think Jeanette might know any of Lily's hiding spots?"

Beth brightened. "She might."

Niall sanded and folded the note. "Let's turn this over to a messenger and go, then."

They found a hack near Charing Cross, and it didn't take long for them to reach Lake Nemi.

Emelia stepped out of the main parlor when she heard them arrive. "Beth, there you are, at last. You have a caller."

"What?" Beth looked confused. "Who?"

Instead of answering, Emelia merely swept open the door.

Beth moved to the threshold, then stopped in her tracks.

Curious, Niall stepped up behind her. Over her shoulder, he caught sight of Rob McRae getting to his feet, a curiously humble look on his face and a bunch of daisies in his hand.

With a sound that was nearly a sob, Beth started moving. "Oh, Rob!" She threw herself in his arms and started to cry.

Niall's friend bent over her, murmuring reassurances, while Niall exchanged glances with Emelia.

He leaned down to whisper, "Kara is going to be so annoyed that she missed this."

⧫

"SET US ASHORE at the stairs near the Waterloo Bridge," Stayme told the wherryman. He glanced back at Kara and Gyda. "I'll need to look in my files to see if I can dig up anything about Royston or the mills where he was previously employed."

"We should go to Bedford Street," Kara said. "Mr. Chambers might be able to tell us where Royston is staying."

"You promised the duchess that you would be circumspect," Gyda reminded her. "We should take Beth along. She's good cover, and we won't look like we are searching out Chambers." Her tone darkened. "Or hunting Royston."

"You are right. We'll drop Stayme off in Mayfair, then head to Lake Nemi and on to the charity." Kara looked west toward Whitehall and Scotland Yard. "I wonder where Niall is now?"

She got her answer a while later, when they walked into Lake Nemi. Kara and Gyda both drew to a halt when a glance into the parlor showed Beth standing in a corner, holding hands with Rob McRae, while Niall and Jeanette stood over a table, consulting over the papers spread in front of them.

"Niall! What are you doing here?" Kara moved into his embrace, then darted her eyes toward the corner and widened them into a silent question.

"I know," he whispered. "He was here waiting when we arrived." Raising his voice, he squeezed her again. "There's so much to tell you."

"We have news, too," Gyda said, watching Rob through narrowed eyes. "But not the good kind." She beckoned Beth over. "You go first."

Kara moved over to take Gyda's hand as Beth told of her encounter with Lily. They listened silently as Niall told of their visit to Scotland Yard.

"Lily has blonde hair," Gyda said dully after he finished.

"It's Royston," Kara said. "It must be him."

They shared all they had learned from the women at the mill.

"You cannot go to the charity," Niall said. "Frye and his men are there. They are after Royston. Let's attack from the other direction." He held up a paper from the table where he and Jeanette had been huddled. "Let's find Lily. Jeanette knows where she and her sister live."

Kara breathed a sigh of relief. "Thank you, Jeanette. We must find her, and quickly."

"I'll write out a quick message for Stayme, catching him up." Niall bent over the table again.

"Jeanette, can you get word out to some of the flower sellers?" asked Kara. "Asking them to look out for her and send us word if she turns up?"

"I'll go myself, if I'm permitted?" Jeanette looked to Emelia, who nodded.

"We have to go—it's nearly evening now," Gyda said. "We need to catch the sister at home before she sets out for the night."

"Let's all go." Rob moved to stand behind Beth. He raised his chin when Gyda shot him a quelling look. "Beth won't be left behind. And I won't leave her, not while a murderer is running about." He took Beth's hand. "She has blonde hair too, Gyda."

"I know. We *all* know." Gyda sent a stern look around the room. "We must be careful. This man is accustomed to hurting people. We have to catch him before he hurts Lily or anyone else."

Chapter Fourteen

L ILY'S ROOMS WERE not far. Jeanette placed them in a court off Clare Street, past Covent Garden and on the other side of Drury Lane. Still, when they found a hack as soon as they hit King Street, they hailed it and all piled in. Kara and Niall squeezed inside with Beth and Gyda, while Rob climbed onto the box with the jarvey.

A heavy silence filled the carriage as they set off, but it wasn't as pervasive as the smell, or the heat. Kara's stomach roiled. "Can someone put the window down?" she asked with a desperate gasp.

"It's not late enough for the air to be noticeably cooler," Gyda warned.

"It likely doesn't smell like urine," Kara bit out.

With a glance out at the relatively quiet lanes of Covent Garden, Gyda shook her head. "I'm not sure that's true."

"Gyda, please!"

"I'm sorry, I didn't notice the smell." She looked to Niall. "Did you?"

Niall shook his head, but he put the window down. Kara leaned over him to gulp in fresh air. "Are you all right?" he asked with concern.

She pulled the fresher air into her lungs. "We spent half the day on the choppy river and haven't eaten anything since breakfast, but mostly, I'm worried about Lily."

"We'll find her," Niall said. "We have to."

Kara climbed out first when the carriage stopped at the entrance to the court. Going to stand at the mouth of the alley, she leaned a hand on the wall and breathed deeply.

"We might need the hack again, depending on whom and what we find inside," Niall said. "Rob, will you wait here with the driver and watch who comes and goes from the court?"

"I'll wait with him," Gyda offered. "He doesn't know what Royston looks like. Or Lily, for that matter."

"Oh, should I stay instead?" asked Beth.

"No. You are closest with Lily. If she's there, you should talk with her. If she's not, her sister might recognize your name and be reassured." Gyda shot Rob a mischievous look. "Don't worry about Rob. I just want a few words. I'll go easy on him."

Rob looked resigned, but Kara's stomach was still roiling. She headed down the long alley that finally opened onto the court. "That one." She pointed to the door in the corner. It was more faded than the others, and lacked the potted trees and shrubs that brightened up several other doorways in the enclosed court. "That's the one Jeanette described." Fighting back nausea, she went and knocked.

Niall and Beth waited behind her. After a long moment passed, Niall stepped forward and knocked harder. A muffled call came from within, sounding sharp and irritated.

Well, Kara was irritated as well, and extremely worried. She raised her hand and knocked again.

The door was yanked open. A young woman in a ragged wrapper glared out at them with flashing blue eyes. Her honey-colored hair was only half coiffed, with most of it hanging down her back. The cranky look on her face faded, replaced with surprise and wariness. "Who are you lot, then?"

"We are looking for Lily," Kara said carefully. "We need to speak with her, most urgently. Is she here?"

The woman pulled her wrapper more tightly around her. "No."

"May we come in?"

The woman hesitated.

Beth stepped forward. "Please. It is important."

It took a moment, but the woman relented. She held open the door and waved them in.

The place was small, only one room with a hearth and a sofa, and a bedroom with a curtain hung for privacy. The fabric hung half pulled open, and Kara spotted just one bed and a narrow chest of drawers. There was no decor, no bric-a-brac. A teapot rested on a grate in the cold hearth and a chest sat next to it, perhaps holding a crust of bread. There was nothing else.

Beth smiled at the young woman as she closed the door. "I'm Beth Williams. I'm a friend of Lily's. Are you her sister?"

The woman nodded.

"I'm Kara." She gave the girl a nod. "This is my husband, Niall."

"I'm Ivy," the woman said, shifting nervously.

"Do you know where Lily is?" asked Beth.

"No. Not exactly."

A step sounded from the floor above. Niall looked up. "Is anyone else here with you?"

"No. This is it, the extant of our rental." Ivy gestured. "The upstairs rooms are blocked off. They are connected to the house next door, now." She grew suddenly impatient. "Lily is not here and I am getting ready to go out for the evening. Why are you looking for my sister? Has she done something? Is she in trouble?"

"Not that kind of trouble," Kara answered. "But she might be in danger. We fear she is missing."

Ivy tossed her head. "She's not missing. She's just gone off with ... her beau."

"With the man who gave her that new smock? Do you know who he is?"

"Some gentry cove that works with that charity?" Ivy shook

her head. "I don't know why she was so excited over that thing, in any case. Even if it does have a matching jacket, it's a child's dress. It's not suited to her. Not anymore. If he wanted to win her over, he should have got her a proper gown, or a trinket. A bit of jewelry, perhaps." She sighed. "But Lily has always had her own ideas."

"Turning from flowers to prostitution is not her idea, though, is it?" Niall asked flatly. "She has been trying her best to avoid it, hasn't she?"

Ivy flushed. "Indeed she has." She placed her hands on her hips. "And while she delays, do you know what she brings home at the end of the day?"

Niall shook his head. "No, I'm—"

"After buying flowers, splitting them into bunches, plus the rush to tie them with, paper to wrap them in, the spare ribbon, and other sundries? Sixpence a day! That is generally her total earnings. Now, it's a bit more when oranges is in. Maybe ninepence a day then, but that's not much over a month in the year, is it?" She gave him a scathing look. "Do you think you could live on sixpence a day? Three shillings and six a week? Our rent is near on to seven shillings a week, as it is."

"No, I—"

But Ivy was on a tear, her eyes wild with anger and fear. "This place is bare, I know, but it's safe. The door bolts. There's no pimps nor gangs ranging in the streets. I can bring my customers here, if I must, and I got a deal with the landlady's son. He listens to make sure I don't yell for help, and after thirty minutes he comes and ushers them out, if they are wont to stay too long. Do you think I can get that sort of arrangement anywhere else? If I lose this place, me and Lily will end up in one of the rookeries, and what do you think will happen to us both there?"

Kara knew. They all knew. The rookeries were crowded, filthy, disease-ridden areas, where even the police feared to tread.

"Listen," Ivy said, "Lily is not going to be able to pass for a little girl for much longer. A girl can charge a fortune for her first time. She might as well make something off it, rather than have it stolen by some blighter who traps her in the street."

Kara swallowed heavily. "Unfortunately, Ivy, we think the man who gave Lily that smock is a … bad man. Someone who has hurt young girls like Lily before."

"What? No! She said he was sweet on her!"

"She wouldn't be the first to believe so," Kara said gently.

"But she said he had courtly manners, and brought her treats. He took her on a picnic in the park, once, like she was a real lady. She came home that evening and didn't want her tea." Ivy stared blankly, clearly remembering. "She said she was full up. Not hungry a bit." The girl blinked at Kara. "Can you imagine? I cannot remember the last time I wasn't hungry." After a moment, she shook her head. "Wait. You said he hurt other girls? Do you mean … hurt? Or—"

"He's killed before," Niall said starkly. "Which is why we need to find her as quickly as we can."

With a moan, Ivy sank down onto the sofa. "Oh, saints alive. It *is* my fault, isn't it? I should have known." Her head dropped into her hands. "He said he was going to set her up as his mistress—but in Blackfriars? What kind of man sets his fancy piece up there?"

"Blackfriars?" Niall repeated sharply. "Do you know where?"

"No." Ivy looked up. "Wait. It's in a court, like this one. Enclosed. I was so mad when Lily mentioned it, because as she spoke, I realized it meant her man knew where we lived. But it must be near the river, because Lily said she could still smell the stink of it there."

Beth made a sound of dismay. "Oh, no. How many places could that be?"

"Quite a few." Niall sounded grim.

He began to question Ivy, looking for any further helpful information. Kara, though, was stepping away on silent feet. The rising despair and anxiety was not helping her nausea. She slipped out the door while the others were caught up in their conversation and barely made it to the neighbor's potted tree in time. She bent over it, retching violently even though her stomach was largely empty. Her body was racked, heaving helplessly—until, suddenly, it was over. The retching stopped. Her nausea eased.

Straightening, she wiped her mouth with a handkerchief and marveled at how she abruptly felt utterly normal—and hungry.

Behind her, the door was yanked open. "Kara?" Niall came to her, looking concerned.

"I just needed a bit of air. I'm fine now."

Behind him, Beth was lingering in the doorway, speaking quietly to Ivy. "She knew nothing else helpful?"

"No."

Kara heard his frustration. "I have an idea." She stepped over as Beth moved to join them. "Beth, your friend, the volunteer at the Waif's Wardrobe, the one who is an artist?"

"Yes?"

"Has he, perhaps, made a sketch of Royston?"

Beth's eyes widened. "Surely he must have. Oh, I hope so!"

Kara nodded. "We need to find out. That would help speed up the search through Blackfriars."

They were nearly to the road where Rob and Gyda waited with the carriage when Beth grimaced. "But what of Detective Frye?" She glanced around at the gloom of the advancing evening. "Is he still there at the Waif's Wardrobe, do you think?"

Niall nodded. "He might be, depending on whether they've found Royston. If they haven't, he might have left a man or two behind there, in wait for him." Kara felt Niall's glance fall on her. "It would probably be better if we did not show our faces."

Gyda was watching for them. Rob was leaning against the back of the carriage, but he straightened when they emerged. "Did you find her?"

Beth shook her head, and Niall shared what they had learned. "Blackfriars it is, then. We'll go door to door, if necessary."

"Let me take Beth to the charity," Rob offered. "It's completely natural for her to spend her evenings there. She can see if she can get a sketch of the man, while you two scout the area and find likely courts located near the river in the area. We'll meet you there, and we can all start searching."

"That's a good idea. Thank you, Rob." Kara leaned against Niall for a moment, then looked up at him. "We can drop them off, then continue to Blackfriars." She pointed a finger at Gyda. "But the windows stay open."

NIALL WAS SURPRISED when Gyda opted to disembark at Bedford Street with Rob and Beth.

"Lake Nemi isn't far. I'll go and check in to see if Jeanette is back or if she's sent word back. Maybe one of Lily's friends has shared something." She looked at Niall, then at Rob, and back again. "What do you think? Meet again in ninety minutes? At the bridge?"

They all agreed. Niall climbed out to have a word with the driver as the others scattered. He hopped back inside to find Kara tucked into a corner with her head lolling back against the seat. "Leave the windows open," she said preemptively.

"I'm growing concerned about you," he said, sitting across from her. "It's not even that smelly in here."

"It most definitely *is*." Suddenly a loud rumble of a gurgle erupted from her stomach. Her eyes widened in surprise and Niall laughed.

"That's it. We are going to stop along the way and feed you."

"We cannot go to Maisie's," she objected. "Not if we are in a hurry. We'll hurt her feelings if we do not stay to visit."

"I've already asked the driver to stop at the Eagle."

"We don't have much time—" she began.

He held up a hand. "You don't even need to go in. I'll just go straight to the kitchen and ask Bruce to make you a packet of bread and cheese, perhaps some cold meat, if they have it."

Kara's stomach growled again, and they both laughed. "Thank you, Niall." She raised a hand to beckon him over, and he slid onto the bench next to her.

He tucked her in under his arm, and she might have dozed for the few minutes it took to reach the tavern, but she was wide awake and appeared recovered as they set off again, heading east. She split one of Bruce's buns, filled it with cheese, and took a huge bite. "So, Rob and Beth!" she said, once she'd swallowed. "What happened? Tell me everything!"

Niall gave a helpless laugh. "I hardly know! Beth and I arrived at Lake Nemi after we left Scotland Yard. Rob was waiting in the parlor with his hair slicked back and a fist full of daisies. She took one look, launched herself at him, and they've scarcely stopped touching or looking at each other since."

Kara stopped chewing. "Sometimes it hits you out of the blue, just like that. I seem to recall launching myself at you, once."

"Our first kiss," Niall said fondly. "Did you think I'd forget it?" He sighed. "Unfortunately, I was a bigger fool than Rob. From the besotted look on his face, I'd say they will quickly be betrothed."

"To be fair, he doesn't have the same sort of tangled web of secrets and family ties to deal with."

"No, he can marry to please himself without worry, and I know his family will love Beth." He grinned. "No doubt we will be heading to Scotland for a wedding soon enough, and then you will see what a true Scots party can be."

She smiled. "I cannot wait."

Niall took a piece of cold ham for himself, thinking as he chewed. "I hope it's true and they sort themselves out, but we have to concentrate on finding Lily. And Kara, you heard what her sister had to say. We cannot leave them in such straits."

"No," she agreed. "Something must be done. Ivy, perhaps, might be happy to take a position in service, much in the same way as Jeanette." Her face screwed up. "But Lily? I cannot see it."

"Nor can I, but I was thinking …"

Kara raised her brows at him and waited.

"Perhaps she might do working for Stayme? She's quick. She thinks beyond the usual straight lines. She knows how to handle herself in the streets. You know he trains up certain men and women to be his eyes and ears."

"Oh, yes," Kara breathed. "That's a perfect idea, Niall. *She sees things*—that's how Beth described her once. We have to find her!"

"Yes," Niall said, grim determination feeling like a lead balloon in his gut. "And here's the bridge. Let me speak with the jarvey. We'll start a couple of blocks to the west, stick to within a few blocks north, then head east, making a list of possible enclosed courts."

Kara nodded. "Let's go, then."

They had identified four likely spots by the time they met up with the others at the bridge. Beth had indeed found a sketch, but Jeanette had told Gyda that none of the girls she knew had seen or heard anything from Lily.

"We'll start at the easternmost court, I think," Niall told them. "We'll leave Wardrobe Place for last, because it is farthest from the river, and it's also likely too nice a spot for Royston's intended purpose."

"How do we mean to go about this?" asked Rob.

"I suppose we should approach anyone we encounter in the right area, show them Beth's sketch, and tell them we are looking for a man who has recently rented rooms, and might perhaps have lately had a young woman join him."

"It's dark," Kara said. "We wouldn't be able to see the sketch ourselves if not for the carriage lanterns."

"We'll take one of the lanterns along." Niall shrugged. "And if all else fails, or there is no one to ask, we'll just start knocking on doors."

"With five of us knocking, we should get through each enclosed court pretty quickly," Gyda said.

"What do we do if we knock and Royston answers?" asked Beth.

Niall considered. "Trip him. Knock him down. Sit on him and start yelling. Rob and I will come running."

"Can you manage that?" Rob asked her solicitously.

Beth shot him a hard look. "Lily needs us to manage."

"True enough." Rob gave way at once.

They squeezed into the carriage and Niall directed them to the first spot, just off Water Street. The houses here were smart, but uniform. They encountered a gentleman on his stoop, locking his door behind him. He glanced at the sketch and shook his head before hurrying on his way. They went door to door, but had no better luck.

"Do not get discouraged," Niall cautioned. "We eliminated that one quickly. On to the next."

Piling into the carriage again, they headed west to the next place, a smaller court near Printer's Square. The houses at this one were significantly dingier, almost shabby. They were tall and flat-roofed, and likely all broken up into rental rooms. As they paused to map out a strategy, a young man entered the close, whistling as he came.

Niall hailed him, showed him the sketch, and explained their quest.

"Oh? Yeah." The young man leaned closer to examine the sketch. "Yes. I know him, but Royster, whatever you said, that's not his name. His name is Miller. At least, we all thought so."

"We?" asked Niall.

"All of us at Number Seven." The young man indicated a large, rambling house near the inside corner of the court. "Miller took the ground rooms a couple of months ago, though he don't seem to be around much. I remember, because he was particular about it being on the ground floor, and Mrs. Cranby—that's the landlady—is very particular about who takes those rooms, as they are so close to her own. He convinced her, though."

"You are sure this is the same man?" asked Niall.

The young man looked at the sketch again. "Yeah. That's him. There's more than a bit o' talk about him, what with him being the only boarder not theatrical."

"Theatrical?" asked Gyda.

"Yeah. You know, part and parcel of the halls or theatres, in some fashion. We all are, on account of old Cranby being a former opera dancer. We got us a grand mix of folk, from a mentalist, to pit players, dancing girls, even a ballerina. And me!" He said it with a grin, his face oddly shadowed in the lantern light. "I work the ticket box at the Star. The new chap, though, he's the only industrial-type bloke we got."

"Have you noticed a young lady with him lately?" Kara asked.

"Nah. And I woulda heard about it. Old Cranby keeps a sharp eye out for that sort of thing."

"Would you mind pointing out the landlady's rooms?" Niall asked politely. "We might as well leave a message with her."

"Oh, aye. Sure enough. Come along, then." The young man gestured, and they all fell in line like a row of baby ducks.

Niall took the rear, keeping Kara close in front of him as they filed through the door. When the young man veered to the door at the right of the narrow stairs, Niall nudged Kara to the left. He lifted his chin toward the other set of rooms.

She understood, and ducked into the shadows as the young man lowered his voice.

"I'll leave her to all of you," he said, backing toward the staircase. "She'll jaw your ear off, telling you about her days on the stage. You'll get a nice spot of tea out of it, but mind, get in and close the door behind you, quick now. Old Cranby is forever chilled, even in the height of summer."

Niall raised a finger, and they all waited while their young guide went whistling up several flights of stairs. Once his tune was cut off behind the closing of a distant door, Niall moved them all swiftly into the shadows of the other side of the hall. The lantern Rob still carried showed Kara knelt before the other door, the lockpicks she carried in her altered skirts already engaged.

"Just a moment," she whispered.

Niall had just enough time to note that there was no light coming from under the door before she spoke again.

"There!"

Taking her hand, Niall pulled his wife up and set her behind him. He put his hand on the door latch and looked back, silently ensuring that everyone was ready.

Eager and expectant faces looked back at him.

Raising a finger to his lips, he swung the door open. They all hovered, staring into the dark silence. Niall indicated that they should wait, then crept forward on quiet feet.

As his eyes adjusted, he could make out a few shapes of furniture. Nothing moved. He heard not a sound. Another door beckoned, but the smaller bedroom sat just as dark and empty. "Come on in, then."

They all filed in. Rob opened the lantern wider and Gyda found a lamp to light. Together, they stared around at the place. There was a thin rug and several pieces of plain furniture, but the coal bucket was full and the pair of chairs before the hearth were upholstered, if a little shaggy. And on the walls hung a great many framed pieces. Peering closer, Niall realized they were trade bills hawking music hall shows and portraits of performers.

Beth bit her lip. "As sad as this is, Lily probably finds it homier than her sister's rooms."

"But where is she?" Kara said, sounding frustrated. "Have we even got the right spot?"

"It's the right spot," Gyda said. She stood before a tall chest of single drawers.

"How do you know?" asked Niall.

In answer, Gyda reached into a drawer and pulled out a thick wooden dowel with two rounded, flat ends and a hole through the middle. "The drawer is full of them."

"What are they?" asked Beth.

"Bobbins," Gyda answered grimly. "The sort used in cotton mills."

Beth abruptly sat in one of the stuffed chairs. "Why isn't she here? Where is she?"

"Let's spread out," Niall suggested. "Search everything. Under each cushion and in every nook and cranny. Let's see if we can find a clue as to where they might be."

He helped Gyda move the chest of drawers once she had been through it, but the space behind it was clear, if dusty. Niall straightened, though, when he heard a strange, strangled sort of sound from the bedroom. "Kara?" He dashed into the other room, his heart in his throat. Had he missed something? Someone?

But no. Kara stood alone in the small room. On the other side of the narrow bed stood a washstand and a wooden chair. At the foot sat a simple locker. A case had been set atop it. Niall wasn't sure if it had been left open or if Kara had opened it, but she stood, staring down into it, her face gone white as a sheet.

"What is it?" He hurriedly stepped in behind her to peer down, but wasn't sure what had spooked her.

"Gyda," she called, her voice wavering.

His friend and assistant was there in an instant, and she too whitened as she noted the contents.

Niall stared down. It was a case full of smaller cases. Some small, some a little larger. Each was a box with a lid, but each box had been nestled inside the lid, as if leaving the treasure inside on view.

Except they didn't appear to be treasures. One was a coin. Several contained ribbons. There was a small book of verse, a bracelet …

"A simple thing," Gyda whispered, lifting a necklace from its box. "Twisted leather and a green stone pendant."

As she looked up into Niall's face, Kara's eyes filled with tears. "Royston gave this to Mary's sister, Maggie. The one she has come looking for."

"The bracelet," Gyda said hoarsely. "Mary said he gave the first girl at the mill a bracelet. They found her in the water." She looked at all the trinkets. "Does this mean …? Do each of these represent a girl?"

A dead girl, was what she meant.

"There is one more box," said Niall.

The lid was still on that one. Kara reached for it with shaking fingers. "I cannot," she whispered, drawing her hand back.

Before Niall could move, Gyda reached out and lifted the lid.

No one made a sound.

Finally, Niall lifted out the soft green smock that had been folded inside. Recalling Beth's descriptions, he shook it out and turned it so that he could fold down the bit around the button-hole, where the shoulder strap would fasten. It shone in the dim light, the bright, pink-striped lily that had been lovingly embroidered there.

"Oh, no," Kara moaned.

"Is that …?" Beth stood on the threshold, staring at the smock in Niall's hands. "Are those Lily's things?" She came forward to look in the case. She frowned—and then it registered. "The girls at the mill. The bracelet. The necklace." She went completely pale. "He's … He's …"

Niall began to fold the smock up again. When he started to put it back in the case, Beth tried to stop him. "No," she said sharply. "No! Don't put it back. That means—" She stopped, horrified.

"We must," Niall said gently. "We have to put everything back the way we found it. The police need to see it that way. They need to hear the story about the mill in Manchester. We need to go to Wooten."

"It's so late," Kara said, sounding weary with worry and grief. "Surely he's at home. Should we wait until morning?"

Niall shook his head. "I'd say the odds are high they are all still at the Yard." He considered. "Even if Wooten or Frye are not there, there will be men there familiar with the case. We need to let them know about this place, and discover what they found when they went to the charity."

"Perhaps they have Royston," Rob said from the doorway. "Perhaps that's why he's not here."

"Then where is Lily?" Beth demanded. She glanced back at the case, dread and certainty warring in her expression.

"Maybe they have her, too?" Rob offered.

Beth didn't answer. She just stared into the case. "He needs to be stopped."

"He does," Niall agreed, wholeheartedly. "Let's go see if the police have him."

Chapter Fifteen

Kara was surprised when Beth slid onto the bench next to her in the carriage. The girl pulled Rob in to sit on her other side when he would have climbed onto the top with the driver. She clenched Kara's hand, and they all sat in silence as they rumbled their way toward Scotland Yard.

Traffic was light this late. They made good time. Dread settled in Kara's chest as they drew closer, but her nausea did not return, thank goodness. But the question rattled in her brain. What if the police did not have Royston? What would they do then?

Niall had been right—Scotland Yard bustled with activity, despite the late hour. When they asked for Wooten, they were told he was in his office, trying to snatch a quick nap.

"Should we wake him?" Kara wondered aloud. "He must be exhausted."

"Is Frye here?" Niall asked the constable.

"No, sir. He went home after they failed to find the suspect at the charity house."

"There's one question answered," muttered Niall.

"Why didn't Wooten go home?" Gyda asked sharply. "Is there something else afoot?"

"I believe Inspector Wooten sent some of his men in search

of a charity employee. He's waiting to hear back, but he took the chance to grab a bit of sleep."

"We'll have to wake him," Niall said. "We have news."

They waited where the constable left them, then they all trooped through to the inspector's office when the officer came back to fetch them. Wooten, in his shirt sleeves, was yawning and stirring a cup of coffee. "Come on, come in," he said. "Royston was not at the charity, nor were his records included in the files in the office. But I recalled what you said about his secretary, so I sent men to find Chambers and ask if he might know where Royston is staying. They have yet to return. Poulter said you have news, though?"

"We know where Royston has been spending some of his time," Niall answered. "Although I suspect he has another space of his own. This was more in the way of a love nest." He paused. "We found something there."

"Something you should see," Kara added.

Taking turns, they told Wooten about everything they had heard and found.

The inspector had paled a little by the time they finished. "If what you believe is true …" He grabbed paper and started to scribble. "We need to make enquiries in the places he lived and worked before Manchester, as well." He looked around at the lot of them. "You should go home and rest. You all look knackered. We'll check out the rooms you found, as well as his others, once we track down Mr. Chambers. I'll send word as soon as we hear anything."

Kara felt too tired to argue. "We should spend the night at the rooms on Adams Street. Send any messages there."

"I'll stop by Stayme's in the morning. He might have turned something up," Niall said with a yawn.

Gyda stepped up. "Kara, we need to see Mary in the morning. Tell her about the necklace we found."

"And what it means," Beth said savagely. "She'll want to know."

In the silence that followed, they all heard the pounding of footsteps in the passageway, drawing near. "Sir!" The constable, Poulter, threw open the door. "Come quickly! There is word."

"Royston?" asked Wooten, reaching for his coat.

"No, sir. It's word from Wapping. They have found the body of a girl in the river. She washed up at the Wapping Old Stairs. They've got her at the Town of Ramsgate."

FEAR HAD CHASED away all signs of Kara's fatigue. After a short but fierce disagreement, Wooten had agreed to let them come along, *for the purposes of identifying the body*, as he explained to the constables accompanying them. Niall had sent off the jarvey and his tired horse, with his returned lantern and a fat purse in payment for his long night. Now they were squeezed into an open police wagon with Wooten and his men, on the long, bumpy, chilly ride to Wapping.

Rob had tried to convince Beth to go home instead, but her response had been colder, even, than the night air. The sky started to lighten as they rumbled by the Tower of London, and the shore birds had begun to call by the time they turned onto the Wapping high street.

"I've been to the spot before," Niall told Kara quietly, referring to the pub known as the Town of Ramsgate. "It's old. Very old. It's one of a few spots that claim to be the location of the Execution Dock, the place where pirates, smugglers, and other thieves and criminals were hanged or staked out to drown."

Kara shivered. "Not exactly a charming claim to fame."

"But better than no claim at all," Niall said with a shrug. "At least for a business."

They pulled up before the place. Several of the policemen went down the narrow alley leading to the stairs. Everyone else followed Wooten inside. They were met by the landlord, who tried to quickly usher them through the taproom covered in handsome, carved paneling, toward the far end of the house. "We don't want everyone to see the place overrun with the police," the man said nervously.

"Nonsense," Rob scoffed. "Tell your cook to start cracking eggs. Everyone will be stopping in for breakfast, hoping to find out what's happened."

The thought seemed to cheer the tavern keeper, but he sobered as he stopped outside the door of a private parlor. "We have her laid out in here."

"I'll send one of my men for the coroner after we've seen her," Wooten said. "We have a girl gone missing, and we just need to know if it is her."

With a nod, the man opened the door and stood back to let them pass. He closed it quietly behind Kara as she was the last to shuffle in.

The body lay on a table in the middle of the room. She'd been covered with a sheet. The inspector looked to make sure everyone was ready before he pulled it back to the figure's shoulders.

It was Lily.

The truth of it registered with Kara even before Beth's sob rang out into the quiet. The girl covered her mouth with a hand, whirled, and fled the room.

Gyda stopped Rob from following as the door slammed. "Give her a few moments."

Kara's gaze was fixed on Lily.

"She wasn't in the water long," said Wooten quietly.

He must be right. Lily looked like she was sleeping—until one noticed the ring of purple finger marks against the fair skin of her neck. But this was not Kara's first glimpse of a body pulled from the river, and at least Lily's expression looked calm, her face unmarked by pain or fear.

"It is her, yes?" asked Wooten.

Kara nodded along with the others. Tears welled, but she

fought them. Gyda looked fierce. Niall looked like stone. Rob looked sorrowful, but kept glancing toward the door.

Kara drew a long breath. "I'll go talk to her."

"I'll come with you," Gyda said.

Side by side, they left the men to the business of the dead, and went to find their friend.

It took several minutes, but at last they found their way down the narrow alley to stand at the top of the Old Wapping Stairs. The river stretched before them, shining in the early morning sun. This far down in Wapping, it would be Rotherhithe on the far shore. The tide was out, leaving all the stairs and a short flagstone walkway visible, most of it coated in slick mud.

Beth stood at the end, on a stretch of the rocky shore, the water lapping at her feet.

They went carefully to stand beside her, flanking her without saying a word. The view was lovely, with the city waking up, and the river kissed by the sun, and the kingfishers diving for their breakfast in the shallows.

Beth stood stiff and unbending. Her tears had dried. She stared out at the water in implacable silence for several long minutes. "Lily was smart," she said finally. "Everyone knew it. She was quick, wily. She could size a customer up in seconds, and know how best to convince them to buy. Even the constables commented on how savvy she is—was."

She paused, watching the water on the move. "She's gone now. She's part of the river, of the sky. She's free to roam the streets or sit in the theatre or to pass on to better things. It's easy to think that it was just her circumstances that led to this. That fate had her body ending up on a table in a pub while her spirit has to learn to say goodbye to her sister, her city, her friends. But Lily was *smart*," she repeated. "She had to know what Royston was. She had to know where he got that smock."

Kara felt, more than saw, Gyda shift uncomfortably on Beth's other side.

"No doubt Royston offered up some story to explain it

away," Beth continued, "but I think Lily knew. And I think she told me the truth. She told me she was making her own choices, remember? I think she did. I think she chose her own fate." She gestured back to the pub. "I think she chose *this* fate because she didn't want to live the one she was being pushed into."

Kara stood silent, appalled. Could Beth be right?

"How many others are out there?" Beth's tone was full of passion and outrage now. "How many others feel so desperate, right at this moment? Someone is out there now, feeling as if there is no way out for them." Her chin lifted. "I'm going to do something about it." She glanced at Gyda, then at Kara. "I'm going to fight." She turned abruptly to face the stairs. "But first, I need to sleep. We are done here, are we not? We all need to sleep."

Beth stepped back onto the flagstones then, heading for the stairs and the pub.

"Is she right, do you think? About Lily?" Kara could not keep the anguish from her tone.

"She knew Lily better than most," Gyda said. Her eyes narrowed as she watched Beth climb the stairs, her back straight. "I think I had better go and have a word with Rob."

Chapter Sixteen

"My men have interviewed the fishermen who found the body and the witnesses who watched them bring her in," Wooten said. "I'll wait here for the coroner's man, but the lot of you might as well go home. The landlord says there is a livery down the street. They likely have a traveling carriage big enough for you to get the ladies home in better comfort than the police wagon."

"It's a good idea," Niall said with a nod. "I'll make the arrangements."

In less than an hour, they were all bundled in a relatively roomy coach and heading west again. Kara fell asleep at once, her head on his shoulder. Beth stared stonily out the window while Gyda kept a watchful, assessing eye on her.

They went first to Lake Nemi. The sun was high and the morning half gone by the time they arrived. Kara stirred awake to bid the others a good day's rest. Rob handed both Gyda and Beth out of the carriage. He paused to turn back while the women headed for the door. "I'm going to stay here," he said quietly to Niall. "Gyda thinks we both need to keep an eye on Beth. She's going to clear it with Emelia."

"It's not a bad thought," Niall mused. "We'll go to Adams Street for a few hours' rest, then we'll meet you all back here so we can decide our next course of action."

Beside him, Kara had leaned forward to stare out the window. "There is someone in the servants' stairway."

She still sounded sleepy. Niall glanced past Rob's shoulder. Gyda had gone into the house, but Beth had paused on the walk, glancing back at them, perhaps waiting for Rob. Niall noted the gray tweed cap of the man climbing out of the servants' stairwell entrance and rounding the corner at the top with his hand on the railing. "It's likely a grocer, isn't it?" he answered his wife. "Speaking with the cook, perhaps."

But Kara was suddenly alert and awake, leaning out to push Rob aside, staring at the man in the cap, who had turned to approach Beth.

Niall saw Beth stiffen at the same time he heard Kara gasp.

"It's him!" She gave Rob a push. "Help her! That's Royston!"

Rob whirled as the man in the cap grabbed Beth's arm and started to pull her back the way he'd come, away from the carriage.

"Holy Mother of—" Rob shouted, and started to run. "Oi! Get your hands off her!"

Frantically, Niall pulled Kara out of the way and leapt out, setting off after his friend.

Royston tried to pull Beth into a run, but she dug in, dragging her feet and screaming curses at him. With a shout of frustration, he flung her away, snarling at her, then turned to flee.

Rob pounded after him.

Niall paused to steady Beth on her feet. "Are you all right?" At her breathless nod, he let go and set off in pursuit of the other two.

Odin's arse, Royston was faster than Niall would have suspected. He'd pulled ahead of Rob as they ran down the pavement on New Street.

Niall realized why as Royston plowed through a group of nannies and their charges, and Rob was left to dodge through the confused, irritated crowd. Niall veered around them and was on

Rob's heels as Royston turned right into St. Martin's Lane.

They followed, pulling up a bit as they hit the increased traffic, both pedestrian and in the street.

"Where is he?" gasped Niall.

"There!" Rob pointed.

Royston had darted into the street. He danced in the road, ducking between carriages and wagons, suddenly disappearing as he dodged through a break in the traffic.

Rob followed. Niall was forced to draw back to avoid flashing hooves and flaring nostrils as a brewer's wagon barreled by. He dashed on as the vehicle passed, only to find Rob on the pavement on the other side, casting about with frantic movements.

"Damnation," Rob cursed. "Where has he gone now?"

Niall searched left and right, then suddenly spun around, examining the traffic again. "There he is," he called, spotting Royston hanging on to the high, slatted side of the brewer's wagon.

It was a strategy that might have ended the chase, had the driver not slowed to make the turn onto New Street, heading for the slight veering onto King Street and the taverns of Covent Garden beyond. Rob and Niall dodged back through traffic again, bursting across as the wagon made its turn and picked up speed, carrying Royston at a clip along the same road he had just run down.

Niall put his head down and ran faster.

"Wait! Look, Niall," Rob said, breathing hard. "Here comes another!"

Turning his head, Niall saw another brewer's wagon making the turn, then picking up speed. He gestured and slowed up a little, waiting for it to pass. "Now!" he shouted. He and Rob both ran into the street, then leapt, reaching out to grab on to the wooden slats. He scrambled to get his feet a solid purchase, then heaved a sigh of relief.

He hung on, breathing heavily and offering up a reassuring wave as they passed Lake Nemi, where Kara, Gyda, Beth, and

Emelia stood, perplexed, on the walkway before the club.

"We will get the scabby arse," Rob called.

Niall inched to the side as they made the slight turn onto King Street. He peered at the wagon ahead of them. Royston still hung on. It slowed as King Street gave way to the north side of Covent Garden.

"Bollocks, there he goes." Niall ducked as Royston dropped off his slowing wagon and looked back. "Don't let him see you."

"He'll be heading into the garden," Rob said grimly.

"We'll get him. Get ready to jump … now!"

They hit the roughened cobblestones and ducked behind a meat cart, watching as Royston sauntered deeper into one of the narrower lanes. "He thinks he's lost us," Niall said. "You follow him. Don't let him see you. I'll try to circle around and get in front of him. Then we'll have him."

Nodding, Rob set out after Royston, taking his time and pretending interest in the wares the vendors were offering.

Niall moved quickly, weaving into the chaos and putting some distance between him and the winding lane Royston was following. The market flew by, the air rich with dozens of different scents and echoing with calls of "Buy my fish, fresh caught this morning!" and "Lemons! Bright as the sun!"

Judging that he'd passed Royston, Niall slowed a bit and moved to intersect the man's lane again. He stepped past a coffee seller's stall and casually glanced up the lane, only to curse and brace himself as Royston came barreling toward him, with Rob hot on his heels.

Royston spotted him. The man tried to stop, but slipped in a pile of manure, his arms windmilling as he tried to steer away from Niall. Slipping and sliding, he crashed into a vegetable cart. A pack of dirty urchins jeered, then raced in to snatch up the cabbages that rolled in every direction. Niall went down, too, as he dodged to avoid stepping on one of the street kids. The vendor screamed outrage, insults, and demands, but Royston merely grabbed on, used the man to steady himself, then took off, heading for the clearer streets at the edge of the market.

Niall gave chase again, but Rob was seized by the vendor. "Somebody has to pay!" the man shouted.

On the run, Niall leaned down to grab a rolling cabbage, then another. *Damn.* Royston was heading for a hack waiting at the end of Southampton Street. The bastard was going to reach it before Niall caught him.

Pausing, Niall drew back and threw a cabbage with all of his might. His aim was true. It struck Royston in the back of his head, causing him to lose his balance, stumble, and knock into the side of the hack. He recovered quickly, though, grabbing the handle and screaming at the driver to go. He scrambled inside as the hack took off.

Niall threw the second cabbage in frustration. It bounced off the back of the vehicle as Niall was left, watching it go, taking Royston with it.

KARA WATCHED BETH with a worried eye when the men came back with the news that Royston had eluded them.

"That bastard," Gyda raged. "The hubris of him, trying to take her right out from under our noses. That's it! We are all staying at Lake Nemi until Royston is caught. We cannot risk leaving Beth alone."

Emelia agreed, pledging to make room. Kara knew Gyda was right about protecting Beth. She also knew staying here was not the long-term answer, but she was too tired to argue.

"Beth, it looked like he said something to you, just before he let you go and ran." Niall gave the girl a curious look. "What was it? What did he say?"

"He called me a name," Beth answered with the same eerie calm she'd worn like a mantle since they had seen Lily's body.

"What name?" asked Gyda.

Beth screwed her face into a scowl and lowered her voice into a deep snarl. "'Wicked virago! Just like her. I knew it. Worse than the others!'"

"That's what he said to you?" Kara asked faintly.

"Exactly what he said," Beth assured her. "I'm not likely to forget it."

"Nor are any of us," Kara agreed.

Jeanette entered the parlor carrying a silver tray. "There's a note been delivered. *Cor!* It's been franked by a lord!" She stared down at the vellum in awe. Emelia reached for it, but Jeanette paused. "It's marked *Niall, Kara, or Gyda.*"

"Let's have it, then," Gyda said.

Jeanette glanced over at Kara. She nodded, and the maid bent to allow Gyda to take up the note.

"It's from Stayme," Gyda said. "He didn't know exactly where we would be, so he sent the same notice to several spots. He's found a bit of information on Royston." She frowned over the note. "The man was raised in Sussex by a gentleman farmer. There was some sort of scandal with the mother. She disappeared and the boys were left with the father. Years later, the daughter of one of his tenants was found dead in mysterious circumstances. There were whispers that Royston was involved. Months later, when a village girl was drowned, the local populace again blamed him. His father was magistrate, so the death was ruled a suicide, but it was thought prudent to send Royston away. He was packed off to Cumbria to act as a supervisor in a bobbin mill."

"So he always has a kernel of truth in his stories," Niall mused. "But he's not an owner of either of the mills he claims."

Gyda looked up. "What are the odds that both of those girls were blonde?" she asked darkly.

No one answered.

Emelia sent Jeanette off, and she happily set to work changing linens and setting up cots and pallets. Emelia gave over her bed to Kara and Niall, and took a cot in Gyda's room.

Once again, Kara was too tired to argue. She wrote a note to

Harold and Turner and gave it to the staff while the arrangements were still being made. Rob was insisting on sleeping in front of Beth's door when Kara gave up and went to Emelia's suite. She didn't even undress before crawling into the freshly changed bed. She fell instantly asleep when her head hit the pillow.

It seemed like mere moments later when someone shook her awake. "Kara! Niall! Come on and wake up now. We need to go."

She was warm and cozy and tucked up against Niall's chest. She didn't want to wake, but she was prodded again. "Rob?" She squinted up at him. The room was mellow with afternoon sun. "What is it?"

"It's Beth!" Rob's tone was urgent. "Gyda was right. She is plotting something. I knew she was onto something when Beth insisted on talking alone with Emelia before she slept. It's why I waited until she went to her room to drag a settee into the passage outside her room. And I was right!"

"She woke you, leaving her room? You sleep like a log at the best of times," Niall said groggily. "And none of this can be counted as the best of times."

"Ah, but I used the trick my mam used on us. You recall, when we kept sneaking out to smoke my grandfather's cigars?"

Niall groaned. "You tied a thread from your wrist to the door latch?"

He sat up, but Kara moaned and hid her face behind the pillow.

"I did!" Rob said triumphantly. "And it worked. It woke me when she pulled open the door, but I pretended to be asleep when she tiptoed past me. She went to Gyda's room, then she and Emelia slipped out together."

That captured Kara's interest. Tossing aside the pillow, she sat up too. "Where are they now?"

"I don't know. Gyda followed them." Rob's expression darkened. "I don't understand. That bastard tried to take her. He might try again. Why would she go out without me or you to protect her?"

"They left the house?" asked Niall. He had slept in his trousers, and now he pulled on his shirt.

"Yes. I meant to go after them, but Gyda wouldn't allow it. She said they would spot me in an instant." Rob sighed. "I know she's right. Royston caught sight of me soon enough. But Gyda went after them dressed in boy's clothes. I doubt they will notice her. I've been waiting for word—and she's sent back a message, with an urchin. He says we have to go to the train station. And to hurry our arses."

Chapter Seventeen

NIALL WAS THE first to climb the steps up onto the train platform. He caught sight of Gyda waving frantically from the ticket window.

"Hurry," she called. "I don't have enough coin on me for four tickets, even though Emelia took the last first-class compartment, curse her."

Pausing in the act of pulling out his purse, Niall looked at the train steaming several feet away. "Emelia and Beth are both on board?"

"Did I not just say so?" Gyda gestured toward the front of the train, where the first-class compartments were located. "Get our tickets before the thing pulls away!"

"Where is it heading?" Niall asked, handing over the money to the ticket agent.

"West," the agent answered.

"Are they heading to Bluefield?" Rob asked as the others caught up. "It makes no sense. Why not wake you, then?"

"Not Bluefield, I don't think," Kara said quietly. "But close."

They boarded the second-class car and sat as close together as they could. After the last boarding calls, the screeching of the wheels, the huff of the engine, and all the noise of their departure had ended, Kara spoke softly to explain her guess and the reasoning behind it. "Beth has always been a great proponent of Lake Nemi."

"But I thought Lake Nemi is the name of the club and boardinghouse?" Rob sounded confused. "Didn't we just *leave* Lake Nemi?"

"We did. Emelia named the place after the ancient Greek temple at the edge of a lake, dedicated to the Goddess Diana. Diana is the protector of women and the wilderness, and the goddess of fertility and childbirth."

"And the hunt," Gyda reminded her. "And of crossroads, or choices we make in life."

"She represents many facets of women, and so does the club that Emelia has created, where women may come to relax, to study, to explore their interests without censure." Kara smiled at Gyda. "However, when I was inducted into the club, I purchased a pond a few miles from Bluefield, and we began to use it for ceremonies that bore a resemblance to those of old. They are mostly evenings spent dedicating ourselves to our goals, experiencing a wilder bit of nature outside London, and enjoying each other's company. But we also use the pond, which we also call Lake Nemi, for wind and weather experiments, for entomology studies, and sometimes just for picnics and boating exhibitions."

"But why come now?" Niall asked.

"Beth has always greatly enjoyed all the activities at our lake. I think she gets real peace from the sense of community, and particularly from the ceremonies. I think she wants one for herself."

"A ceremony?" Rob sounded doubtful.

"Protection, perhaps?" Gyda ventured.

"Or strength? I think Beth is preparing herself … for something."

"You heard her. She means to fight." Gyda sounded both proud and worried.

"She doesn't need to fight," Rob objected. "She has me now. I want nothing more than to protect her—from every sort of harm, not just this madman."

Niall reached out and gripped his friend's arm. "Do you love the girl?"

"Yes," Rob whispered. "Saints help me, but I do, and by some miracle, she feels the same. I wasn't sure, you understand. She's shy about sharing her feelings. She's had to hide them, hide herself away, in the past, you see."

"She told you about her family?" Gyda was clearly surprised.

Rob frowned. "Yes. She's been through so much, and yet she has such a quiet, dignified strength, and such a big heart. She's the miracle, truly, to look past her own hurt and to fight so hard to ease it in others."

"If you love her, you have to respect the strength in her as well as the kindness," Niall told him. "It is not an easy thing, loving a strong woman." He grinned at Kara. "It will fair drive you out of your mind with worry, at times, but the rewards are beyond anything you can imagine."

"I don't know how you cope with it all," Rob marveled.

"You are about to find out. Learn fast," Niall advised. "If you don't, you will lose her. And if you don't have the strength to let her fully be herself, then you will deserve it."

Rob nodded, his gaze unfocused as he lost himself in thought.

"But why Emelia?" Gyda asked, sounding a little offended. "Why did Beth not ask one of us?"

"Emelia is the mistress of ceremonies," Kara reminded her. "She heightens the drama and brings the magic." Niall saw his wife bite back a grin. "But Beth is about to discover that what Emelia does *not* bring is the planning."

Niall understood what Kara meant when they reached Hammersmith. Evening's shadows had grown long by the time they pulled into the station and the porters came around to unlock the compartment. They had released the first-class passengers first, of course, so Beth and Emelia were already on the platform when he and the rest of the group spilled out.

Neither woman looked particularly surprised to see them. In fact, Beth merely turned to Emelia, her hand held out in silent supplication. The other woman slapped a coin into it with bad grace. "How could you know?" she demanded of them. "We were as quiet as a mouse in church!"

"I told you I thought it was Gyda slinking into the train station behind us," Beth said. But she aimed a frown at each of them. "I will do what I have come to do," she warned, "and I will not tolerate any interference."

"But what is it that you mean to do, sweeting?" Rob asked.

"It's to be a ritual. At the lake."

Kara's brow rose. "And how do you intend to get to the lake?"

Emelia waved a hand toward the stairs leading from the platform to the street. "We shall take a cart. Whenever we come, they are lined up, waiting to take us all to our temple."

"They are all lined up because I make arrangements for them to be there," Kara said.

"Surely there will be hacks waiting?" Emelia said with a shrug.

"Yes. Hacks waiting to take you somewhere in Hammersmith. You will have a job of it, finding someone willing to travel the six or seven miles to the lake."

Emelia blinked. "Oh."

Niall eyed the lowering sun. "I'll check to see if the livery is still open. If not, I'll ask the tavern to lend us their wood cart."

⇶✂⇷

"THIS ENQUIRY IS in need of better transportation," Kara grumbled an hour later, as she climbed into an open cart for the second time in two days.

"Do you need my coat?" Niall called from his seat on the driver's bench. "It will grow colder, now that the sun has gone down."

"No, thank you, but some springs and a bit of suspension might not go amiss."

"Here's the thing," Beth announced. "This is my ritual and I have rules. And the first rule is that I can have no men at my ritual."

Beside her, Rob straightened. "No men? But we are here to watch over you." He gestured. "Have your ceremony. We will merely keep you safe."

"You may keep watch from a distance—and from beyond the sight line. This is to be a purification ritual, and I won't have it befouled with male vibrations."

"Vibrations?" Rob scoffed. "You sound like one of those spiritualists. Never say you believe in such claptrap?"

"I don't think I truly believe in the seances and such, but I do find some of the concepts interesting."

"Like male vibrations?" Rob asked with skepticism.

"Rob McRae, didn't you tell me that you've seen your grandmother's ghost?" Beth demanded.

"Aye, but ghosts are real! Vibrations are poppycock!"

Beth raised a brow at him. "Isn't it interesting, how much we are learning about each other?"

"Rob might have a point," Gyda said. "What if Royston followed us?"

"Without any one of us spotting him?" Beth asked.

Kara thought about it. "If he had been watching the house for Beth, might he have followed her to the train station?"

"*I* followed her, and I didn't spot him," Gyda said.

"Do you think he's fixed on me?" Beth asked quietly. "Or is he just looking for another blonde girl?"

"I think he wore tradesman's clothes and lurked in the servants' stairwell at the club," Niall said from the driver's seat. "I'm sorry to say so, but for some unknown reason, I think it's you he wants, Beth. But I also think it is unlikely he could have followed you this afternoon. He will be looking for you, though. At least, I believe he will. Which is why we will all go to Bluefield Park when your ritual is finished. It will be much more difficult for him to get near you there."

"We've turned Bluefield into a fortress once before," Kara said. "We will do it again."

They all lapsed into silence for a while. Eventually, Kara's practical brain could not keep quiet. "What will you need for your ritual, Beth?"

"Well, my granddam was a Scot, and she used juniper wood and rowan branches for cleansing, so that's what I'd like to use, if it's possible."

"Bah!" Emelia said. "Wood is wood. We will just pick up branches as we head to the ceremonial site."

"There's no need," Kara said. "Emelia, remember the locked boxes at the edge of the clearing? There is dry firewood, as well as smaller trunks of juniper and rowan. Several of the members researched it when we first began to come out here. They recommended both, as they are used in ceremonial rites. There is also a smaller box of dried cinnamon bark, which was commonly sprinkled in the fires at Diana's original temple, if you'd like to add that."

"Oh, yes. I'd like to include the ancient ways as well. I don't think it can hurt."

"Not like vibrations," Rob muttered.

Not much more was said as they made their way to the pond, until Niall pulled the wagon to a halt. "This is as far as the cart goes. The rest of the way is on the footpath."

"Do you really think it is safe?" Kara asked, going to stand close to him as they all climbed down.

Niall gestured at the intense dark of the woods behind them and the star-filled sky hanging over the lake. Now that the cart had stilled, the songs of the frogs and crickets had begun to sound out loud again. "Could Royston have followed us all the way out here? It's highly doubtful."

"I suppose you are right."

Niall raised his voice. "I know Rob will not be happy unless he is at least within earshot of Beth, so I will stay here with the horses and keep watch. He can sit just out of sight until your ritual is complete, then we are off to Bluefield. It's just a couple of miles away."

Everyone agreed.

"Take the lantern from the wagon," Niall continued. "The moon is too low to do you any good out here. I won't need it, but you will, until you get your fire going."

Kara kissed him thoroughly, then trailed after the other women as they set off.

Rob was on her heels. "I hope they wrap this up quickly," he muttered.

Usually, Kara enjoyed the lakeside ceremonies, but tonight she felt tired and on edge, and she found herself silently agreeing with Rob.

Chapter Eighteen

A ROCK-LINED FIREPIT was centered in the clearing where they held their ceremonies.

"Are you sure we will not need the podium?" Emelia gestured toward the water's edge.

"Not this time," Beth assured her.

"I do like to speak from there," Emelia said wistfully.

"You do it magnificently," Kara told her. "I think, though, Beth is looking for something simpler tonight. And there is no audience, after all. It is just us."

They raided the boxes and set to work laying the fire. Gyda kept stopping to look up at the stars, but between them, Kara and Beth got the fire going. Emelia sprinkled a bit of ouzo around the firepit. She liked to work the strong Greek spirits into the ceremonies, as she said it would honor Diana.

"Hold a moment," Beth said when Kara fetched the branches of juniper and rowan. She looked to Emelia. "Will you call the women, any who might guide and protect us, asking them to witness this?"

Emelia leapt to her feet. "Of course!"

The others settled on the stone benches as Emelia began. Even Gyda's attention was caught as Emelia spoke with eloquence and passion, invoking the female deities of more than one tradition, as well as the ancestors of all the women present, asking for grace, for wisdom, for strength, and for guidance.

When she had finished, Beth stood to exchange places with Emelia. Removing a thin, wrapped bundle from her cloak, Beth placed it on a bench, removed the cloak and folded it, then took off her shoes as well. Standing at the fire's edge, she lifted her face to the stars and drew a deep, long breath before she bent down to add the branches of juniper and rowan to the fire.

A sharp, fresh tang filled the air with the scent of fir. The pop and snap of resin began to sound as the flames grew higher.

"Stay there," Beth warned as she backed up a few steps, then several more. Suddenly, she was running, and as she grew close, she leapt as gracefully as a fawn and hurdled the fire.

Kara and the others gasped.

"Oh, she's doing it again," Emelia said, grasping Kara's arm as Beth whirled and jumped back.

"Twice more, from the other direction," Beth said. Once she had completed four jumps, she stood and raised her arms to the sky. "I am cleansed," she said softly. "No negative spirits can linger."

She wasn't finished, though. Kara watched as Beth went to retrieve the bundle. Taking it up, she went around to stop in front of Gyda. "Keep the wrapping between it and your skin, if you will."

Looking curious, Gyda opened the bundle. "Oh, Beth," she said on a whisper.

Kara teared up a bit. Inside the bundle lay the knife that Gyda had made for Beth, back when she had been so much quieter, shyer, and more reticent. Gyda had decorated it with symbols to remind Beth of her own strength, and of the friends she had made and bonded with, so that she knew she was no longer alone.

"It was taken and used for dark, violent deeds," Beth said. "For a long time, I thought it was my fault, because I hadn't been strong enough to keep it."

Gyda frowned. "No, Beth. You didn't stab Sally Doughty.

You cannot take that responsibility upon yourself."

"You are right. I've grown since then. I understand myself better, and I see the world a little clearer. I've learned I cannot let fear rule me. And so, I will not. It ends tonight." Beth shook her head. "Even if Royston has shifted his focus onto me, I refuse to cower and hide. Nor will I give up, as I am afraid Lily did. I will protect myself. But first, this needs to be cleansed."

Gyda nodded, and Beth took the knife in her hands, facing back to the fire. She edged closer and lifted her hands so that they hovered over the flames, in the path of the smoke.

"Just a moment," Kara said suddenly. She went to fetch the small box of cinnamon bark. Crumbling a piece, she tossed the powder and bits into the fire, where they burst into bright sparks. *"My drops of tears I'll turn to sparks of fire,* as Shakespeare said."

"Yes," Beth said fiercely. "That is exactly it." She repeated Kara's words, then spoke a bit of Gaelic, repeating herself several times as she passed the knife repeatedly through the smoke of the fire. When she was finished, she grasped the knife and brandished it. "All the dark echoes are banished."

She placed a foot on a stone bench and hiked her skirts high. A leather scabbard showed, strapped to her thigh. Securing the knife, she threw her skirts back down and stood straight. "Now I am ready to fight."

Kara and the others let out whoops of joy and pride.

NIALL TIED THE cart horse to a sapling in a spot where it could graze on marsh grasses, if it were so inclined. He perched himself on a fallen log a short distance away, where he could both watch the trail they had followed here, and keep an eye on the stretch of shore where the club held their ceremonies.

He was too far away to hear anything, but he could follow the progress of the lantern down the path, and he did see the bonfire when they got it lit. His mind wandered over their situation as he waited. He wondered what the significance of blonde hair was to Royston, and he spent some time plotting out the changes they would need to make at Bluefield until the man was caught.

They would have to fill Harold in on the danger to Beth, but Harold had come from the streets, and he'd held his own in more than a few of their adventures, as well. He would be another watchful eye in the days ahead.

Niall was just wondering if their solicitors had completed the casework for Harold's adoption when he noticed the sparks flare in the fire at the curve of the lake. A few moments later, the frogs between him and the water abruptly stopped singing.

Niall froze, but a shout rose up from the women at the same moment, and he sighed. He would tease them, in a bit, about being so loud as to silence all the—

He heard the snap of a twig directly behind him, but it was too late. Something smashed into his temple and he toppled off the log.

Chapter Nineteen

"WE MUST STAY until the fire burns down of its own accord and our visitors depart." Emelia waved a hand to encompass all of the circle of light.

The four of them sat together then, huddled around the dying fire, speaking of the women who had impacted their lives in the best ways—and in the case of a few, those who had taught them of the sort of woman they did not wish to be.

Kara found her own thoughts drifting once again to her mother. Looking across the fire at the empty benches, she was comforted by the thought that perhaps her mother might have come to lend her wisdom and strength to them all tonight.

Beth certainly seemed uplifted by her ritual. She appeared calm and hopeful, despite the hovering threat of Royston.

Gyda, though, grew distracted again as the fire burned low and the stars above them seemed to multiply. Abruptly, she clutched Kara's wrist. "Did you see something?"

Kara followed the direction of her friend's gaze to the dark skies. "No. Did you?"

Gyda stood. "I need to go. I'm sorry. I need a moment. Call for me when you are all ready to leave." She fled into the dark, in the direction of the water's edge.

Emelia scooted closer to Kara. "What *is* she doing?"

Kara shrugged. "Adjusting to her loss? Struggling with the idea of a murderer coming after her friend?"

"Yes, yes, but what is it about these late nights spent staring into the sky?" Emelia threw out her hands. "Even in the city she is creeping out into the garden in her night rail. Twice now, she has spooked one of our members into thinking she is a ghost."

"I don't know," Kara admitted. "But it is harmless enough."

Emelia straightened. "Bah! You English! Always pushing down or hiding your feelings instead of screaming your anger or crying an ocean over your sorrow. Well!" She stood. "I am just tired and cranky enough, right now, to go and ask her."

"Emelia, must you?" Kara pleaded. "Let her have her late nights, if that is what helps."

"And so she shall have them, but I will have my answers as well!" Emelia paused. "Where is that bottle of ouzo?"

Kara sighed as Emelia retrieved the bottle and stalked off into the dark after Gyda. Lifting a shoulder, she gave Beth a half grin.

But Beth looked serious as she moved closer. After a moment, she spoke. "Thank you for helping me do this."

"Of course."

"I asked Rob to teach me how to stab a man," she whispered. "He says it is harder than I imagine." She looked worried. "I hope I can manage it, if it comes to that."

Kara took her hand. "Remember what Gyda said when first she gave you that knife, Beth. You need to remember, you are not alone. Not anymore. We will do all that we can to make sure it never comes to that."

Breathing deeply, Beth nodded. "Thank you. I do remember, and it makes me feel stronger." They sat for a moment and stared up at the stars. "What do you think Gyda is looking for?" she asked.

"Charles," Kara said. "In some way."

"But why in the night sky? I would have thought she would look in the museum, or even in a painting or another piece of art." Beth sighed. "Perhaps Emelia will provoke Gyda into telling her. She has never explained it to me."

"Nor to me," Kara said. "She will tell us when she is ready, I imagine."

Beth's gaze had already wandered in the other direction. "Speaking of which, we have taken much longer than I expected. Rob must be ready to scream. Perhaps I will go and invite him and his vibrations to sit by the embers."

Kara laughed as Beth moved in the opposite direction. "Wait! Take the lantern," she called, but Beth just scampered on.

The fire faded while Kara sat alone a few minutes. She wondered what Niall was thinking, over there in the dark. She knew he would not have liked being left, but she also knew he trusted her—and Gyda, too.

When Beth did not return right away, Kara decided she and Rob might have decided to take advantage of the dark. With a sigh, she stood and took up the bucket they kept with the wood, intent on fetching water to douse the last embers.

She'd just reached the edge of the lake when she heard Beth cry out. Her heart stopped. The bucket slipped from her fingers.

With a soft cry, Kara turned and sprinted back to snatch up the lantern before heading toward the spot where Beth had disappeared. It took several moments of silent, frantic searching before she found Rob stretched out on the ground, alone and knocked out cold.

With a gasp, she fell beside him. Thank all the saints, he was breathing. "Rob! *Rob!*" She shook him, but he didn't respond.

Anxiously, she patted his face, even as she looked frantically around for a sign of Beth.

Then she glimpsed it. She brought the lantern closer to Rob's face. A great red circle of a bruise marked his temple. What in seven hells had made that?

Her head came up. She heard a thrashing in the woods. *Beth!*

Think! Think! Checking one last time to be sure Rob was breathing, she left the lantern and got to her feet. She took a step toward the northwest. The sound had come from that direction, had it not?

Yes. There were several more footsteps, quick and furtive.

Walking carefully, trying not to make a noise, she ventured deeper into the wood. Mentally, she reviewed what tools she had in her specialized pockets. Her lockpicks. Matches. Cursing, she wished she'd tucked a blade somewhere, but when she'd last left the house, she'd been going to visit the mill. How had things come to this in just over a day's time?

Moving quietly meant moving slowly, but after a moment, she heard the snap of a branch and a low curse. They were not far ahead of her.

Because surely this was Royston's doing. It must be him. But how had he found them out here?

Carefully, carefully, she placed each step. Glancing back, she could see the light of the lantern through the trees. Hopefully he would think she was still back there. Ahead, she heard a grunt and a few quick steps before another, larger thrashing of brush. She eased closer.

"Stop it!" someone ahead hissed. "I won't tell you again!"

"Let go of me!" Yes, that was Beth, and she'd said it in a snarl.

"Hush now! Do you think I'll let you go? After I've gone to all this trouble to track you down? No." His voice lowered, the tone turned ugly. "You will pay. You must."

"Pay for what? I've done nothing to harm you!"

There was another round of crashing footsteps, then Beth grunted in pain. Kara used the noise of the commotion to creep closer. Crouching down, she could see that she'd drawn abreast of them, two dark figures in the dim light. Royston had shoved Beth's back into a tree and pushed his face close into hers.

"Done nothing to harm me?" He gave a harsh laugh.

"Nothing!" Beth insisted. "I don't even know how you found us, so far out of the city. Or why?"

That seemed to give Royston pause. He pulled away a bit, although he kept her pinned to the tree. "Oh, yes. It was the most fortuitous thing. After you escaped me, and *I* escaped *them*, I thought your friends would surely whisk you away. It made sense that you would all retreat to Sedwick's estate. I decided to anticipate you all, establish myself in the neighborhood so that I could watch for my next chance." He drew a deep breath. "You would have made a mistake, eventually. They always do, you know." He gave a sharp laugh. "Imagine my surprise then! There I was, standing like cattle in third class on that train, when you walked by with the Italian woman! Boarding the very same train! I thought surely it was fate. It meant I was vindicated in choosing you."

"What rot!" Beth spat.

"No, it is true! It must be. How else could I have followed you so easily, out to this forsaken place?"

"You followed because someone in that village was eager to gossip about us, I would imagine."

Royston paused again. "Well, that much is true. Everyone in the stables of that tavern was eager to give their opinion on the wicked sorts of things you and your friends get up to out here. They warned me not to follow you, but they were happy enough to take my money and give me a mount."

"That is nonsense," Beth declared. "What is wicked is the way they feel free to gossip about and judge us, without even trying to understand the truth."

In a flash of movement, Royston grabbed Beth's chin. "There it is again. That mouth," he snarled. "How freely you give your opinions and defend your unladylike ways." Pushing away from her, he took a step back. "Do you know? I almost passed you by. I thought you were a proper woman. Quiet and meek. Keeping to her legitimate place, in the background. Not like that Foulger woman. So loud! So insistent! She would not be silent when she was told. She *would* put herself forward. Always pushing, pushing."

"You killed Glynn," Beth whispered. "You truly did it."

"Well, didn't I have to? It was her own fault. She saw me with Lily. More than once, I gather. She said she wasn't having it. She was going to tell the Duchess of Rowledge. Tell her I was messing about with one of our charity recipients, that I was using my authority within the organization to exert myself on the helpless and vulnerable. Well, I couldn't allow it. I couldn't let them start asking questions. I warned her, but she would not back down." His voice grew distant. "She wasn't like the others, though. She wasn't susceptible to my flatteries. There was no time for preparation, nor time for all the steps of the dance."

"You bashed her head in! And you squeezed the life out of Lily!"

"Yes, Lily. She had me tied in knots, that one, for I could not decide. Was she a child? Or another scourge of a mouthy whore, like the rest of them? I could scarcely decide—until she came to me and said she'd seen the smock, the one Glynn was making for her. I had it tucked away in a drawer in my office. Lily had been sneaking about where she did not belong. She had wondered if I could be the man seen leaving the Wardrobe that night, and so she felt free to touch my things, invade my privacy." He sneered. "Then I knew. She was a filthy, self-serving termagant, like so many of you."

"She was just a girl!" Beth cried. "She had her entire life ahead of her—and you stole it!"

"That girl was surely *not* looking forward to anything in her future," Royston said bluntly. "She scarcely fought me at all! It hardly felt like a punishment, in all honesty, and I admit, it worried me." He put a hand to his brow. "Is it a sin, I wonder, if it doesn't truly become a punishment for her crimes?"

"Crimes?" Beth scoffed.

"She stepped out of her place, didn't she? She asked for things she'd done nothing to earn. She made herself into a threat." He stepped closer to Beth again. "Like you."

Kara saw Beth's chin lift. "In what way have I threatened you?"

"You brought those friends of yours into the charity, pulled them right into the midst of Glynn's death! Yardley would surely have been on his way to his hanging by now, had you not interfered. Had *they* not interfered. You stepped out of your place, too. You started the nonsense of hosting a memorial service, when Glynn Foulger should have just faded quietly away. You are drawing public attention to the charity, which will make it horribly harder to kill! It's not just my plans you've ruined."

Lifting his hands to her shoulders, Royston shook the girl. "Why do you think I came for you in the open yesterday? You ruined any chance of the usual game, the lovely dance. I heard of the police who were at the Waif's Wardrobe yesterday. They were asking questions about me. They came to my home. They questioned my neighbors." He shook her again. "Do you know what that means? I shall have to start over. Again. Under an entirely new identity this time."

Royston turned his head then, and looked back the way they had come.

Kara shrank down.

"Your friend must have turned tail and run for her husband, leaving the lantern as a marker." He laughed darkly. "Much good it will do her. He's in the same shape as your man." He let go of her and puffed his chest out a bit. "No one else knows what an effective weapon a wooden bobbin can be. One good blow to the temple, with just the right amount of force, and you can quash a man good and proper. I learned it from a mill doctor, you see. He told me about it after one of the boys got coldcocked, cleaning beneath the looms. Something about knocking the brain into the side of the skull drops them quick."

"If Rob dies …" Beth seemed unable to finish her sentence.

"They usually do not. But it is no concern for you. We will go on before your friends return. You will cooperate, or I will use my bobbin on *you* and carry you out." He turned to glance back again, and this time Beth was ready. She wrenched free and turned to run.

Shouting, Royston reached for her and missed.

Kara stood as Beth leapt over a downed tree.

Royston lunged out and reached again. He caught the back of Beth's skirt and held on, pulling her up short. She tripped and went down.

Huffing out his anger like a bellows, Royston dragged her back across the log, spun her around, and propped her up so that her back lay against it. Leaning in close, he screamed in her face. "Now see what you have done! You are a betrayer. A cheat! Everything is your fault, do you hear? Just like her! Why do you get above yourself? You are a woman, a vessel of original sin. You are weak. Inferior. Inconstant. Just like Father told you! Everything bad, ugly, and evil in this world can be traced back to you. If only you had just behaved, kept quiet, kept your opinions to yourself, none of this would have happened. It's your fault. All of it, laid at your feet."

Something was happening to Beth.

She'd been defiant before. She'd met Royston's anger with fire of her own and used his inattention to try to get away. But something had changed. Perhaps the horrid words and terrible accusations he was flinging at her? Perhaps it was her position, stretched out beneath him with her skirts half rucked up, while he knelt over her?

Kara couldn't know, but something had doused Beth's fire. She huddled with her face turned away, her eyes closed, and her shoulders hunched defensively. She was flinching, as if every angry word was a blow.

And Royston was loving it, reveling in her obvious fear, relishing her capitulation. "Yes!" he yelled. "You know I am right! You are fickle and weak."

And he was distracted—and facing completely away from Kara.

Now was her chance.

Gripping her longest lockpick, she stood and charged forward, aiming to drive it into the curve of his neck.

Did he hear her coming? Had Beth seen her and given her away? Kara didn't know, but Royston started to turn to face her, and she drove the lockpick into his shoulder instead.

Cursing, he turned and backhanded her, striking her across the face and sending her reeling.

"Damn you," Royston shouted. He yanked the pick from his flesh and flung it away.

As Kara straightened, Royston wrapped his hands around her neck. "Interfering bitch," he snarled. "It didn't have to come to this. Not for you. You are not right for the dance! There is no soaring justice to be had in this. No integrity to be restored by your death."

Pain exploded, unexpectedly sharp. Kara gasped for air. She tried to push him away, her fear rising faster than she would have thought.

"Still, you must die," Royston ground out, pressing harder.

She struck him, aiming for the inside of his elbow, to try to loosen his grip, but he merely tightened his fingers. Her vision started to blur. He seemed immovable. She tried to pry his hands away. She couldn't breathe. Couldn't swallow. Terror bloomed.

"I am not weak."

Kara barely heard the soft words over the ringing in her ears. Her legs were giving way. Through a haze, she saw a small hand grab Royston's shoulder.

With a growl, he tried to shrug Beth off, but the girl held on.

He squeezed Kara's neck tighter. She was falling.

"I am not inferior," Beth said, her voice rising in volume. "Your faults, your problems, your sins—they are due to your own weaknesses and no one else's."

Something warm sprayed across Kara's chest. The stricture around her neck abruptly eased. She dropped to her knees, gasping for air.

Looking up, she saw Royston wore a look of surprise. His hand was clasped to his neck. Blood streamed between his fingers.

"I am strong," Beth said clearly. "I try to be kind." She yanked on Royston's shoulder again, and this time he turned, looking down at her in disbelief. He reached for her with his other hand, but she stepped back, evading him easily.

"Rob said I'm too small and inexperienced to try to stab you in the heart. He said to aim for the vessels in your neck. I am a good listener." She raised her hand, and Kara saw the knife glinting faintly in the dark.

Beth slashed at the other side of Royston's throat and he fell backward, staring up at the sky while his life's blood poured out of him.

Beth moved to stare down at him. "I am a fighter," she said clearly.

Chapter Twenty

APPLAUSE DRIFTED THROUGH the workroom of the Waif's Wardrobe. The place had been transformed. Emptied of most of its tables, boxes, crates, and piles of clothing in various stages of readiness, it was now filled with bright flowers, soft lights, ladies in fine gowns, and crisply clad waiters passing champagne and finger foods.

"Everyone here at the Wardrobe would like to thank you all for your generosity," Beth said from atop a hastily erected dais. "We are beyond excited to announce that we have reached our fundraising goal."

More applause rang through the room. Kara clinked her glass with Inspector Wooten's as he approached.

"Thanks to your generosity, we are now fully funded and able to open our new branch in Yarmouth," Beth continued. "It will be named Glynn's Wardrobe, in honor of our friend, Miss Glynn Foulger, who gave her life to protect our volunteers and our values."

Wooten glanced around at the crowded room. "I see the publicity surrounding the murder did not adversely affect your turnout today."

"Goodness, no. In fact, I would say the opposite is true." Kara gave a nod toward the dais. "Beth has become something of a celebrity. People are eager to donate or volunteer if they can meet her and hear her story."

"She seems to have handled it well, and put it all to good use."

"They have given her Royston's position. She is the manager here now. And she is doing a good job of it."

Wooten glanced askance at Kara. "You know, there is considerable debate—and betting—at Scotland Yard as to whether *you* were actually the one to dispatch Royston that night. Some of the men think Miss Williams is too quiet to have done the deed."

"And what of you, sir?" Kara asked archly. "How did you bet?"

"Scarcely anyone is more aware of, and proud of, your abilities, Your Grace, but I detect a thread of steel in that little girl's spine."

"I am glad to know your instincts are still well honed, Inspector. I will let you set your men straight." She touched her throat, where the bruises Royston had left had finally faded. "It all happened exactly as we told you. Beth saved my life."

"Thank the heavens for Miss Williams, then," Wooten said, raising his glass in a toast.

"Kara!"

She found herself gripping the inspector's arm for balance as Gyda came skidding up to grab on to her.

"Who is that vision in lilac silk? I heard her speaking with someone about the importance of teaching children about different heritages through the world."

Gyda jerked her head toward a group gathered at the portrait of Glynn Foulger sitting on an easel in the corner next to the dais, awaiting its hanging in a place of honor in the new charity building.

"Ah, that is the Countess of Canfield. She is one of the founders of the charity."

Gyda visibly deflated. "Oh. A countess. Is her earl here with her today, then?"

"The lady is a widow, I believe," Kara told her friend.

"Excellent!" Gyda's expression lightened again. "I mean, how unfortunate, for her to be widowed so young. Will you introduce us, please?"

"Of course."

Gyda waggled her brows. "If I find her agreeable, I might just invite her to our picnic."

"I will let you ladies proceed," Wooten said, handing his glass to a passing waiter. "Is the duke about?"

"I think he's following the platter of veal baskets around the room," Kara said with a laugh.

"He's recovered, then? And Mr. McRae?"

"They both have had headaches, but they seem to be coming more infrequently." Kara paused to watch the inspector. "You will be attending our picnic this evening?"

"Neither Mrs. Wooten nor I would miss it," the inspector said. "Indeed, your invitation is the first thing to have tempted her away from our new grandson."

"We will see you at Bluefield later, then, Inspector." Gyda tugged at Kara's arm. "Come along, Kara!"

LATER THAT AFTERNOON, Kara dressed for the evening's upcoming picnic. Niall and Harold were outside setting up games. Turner and the rest of the staff had everything else well in hand, so she went to the ivory sitting room to look over her correspondence. The words kept blurring, however. Closing her eyes, she sighed and rested her head on her hands for a moment.

"Your Grace? Your Grace?" A gentle hand touched her shoulder. "Kara?"

Her eyes opened. She sat up in surprise. "Oh! Turner! I must have fallen asleep! What time is it? I haven't missed the start of the picnic, have I?"

"No, there is still time." He set a tray on her desk. "It's only that Cook just pulled a tray of your favorite salmon puffs from the oven. I thought you might enjoy a few while they are still warm."

"Oh, how kind you are. That reminds me, Turner. We must be careful to keep things cordial between Cook and Maisie. I know they are rivals for Harold's affections and appetites, but this is the first time I've been able to coax Maisie to Bluefield, and I want it to go well."

Kara's gaze fell upon the salmon puffs at the same time as the smell registered. Her stomach abruptly revolted and she hastily stood and backed away. "I'm sorry." She turned away. "Oh, heavens. I'm afraid I don't have an appetite at the moment."

Turner whipped the tray away at once. "Forgive me, Your Grace."

"No, no! It's me, I'm sure! My appetite has been fluctuating lately."

Turner opened the door and called for a footman to return the tray to the kitchens. He came back and looked at Kara carefully. "I did notice that you seemed to be disturbed by the duke's kedgeree yesterday morning."

"I was, wasn't I?" Kara laughed. "Perhaps I have just gone off fish."

"Perhaps," Turner said gently. "Food aversion can be a symptom—"

"Oh, no. I'm not ill, I am sure. Do not fear, Turner. Perhaps it is only a delayed reaction to all the excitement."

"Perhaps. Will you sit, Your Grace?" He patted the back of a chair by the hearth.

"Just for a moment. Join me? We'll hide out for a few minutes before we tackle the rest of the picnic preparations."

"Thank you." Turner sat, then cleared his throat. "I thought I might ask … It's just that I often found your mother asleep at odd times—"

"Oh? Did you?" She was touched—and relieved—to hear her

mother had displayed some odd tendencies, too.

"It happened often, Your Grace, when she found herself … in expectation."

"Of what?"

"Of you, Your Grace."

"Oh!" Kara flushed. "Oh!" She clapped both hands over her mouth. "You mean … You think … That I … That we …" Abruptly, she started to cry. "Turner! Do you think? A baby?"

He blinked furiously. "I think that you might wish to consult with Elsie."

"With Elsie?" Kara frowned. Her maid? "Oh! Oh! Yes. Let me think." She started to shake. "Oh, Turner! I think you might be right!"

The butler stood, and so did she, and suddenly she was in his arms and they were both crying and hugging each other close. Eventually, Turner stepped back and offered her a handkerchief. "May I say how very happy I am for you? For you both."

"Yes! I must tell Niall!" She hugged Turner once more before they both left the sitting room, only to find that the first picnic guests were arriving.

Kara floated through the evening, her heart full and her pulse pounding in excitement and anticipation.

It was a lovely party. Harold was in fine form, making everyone laugh and eating his way through the tables of food. Her cousin Joseph came, and he brought along a Miss Steene and her parents.

"She seems lovely," Niall whispered, after the group of them wandered away to play a round of croquet. "Dare we hope?"

"Joseph deserves to be happy. I'm daring," she whispered back, staring at her husband and wishing she could drag him away to tell him.

But Josie Lowe was being appealed to for a song, and she soon had everyone both laughing and crying. It was a relief for Kara to have an excuse to vent a little of what she was feeling. Gyda, too, seemed to feel Josie's sad song strongly, but Kara watched her closely, and she seemed to recover.

Kara strolled over to ask, "How did you find the Countess of Canfield this afternoon?"

"I liked her immensely. She has a daughter, did you know?" Gyda said.

"Oh. No, I didn't."

"The girl is obsessed with her father's family's Russian ancestors and Russian folklore. The countess told me some interesting stories."

"How nice." Gyda was intensely proud of her own Norse blood, so she would approve of such an interest.

"Kara, do you think Niall meant it, when he said I could use his little forge in Scotland?"

Kara's interest instantly piqued. "Yes, absolutely." She paused. "Do you think you are ready to begin your work again?"

"Perhaps. I think I'd like to be up there, alone for a while, to think about it."

"I think it's a lovely idea."

Kara was called away then, but her heart felt lighter for her friend. She moved through the party, keeping check.

Cook and Maisie had circled each other warily, but now Kara saw them sharing a bottle of wine with Emelia and joining together to argue that English cuisine could not be *so* much worse than Italian.

Miss Henrietta Moseman stopped Kara to fill her ears with raptures about her latest beau, while across the way, Mr. Arthur Towland filled Niall's with excited descriptions of the latest rare book he'd found for the library in the Druid's Grove.

And to cap the evening off, Rob McRae got down on one knee and formally asked Beth to marry him.

Thankfully, she said yes.

It was the perfect end to a wonderful evening. The moon had sunk low when Kara and Niall waved goodbye to the last of the guests. They stood for a moment in the drive, drinking in the peace of the night.

They both sighed when they spotted Gyda heading out alone into the gardens.

"It was a night like this when we first kissed," Niall said. He shifted Kara over a few steps. "Right … about … here."

She grinned as he bent over her and proceeded to remind her just how it had gone.

"Well," he said, when they broke apart, "that's the curtain down on a successful event. Now, shall we take some time for ourselves?"

"Yes." Kara nodded. "I rather think we should."

Niall took her hand and walked backward toward the house. "Shall we get in some practice? While we have the chance?"

She resisted the tug of his hand. "Actually, I don't think we need to practice."

"Don't we?" He was clearly trying not to sound disappointed.

"No." She grinned at him, so relieved and happy to finally be able to share. "I think we've finally got it right."

"Oh, but …" Niall stopped. "Wait, are you saying …?"

"Yes. I think I am."

Niall gasped. "Kara? Truly?"

"I think so." She told him what had happened earlier with Turner, and they both laughed, before he picked her up and spun her around until they were both blissfully happy and dizzy.

"I suppose it's a sign of a sad dearth of female guidance, isn't it? When your butler and right-hand man has to inform you of your condition?"

He kissed her gently. "I think your mother knows, even if she couldn't be the one to share it with you." Kara teared up again when he spread his big hand over her belly. "And this little one will have no such lack of guidance, love, or care."

She pulled him close, and they stayed that way for several long minutes—until they both jumped when a scream came from the garden. "Kara! Niall!"

"Gyda?" Kara said. Holding hands, they ran to where their friend was turning and spinning in dizzying circles.

"It's Charles," she cried. "At last, it's Charles!"

"Gyda?" Niall sounded concerned. "What do you mean?"

"Look up! Look up! There!"

Kara caught the flash of a shooting star in the darkest part of the sky. Gyda took her hand and flung the other one skyward. "Charles and I, we always sat outside in the dark. It's where we did our talking and planning. And we so often caught sight of a shooting star. Ridiculously often! He said it was a sign. A sign that we were doing the right thing. That even if we were apart at night, we could look up and know—we are together, and everything will be all right."

"That's lovely, Gyda," said Kara.

"Yes, but don't you see? I hadn't seen one since he died. *Not a single shooting star.* But now, look! There's one! And another!" She dropped Kara's hand and flung herself on the ground, staring upward. "The sky is full of them!" She sat up. "Do you understand? I think it means he is well. I am fine. We are still together. We always will be, in some way. I think it means everything is going to be all right."

Niall wrapped Kara in his arms, and she sighed in utter contentment.

"I believe you are right, Gyda," he said.

Kara agreed. "We are going to be fine. All of us. We are together and all is going to be well."

ABOUT THE AUTHOR

USA Today Bestselling author Deb Marlowe grew up with her nose in a book. Luckily, she'd read enough romances to recognize the hero she met at a college Halloween party – even though he wore a tuxedo t-shirt instead of breeches and boots. They married, settled in North Carolina and raised two handsome, funny and genuinely intelligent boys.

The author of over twenty-five historical romances, Deb is a Golden Heart Winner, a Rita Finalist and her books have won or been a finalist in the Golden Quill, the Holt Medallion, the Maggie, the Write Touch Reader Awards and the Daphne du Maurier Award.

A proud geek, history buff and story addict, she loves to talk with readers! Find her discussing books, period dramas and her infamous Men in Boots on Facebook, Twitter and Instagram. Watch her making historical recipes in her modern kitchen at Deb Marlowe's Regency Kitchen, a set of completely amateur videos on her website. While there, find out Behind the Book details and interesting Historical Tidbits and enter her monthly contest at deb@debmarlowe.com.